BURN THE ENGLISH MUFFIN!

"It's going to be all right," said Pendlebury, uncaring at the emotion evident in
his voice. "They haven't called it off.
They've brought it forward. It's tonight."

Gilbert half stood, imagining the need to
respond in a hurry, but Pendlebury waved
him down, content he was in charge of the
situation once more.

"Everyone is in the right place," he said.
"There's no hurry. It'll all go just as we
planned."

"What about the Englishman?" queried
Gilbert.

"Kill him," said Pendlebury positively.

CHARLIE MUFFIN U.S.A.

BRIAN FREEMANTLE

BALLANTINE BOOKS • NEW YORK

Copyright © 1980 by Innslodge Publications, Ltd.

This book has been published in the United Kingdom as CHARLIE MUFFIN'S UNCLE SAM.

Library of Congress Catalog Card Number: 79-8019

ISBN 0-345-29440-8

This edition published by arrangement with Doubleday & Company, Inc.

Manufactured in the United States of America

First Ballantine Books Edition: December 1982

To Leslie Thomas, who said it wasn't easy.
And to Diana, with love.

Prologue

TSAR NICHOLAS II of All the Russias and his desperately ill heir, Tsarevich Alexei, had less than three months to live when the specially guarded Imperial prison train arrived at Ekaterinburg on April 30, 1918.

A year earlier, the Tsar had abdicated in favor of the government that preceded Lenin. In the first few months, under a semblance of a government, respect had lingered for someone whom most Russians regarded as a near God. By April the Bolsheviks had taken control. Little respect remained.

In Ekaterinburg it was predictable. Ekaterinburg is a mining town in the heart of the Urals, and from the Urals Lenin had drawn the fiercest support for his revolution. The coming of the Imperial family had been kept secret, but inevitably there had been rumors. The carriage from the station to Ipatiev House, where they were to be held, was jeered and spat upon, and initially the guards were as much to protect them from mob violence as to prevent any rescue attempt.

At the time of his abdication, Tsar Nicholas had been the richest man in the world. Still with him at Ekaterinburg was a trainload of personal possessions he had been allowed to assemble. Had he survived the Russian revolution, the priceless contents of that baggage train would have ensured a life as luxurious as any he had known throughout his fifty years. Among the treasures was a stamp collection. Befitting the world's richest man, it was worth a fortune, 1,274 items carefully annotated and cataloged in a set of hand-tooled leather albums.

Its creation had been conceived as early as 1907, when Nicholas had decided that three hundred years of Romanov suzerainty should be celebrated by a stamp issue depicting the emperors and empresses of the dynasty. Work had begun in 1909, and at every stage during the four years it had taken to create, the Tsar was involved, making his personal choice of the drawings and the essays and the specimens. It had been issued on January 2, 1913, by which time he had already ordered his personal philatelist to prepare for him a unique collection. It included the original drawings and artists' sketches, the rejected essays, heads, and frames, in black and in every other color that had been attempted, samples of those color trials, the final design, and the projected but unadopted overprint for use in the Grand Duchy of Finland, then under the Tsar's control. There were also the first prints of every issued stamp, in blocks of four.

The first guard commander for the Tsar, Tsarina, and their five children at Ekaterinburg typified both the local feeling and that of the Bolsheviks, who had erupted in hatred to overthrow three hundred years of blinkered, misguided Romanov rule. Alexander Avdeyev was a bully and a drunk, a former fitter in a munitions factory who insisted on eating with the Imperial family and on one occasion elbowed the Tsar in the mouth, stretching across the table to seize some food. Pilfering the royal treasures had started before Ekaterinburg, at Tobolsk, but under Avdeyev's command the stealing was allowed to go unchecked, at times even encouraged, like a game, because of the distress it caused the Tsar. But five weeks after their imprisonment at Ekaterinburg the stamp collection was intact; those who were stealing were peasants who wore rags, and the fine linen and jewelry and silver and gold had more obvious value. Stamps were just pieces of colored paper.

After three months, Alexander Avdeyev was replaced by Yankel Yurovsky, the regional commissar for justice and a member of the Cheka, the secret police force through which the Tsar had formerly controlled his country. Yurovsky showed the Imperial family more respect and stopped the guards making crude, sexual insults toward the Grand Duchesses Olga, Tatania, Maria, and Anastasia. The stealing he didn't bother about.

By July 14, 1918, rescue was very close for the Tsar and his family. Headed by two superbly trained and led Czech regiments, the White Russian Army had almost surrounded the town. In their cream stucco two-story house on Voznesensky Avenue, the Imperial family could hear the constant crump of artillery, hourly getting nearer. It was audible, too, in Room 3 of the Hotel America, which was the Cheka headquarters and where Yurovsky sat in permanent, emergency session with three other members of the Ural Soviet. Alexander Beloborodov, the chairman of the Soviet and the man who had received the Tsar, his family, and the treasures in April, nearly always controlled the meetings. His deputy, Alexei Chutskayev, had dealt with the British inquiries over the Tsar's fate and was frequently asked his opinion about foreign concern for the family, particularly for the German-born Tsarina, Alexandra. The fourth man, Chaya Goloshchokin, was the regional commissar for war who had just returned from Moscow after meetings with Lenin and Trotsky about what to do with their royal prisoners.

On July 16 Tsar Nicholas, just fifty, and his hemophiliac son, Alexei, just fourteen, were shot and bayoneted to death. In the early morning darkness, the Tsarina and her four daughters were taken from Ipatiev House to a railway station on the outskirts of the town and put aboard a shuttered carriage which took them two hundred miles northwest of Ekaterinburg, to the provincial capital of Perm, where they were kept isolated from everyone and their presence never confirmed officially.

As their train left Ekaterinburg, it passed the royal baggage cars. Some of the locks were already visibly smashed in the scramble to loot the Imperial family possessions, which, because of the speed of the Bolshevik retreat, had to be left behind.

The White Russian officer who half guessed its importance and believed the Tsar still to be alive paid three loaves of bread and a packet of salt to retrieve the stamp collection from a disappointed peasant who had thought the album contained bank notes. A Swedish consular official, at the time as ignorant as the officer of the fate of the Tsar, smuggled the stamps to the Latvian port of Riga, for their eventual return to their rightful owner.

It was eight years before it was heard of again. To the surprise of the philatelic world, the Romanov Collection unexpectedly appeared for display and sale in New York in 1926. In the mid-thirties it was put on exhibition again, this time in a restaurant in London's High Holborn and then at Selfridges, the Oxford Street store. There, a twenty-four-hour security guard had to be established because of Bolshevik threats to destroy it.

Before the outbreak of World War II, it again went to New

York, once more to be sold. It was broken up, large sections going to individual buyers.

It was not until after the Russian revolution that the second, 925-item collection of proofs and essays of the Imperial collection had been found to exist. Richard Zarrins, director of the Imperial State Printing Works and the man who had supervised the Romanov issue, formed it from the material left over after the Tsar had had his collection assembled. In 1967 the Zarrins stamps—like the Tsar's collection before it—reached America, to be sold by a New York dealer. After that, like Tsarina Alexandra and her four Grand Duchess daughters forty-eight years before, it vanished.

For the avid philatelist, it is a fascinatingly unique collection. For some, even worth committing crime to possess.

CHAPTER 1

ON THE day that his attempted destruction began, Giuseppe Terrilli ordered the killing of three people. One had to be allowed to die slowly, as an example to other recruits who were not careful enough. It took five hours, for the last two of which the man became insane. It was a good example.

Terrilli, who was 1,500 miles away on his Miami estate, lunched in his customarily spartan manner: just cottage cheese, salad without dressing, and mineral water. Not once did he think of the people who were dying. It was a business matter, being satisfactorily resolved and therefore no longer necessary for any further consideration. Giuseppe Terrilli regarded such detachment as essential for the business he conducted.

The man who set out to be Terrilli's destroyer never discovered the example killings. It would have been difficult, because Dean Warburger was in the Director's office at the FBI headquarters in Washington and the murders were in the northern Colombian province of Guajira.

But Warburger had learned that day of something else, and his initial excitement was such to prompt a four martini and lobster au gratin lunch at the Sans Souci. By four in the afternoon, Warburger had a bad headache and realized that the intake was dangerous as well as premature and the proposal probably impractical. He authorized a feasibility study anyway.

It was the first time, after almost a year of exhaustive investigation, that he had become aware of Terrilli's interest in philately. And Warburger, who was determined to make his directorship of the FBI as legendary as that of J. Edgar Hoover, thought he had known *everything* that it was possible to uncover about Terrilli. Warburger usually disdained any dictum by which Hoover had ruled the Bureau, but on this occasion he made an exception. Hoover said that personal secrets were weaknesses. It was the hope that Hoover was right which had caused the early Sans Souci celebration.

It took six weeks to steer the Lady McLeod of Trinidad

toward a dealer through whom they discovered Terrilli had bought in the past. Warburger only became really excited when Terrilli made the purchase, because he had ensured that the theft of such a rare stamp as the Lady McLeod had been widely publicized. Having confirmed the weakness, Warburger refused to hurry, recognizing it as possibly the only chance he would get. The indictment had to be unbreakable, with Terrilli provably involved in a crime. And that meant the bait had to be spectacular.

It took a further two months for Warburger to determine upon the Romanov and Zarrins collections. They were unusual enough and their disposal in America between 1926 and 1967 meant they were traceable by the Bureau.

Warburger was an expert in the internal government of Washington, which meant it would have been unthinkable of him to confine the operation only to Terrilli's arrest. There had to be political side benefits, and he employed himself on obtaining them while his agents traced the stamps to their scattered ownership. By the time Warburger had the location of nearly every item, he had a senator ambitious to be Attorney General set up as a front man and the protection of the FBI hopefully guaranteed for several years.

It was a full twelve months from the Sans Souci hangover before Warburger was completely happy with the preparations.

"There's nothing I haven't anticipated," he boasted to his deputy, Peter Bowler.

At that stage it would have been as difficult for him to predict the involvement of Charlie Muffin as it had been to learn of the Guajira killings.

Charlie Muffin, who was a realist and therefore aware of the social gulf between himself and Rupert Willoughby's friends, was curious at the reason for his invitation. He still went to the party, of course; a man officially listed as a dead traitor by the intelligence services of both Britain and America and wishing to remain that way doesn't get out much and Charlie liked company, even company which seemed to regard him oddly.

Realist again, Charlie accepted that it wasn't their fault. It had always been the same, whenever he'd worn a black tie. He had rented the dinner jacket and everything that went with it, even the shoes, which pinched. He had expected the discomfort with his feet, because they usually hurt, but he had hoped for more success with the suit. Inside the jacket, he had found a raffle ticket for the Henley regatta, with a telephone number on the back. Perhaps there would be some compensation in the reply when he called the number.

Very early in the party Charlie had discarded his champagne, because the bubbles gave him wind and he genuinely didn't want to fart and reduce the chances of his being invited again. But he hadn't realized the combined disadvantages of not having a glass in his hand and looking like he did in a rented outfit.

Since he had entered the two-floored apartment off Eaton Square in which a smaller group of people had already eaten and to which a larger number of guests were now arriving, for an after-dinner party, several people had half turned to him, as if expecting him to be carrying a tray of drinks. Once, rather than interfere with the conversation of a rather angular, flat-chested woman who had gestured at him, Charlie had taken her empty glass so that she could use the otherwise occupied hand to finger-wave some point to a frowning man whose photograph Charlie recognized from one of those blown-up displays outside the Old Vic.

Charlie became aware that Willoughby had witnessed the episode with the angular woman and wandered toward the Lloyds underwriter, who was standing immediately before the elevator from the first floor, to receive the people when they arrived.

"Sorry about that," apologized the man. He was much taller than Charlie and stooped, attempting to minimize his embarrassing height. It gave him an odd, hunched-back appearance.

"Doesn't matter," said Charlie. He looked to where the woman had begun another hand-moving story.

"She's wasting her time," he added. "That guy's a poof."

"So I believe," said Willoughby. "Would you like another drink?"

Charlie shook his head in refusal. He was quite proud of how well he had conquered the booze habit. It had always been worse when he was bored: and he was very bored now. Sometimes he wondered if it was even necessary still to take precautions against detection. The doubt never lasted long. There was never a moment of his waking life when he could properly relax. His exposure of the incompetence of the British and American services had been too complete and the Soviet propaganda too embarrassing for him ever to believe himself safe.

"Nice party," he said.

Willoughby smiled at the politeness. "Clarissa likes these sort of things," he said, his voice that of a man who knows he is criticized for allowing his wife's indulgences but can't stop permitting them.

As if on cue, the woman appeared through the crush of people, bright smile attached like a badge, head twisting from side to side in permanent greeting and chirping cries of apparent delight and surprise at the people she saw. Frequently she stopped, offering her cheek to be kissed. She was not a particularly tall woman and her face was chiseled by the perpetual diet. Her hair bubbled in a current style, which tended to accentuate the appearance of thinness, and her dress, which Charlie assumed to come from the latest designer to be lionized by the society rich, was layered in tiers of brightly colored chiffon, which bounced, featherlike, as she moved. She looked like a bird in search of a nest. A slim cuckoo, perhaps. No, more like a bird of paradise.

She greeted her husband as if he were standing alone, and Charlie realized that like so many others, she believed him to be one of the extra staff brought in for the evening.

"Millie says the ambassador *is* coming. And that he's trying to persuade the princess, too."

The scientist who perfected a cancer cure would probably have a matching note of triumph in his voice when he announced the discovery, decided Charlie. He wondered if Clarissa Willoughby would be a difficult person to like; he would try, for her husband's sake.

"Good," said the underwriter, unimpressed and showing it. He turned, making the woman aware of Charlie.

"This is the person whom you particularly asked to meet," he said in introduction.

Clarissa focused on him for the first time. She squinted, not frowned, when she was curious, Charlie saw.

"Who . . . ?" she said doubtfully.

"He helped us over the Hong Kong problem," enlarged the underwriter.

"Helped" seemed such an inadequate word, thought Willoughby. It was easy for him to understand why his father, when he had been head of the intelligence service, had regarded Charlie as the best operative he had ever had. Willoughby doubted if anyone else could have isolated the liner insurance fraud which would have bankrupted his firm for £8 million. Clarissa had openly announced her intention to divorce him if it happened. Sometimes Willoughby wondered if he should have been as grateful to Charlie about that outcome as he was about everything else.

"You're that *fascinating* man!" exclaimed the woman.

"I represented the company in Hong Kong," said Charlie modestly. Clarissa Willoughby was someone who constantly talked in italics. She probably shouted at foreign airport porters who didn't speak English, too.

"And were *brilliant!*"

"Lucky," qualified Charlie.

"I always think people make their own luck," said the woman.

Italics and clichés, thought Charlie.

"There were some people who weren't quite so lucky," he said. A whore, named Jenny, Charlie recalled. And an Englishman ostracized because he had loved her. Their graves would be neglected, he guessed. It would offend the Chinese, who attached great importance to their ancestors and to whom cemeteries were places to visit on holidays, like picnic parks. It could easily have been him in that cemetery, overlooking the New Territories and the Chinese mainland. He had allowed Willoughby to invoke the loyalty and respect he had felt for the man's father and come nearer than at any time in five years to discovery from the CIA.

Charlie became aware of her examination and thought how strange it was that people usually did that, as if in search of something they couldn't understand. Instinctively he started pulling in his stomach and then stopped, annoyed at himself. Bollocks, he thought, relaxing so that the rented suit bulged again. Why should he try to impress her?

"You're very different from what I expected," she said.

"Shakespeare probably stuttered," said Charlie.

"What?" frowned the woman.

"And disappointed people, who expected brilliant conversation," said Charlie laboriously. She would be a difficult woman to live with.

"I didn't say I was *disappointed,*" she said coquettishly.

The elevator arrived with more guests and she jerked toward it. The ambassador and the princess? wondered Charlie.

"We must meet again, when there's less people. Dinner perhaps," she invited, hurrying away.

"That would be nice," said Charlie, aware she hadn't heard. She probably hadn't intended the invitation, either.

Willoughby did not go with her.

"I'd like us to meet soon, Charlie," he said, taking up his wife's remark.

"Why?" asked Charlie. So there *was* a reason for the invitation, he thought, unoffended.

"What do you know about stamps?"

"Nothing," said Charlie.

"We've been approached for a rather unusual cover," said Willoughby. He looked after the disappearing figure of his wife.

"Politician in Washington; his wife is a friend of Clarissa's, actually. They want cover for an exhibition. Value is put at three million pounds."

"That's a lot of stamps."

"It is, as a matter of fact. Unique, too. Nearly all the collection of Tsar Nicholas II. Plus part of a second collection created by someone else attached to the court that fills in the gaps."

Charlie turned so that he was directly facing Willoughby. There was a look of pained rebuke about his expression.

"I don't think it would be a good idea for me to become associated with anything connected with the Soviet Union, do you?" he demanded.

Willoughby had anticipated the reaction. The inept army generals who had chosen Charlie for sacrifice during a Berlin border crossing had been those who replaced his father in the department and led to the old man's alcohol-induced suicide. So he had wanted revenge as much as Charlie. To anyone else, setting the department heads of M16 and the CIA for humiliating Soviet arrest and then even more humiliating exchange for an imprisoned Russian spy master could only be construed as traitorous. Charlie had been lucky to escape the combined pursuit of both agencies. No, not lucky. Clever. It had cost him a lot, though. The assassination of his wife. And the permanent uncertainty of being discovered. Willoughby looked at the other man pityingly. Charlie Muffin might have survived, on his own terms, but he'd created a miserable life for himself.

"Surely there wouldn't be any harm in discussing it?" said the underwriter hopefully.

"Or purpose," said Charlie. It was a conversation very similar to this which had sent him to Hong Kong.

"A discussion might help me decide what to do."

"Haven't you offered cover yet?"

"Yes," nodded Willoughby. "It's the protection I'm concerned about."

"We can talk about it," agreed Charlie, his voice indicating that was all he was prepared to do.

"How about tomorrow?"

Charlie frowned at the pressure. "All right," he agreed. It would be a way of filling another day. Since Edith's death, he had been very lonely.

"I'll remind Clarissa about that dinner invitation, too," promised the underwriter.

"Fine," said Charlie. He wondered how he would enjoy a concentrated period in the woman's company.

"Tomorrow, then?" pressed Willoughby, as if he doubted Charlie's agreement.

"Eleven," said Charlie. "But it's only to talk. I don't want to become involved."

"I understand," said Willoughby.

He didn't, Charlie decided. He left the party as early as he considered it polite. Clarissa Willoughby was at her station by the elevator, blank to everything except the hoped-for arrival of guests she considered important. From her reaction to his farewell, Charlie guessed she had forgotten him already.

There were taxis going to and from Chelsea and Victoria, but Charlie walked, despite his pinched shoes, more confident of isolating any surveillance.

It took him over an hour to reach his apartment in Vauxhall. He had searched a year to find it, a high-rise apartment building that thrust permanently black beside the Thames because it was on the leeward side of Battersea power station and got all the smut, regardless of what everyone claimed about the Clean Air Act.

It was the sort of building frequently criticized as socially wrong at inquests on people who discarded themselves from the top, depressed by the anonymity and loneliness. It was precisely for its anonymity and the fact that nobody was interested in him that had made Charlie take it. The apartment was boxes within boxes, a sitting room with a dining annex, just one bedroom, a bathroom, and a toilet. The window to the fire escape was always ajar, winter or summer, for easy escape.

It was only when the jacket that he pitched toward the chair missed and landed on the floor that Charlie remembered the raffle ticket and the telephone number. He retrieved it, stood gazing at it for a few moments, and then shrugged. Why not?

Someone as alert as Charlie should have recognized it, from the speed and professionalism of the answer, but his mind was still occupied with thoughts of stamps and insurance cover arranged through social friends, and so he initially missed the husky sensuousness.

"Believe we met at Henley," he said brightly.

"Henley?"

"Boat races the other week. Remember me?"

There was a pause, for both of them a time for realization. The woman spoke first, because it was her business, after all.

"Same as last time," she said briskly. "If you want to wear that funny cap and striped blazer while we're doing it, it's kinky so it's an extra five pounds. And the ruler is another five pounds, too."

"I need another sort of relief," said Charlie for his own amusement. "I've got aching feet."

"Try a fucking chiropodist," said the voice, no longer husky or inviting.

He frequently had, remembered Charlie. The last one had individually wrapped his toes in little cocoons of cotton wool and put an additional three pounds on the bill. Perhaps that was kinky, too.

CHAPTER 2

LIKE THE drawbridges that were the only entries to the castles of medieval times, a set of bridges staples the island of Palm Beach to the Florida mainland, with Lake Worth forming the moat. Only very rich people ever lived in castles and only very rich people live in Palm Beach. Perhaps in unconscious envy of medieval times, when the divisions of wealth between those who had and those who did not was more clearly defined, a few of the residents have actually invoked castellated architecture for their mansions, which jut, ridged and angular, among the more traditional hacienda constructions which show the Spanish influence throughout the state.

An eccentric newspaper magnate who had been a personal friend of Henry Morrison Flagler, the Standard Oil founder credited with the single-handed development of Palm Beach as the resort it now is, was responsible for just such a construction at the end of a small but usefully private road that loops off Ocean Boulevard. Even in a society accustomed to grandeur, the building was regarded as something unusual, transported as it had been stone by stone from the French countryside where it had been originally built as a fortified chateau, three centuries before. While retaining perfectly its outside design, the newspaper magnate had permitted some interior improvements, like modern plumbing and air conditioning, and the man who had succeeded him in ownership had further added to the amenities. One such innovation had been to introduce the electrification to the surrounding fencing and then to attach spotlights at strategic points, so that at the touch of any one of five switches, the grounds could be bathed in a blaze of revealing light and protected by sufficient volts to kill a man. While elsewhere this might have been regarded as a little strange, paranoiac even, in Palm Beach it was accepted by neighbors, who knew how the possessions of the wealthy are coveted by others. For some, it would have been comforting to know that at night the mainland bridges could have been raised, to keep out intruders.

Giuseppe Terrilli was known to be wealthy. While not as outgoing as his predecessor in the castle, Terrilli was a respected member of a community where such an attitude is achieved by making exactly the right contributions to the charity functions staged at the Breakers Hotel, financing a cultural week at the music auditorium, presenting a Modigliani to the Norton Gallery of Art, and actively serving on the committee of the Palm Beach Round Table and attending every event put on by them at the Paramount Theater.

There was further respect in that Giuseppe Terrilli chose to be an all-year resident and not one of those who took off for the summer, when the climate and humidity became somewhat bothersome to those who had money to guarantee their every comfort. There was an obvious reason, of course. All of Terrilli Industries was based in and around the state.

The construction division responsible for so much real estate development—and for the built-at-cost school for underprivileged children that he had so modestly declined to have named after him—was less than an hour away at Fort Lauderdale. The air charter and transport fleet was even nearer, at Palm Beach International Airport, and from there it was little more than an hour to the excellent airport at Tampa. On the Gulf Coast, where the ports are geared for freight work, there was the sea division, with a fleet of container vessels moving throughout the South American countries and using the easy access to the Panama Canal to work the West Coast and the Far East.

Terrilli involved himself just sufficiently in civic affairs but at the same time managed to remain a private, unostentatious man. To some in Palm Beach, the house seemed strangely out of character. But it was an oddness that didn't trouble them for long: Moguls are allowed their eccentricities, and apart from the house, Terrilli was the most conservative of men. No one remembered being told his age, but it was guessed at around fifty, and if there was talk at all now that he was completely assimilated within the enclosed community, it was at coffee mornings or whist functions at which still disappointed women sometimes wondered why such an attractive, courtly man remained unmarried.

There had been a wife. There were some who could remember her, a diminutive blonde already showing the eaten-away signs of the illness from which she had died five years before and bearing little resemblance to the vibrant, almost glittering woman whose photograph was so prominently displayed in the unusual home. After a respectable period had been allowed to elapse, so there would be no intrusion into his mourning, there had been a flurry of invitations. At the affairs for which he had accepted, Terrilli had been courteous but reserved, never once hurting the feelings of the women whom he gently rejected, always making it seem that the reluctance was belatedly theirs rather than his own.

Now, after so long, the regret had almost left the voices of those who gossiped. There was a romance about the man's decision to remain faithful to the memory of one woman, sad though it may have been for those who had so briefly hoped.

A basement gymnasium had been another improvement Terrilli had made to the castle, and use of that, together with his fairly frequent appearances on the Breakers and sometimes the Everglades links, accounted for his slim, lean figure. In a climate of constant sunlight, which encouraged brightness, his dress was always subdued, rarely going beyond gray or black, which tended to heighten the side-grayness of his hair already brought out by the deep, year-round tan. His car was a Rolls-Royce, of course, but without the blackened windows favored by some but which looked theatrical. When Giuseppe Terrilli was chauffeured around the tiny island, he was plainly visible, head usually bent over the market section of *The Wall Street Journal*.

There were many things about Terrilli of which the admirers in Palm Beach were entirely ignorant. They didn't know, for instance, of the stamp collection housed in a vaultlike room, very near the gymnasium but insulated from it, so that the temperature remained a constant, undamaging sixty-eight degrees.

Or that such was the intensity of the man's interest that there was never a day when Terrilli did not spend at least two hours hunched, oblivious to everything but the tiny squares of paper before him, in his subterranean chamber.

Such a natural hobby would have caused little surprise in

a community where an eighty-year-old millionairess collected piranha fish and another kept an alligator tank in her bedroom.

But they would have been truly amazed to know that Giuseppe Terrilli was one of the top five Mafia figures in the United States of America.

Increasingly Warburger was coming to regret his decision to concentrate on Senator Kelvin Cosgrove and his aspirations to become Attorney General and leave the final personnel selection to his deputy. Peter Bowler appeared to think the entrapment of Terrilli would be simple, after so much advanced planning.

"Jack Pendlebury!" echoed the Director. "Oh, come on!"

"He's one of the best operators we've got," persisted Bowler. "And that's what we need more than anything else because of the low profile we'll have to keep. He's damned efficient, he's devious, and he comes from Texas."

"Cosgrove hasn't said he wants anyone from his home state."

"It wouldn't hurt, surely?"

"He hasn't seen Pendlebury," insisted Warburger. He tried to think of objections beyond those he had already made.

"He cheats on his expenses, too," he added in sudden recollection.

"Cosgrove and Pendlebury won't have to live in each other's pockets all the time," said Bowler. "And he's no worse than some others I've known with his expenses."

"There'll have to be some contact. And Cosgrove won't like it. There must be *somebody* else," said the Director.

"I've run the check through the computer, taking us back as far as eight years. Pendlebury is the only supervisor whose operational life has kept him far enough away to reduce the risk of his being identified."

"The only way Pendlebury is likely to be identified is for vagrancy," said Warburger.

"He's exactly right," argued Bowler. "If you notice him at all, it's out of pity."

"I don't like it," said Warburger stubbornly. "The man makes me uneasy."

"I'm made far more uneasy at the thought of the whole thing going down the tube from something as simple as one of our people being spotted. Let's not forget how organized these people are."

Warburger nodded at the remark, recognizing its truth. The Director was a man who believed in statistics, and the statistics were unarguable that for years now, crime was paying. That's why this one single operation was important; the tremor it would send right down through the structure of organized crime would register about 9 on the Richter scale.

"I want it cleared with the senator, so there'll be no offense," warned the Director reluctantly. "And if he agrees—and only if he agrees—I want Pendlebury briefed so thoroughly he'll think he's being programmed to be Pope."

"Of course."

"And try to see he smartens himself up a bit. He's like a mobile slum."

"I'll try," promised Bowler without conviction.

"Tell him something else, too."

"What?"

"He'll realize how important this is. He's a cunning bastard. Make it clear the petty cash isn't limitless. I'll want receipts for everything . . . in handwriting other than his own."

At that moment, the subject of their conversation was in Tijuana, in the sort of bar that tourists shun, because there is never an attempt to clear the cockroaches from the toilets or even put in paper towels, because the water doesn't work anyway. He was sitting forward on the stool attentively watching the barman mix the margarita, widening the gap between his thumb and forefinger to indicate the amount of tequila he wanted. Pendlebury had declared the first to be like mosquito piss and knew the barman was annoyed and would try to cheat on the measure.

The taco came as the drink arrived. Pendlebury heaped the relish on top of the beef, heavy with the chili and the onions, and as he lifted the envelope to his mouth, a mixture of ketchup and mustard fell away, ricocheted off the lapel of his crumpled fawn suit, and then spread itself in a splash over the left leg of his trousers.

"Shit," said Pendlebury.

He paused for a moment, examining the deepening stain, then went back to his food. They were the best tacos in Tijuana and better eaten hot: He could always try to scrape the stain off with a knife after he had finished.

"Drink better this time?" asked the barman, at last recognizing that Pendlebury wasn't an amateur.

"Great."

"Ready for another?"

"Why not?" said Pendlebury. It would be far too hot to walk about outside for another hour, at least. Maybe even two.

"And I'll want a copy of the bill," he added. "Several, in fact."

CHAPTER 3

JACK PENDLEBURY had tried to formulate all the alternatives but had decided, with a regret which came as something of a surprise, that he had been recalled to Washington to be dumped. Sure, there were things that didn't add up, like why bother to bring him to the Capital when it would have been as easy to sack him on station, with one of those letters that looked as if it had been signed by the Director but came in fact from a machine that could perfectly create a facsimile of the man's signature. But sometimes they did inexplicable, illogical things. Perhaps it had been decided to make an example of him. Belying the overfed, country-boy appearance which was rightfully his, because he had been born and raised on a Tennessee homestead, Jack Pendlebury was an astute man. A lot of people went so far as to say a smart ass. And he had known for a long time that he didn't fit a department in which men were expected to have button-down minds with their button-down shirts, following procedures as if the job they did was a game, which had rules. People who made their own rules were suspect.

Betty wouldn't be sorry, he knew. She'd worry about where the money would come from, of course; she was very conscious of money. But she had never liked the job. She had been frightened he might get hurt, never quite believing that he'd only ever fired his gun on the practice ranges, when the regulations demanded it, and that on the three occasions in his operational life when someone had fired at him, he'd kept as flat as hell, letting everyone else do their John Wayne impressions. It was still nice to have a wife who thought he was brave, though.

The security guard held him at the front desk, as if he did not believe the green identity card he produced, calling up to Bowler's office to confirm that Pendlebury was expected and even then seeming reluctant to accept that he was an employee of the Bureau.

"Where's the washroom?" asked Pendlebury.

The man nodded further into the building. "First past the elevators."

Pendlebury went toward it, still feeling the uncomfortable wetness near his crotch. If it hadn't been for that damned bloody mary, he'd have looked quite presentable. He'd had the suit cleaned and sat all the way from Houston with his jacket off, so it wouldn't get creased. They had actually been circling Dulles Airport when the stupid bastard in front had put his seat back and Pendlebury had got the drink in his lap. Hadn't even had time to taste it, which was another cause for regret. With more room than he had had in the aircraft toilet, Pendlebury tried to sponge away the stain, but the dampened paper towel began to disintegrate, shedding itself over his trousers. Sighing, he picked the bits off as quickly as he could, aware that the deputy would be wondering where he was.

There was a further check, on the top floor, and Bowler was standing impatiently just inside his office when Pendlebury entered.

"The Director's *waiting!*" he said. He made it sound as if they were late helping Moses down with the tablets.

"Sorry," said Pendlebury. Warburger wouldn't *personally* fire him. What the hell was it, then?

"I've gone in to bat for you on this one," said Bowler as they hurried along the corridor.

"What?" demanded Pendlebury. Bowler didn't know him, any more than Warburger did. Whatever support Bowler had provided, it had been for his own advancement. He thought the man's use of the baseball metaphor was juvenile, too. He wondered if it had anything to do with his peculiar name.

"Director wants to tell you himself," said the other man. "For God's sake, don't foul it up. What happened to your suit?"

"Something spilled on the plane."

"Thought you might have had time to buy another one," said Bowler, and Pendlebury stared at him in amazement, aware the man was completely serious.

"Don't have any weddings or funerals coming up," he said.

Bowler entered the Director's office ahead of him, shaking his head as if in some personal sorrow.

Warburger was standing, just as his deputy had been. There was only the slightest pause, as if the gesture might be forced, and then he came forward, offering his hand. Pendlebury took it with cautious curiosity.

"Good to see you again, Jack," greeted the Director, who had never met him before.

"Thank you, sir," said Pendlebury. He was conscious of the other man's examination and the slight twinge of distaste at the wetness around his groin. He wondered if the man suspected him of peeing himself.

Warburger held back from asking, instead leading Pendlebury to a seat near his desk. Bowler was already waiting, near a chair which Pendlebury assumed was his by custom.

"Got a big one for you," announced Warburger, back in his own executive chair, but leaning forward from it urgently. "The biggest."

Pendlebury decided Warburger would always talk with intense enthusiasm, in the hope those whom he was addressing would become infected by the feeling and work the better for it.

Warburger seemed to expect some response, but Pendlebury couldn't think of anything to say. Finally the Director continued: "What did you think of those Chicago auctions?"

"Brilliant," said Pendlebury honestly. He had never been able to understand how the second one had worked so well, after so many criminals, a lot with provable Mafia connections, had been scooped up in the first phony warehouse sale of stolen goods that the FBI had staged. Greed, he supposed. Often Pendlebury thought that psychiatrists and psychologists were wrong and that greed superseded sex or hunger as man's primary motivation.

Warburger smiled, pleased with the assessment. "We're going to put on another one," he said. "Just for one man. We're going to get Giuseppe Terrilli."

"You've got to be joking!" said Pendlebury, aware the moment he spoke that he'd lost the goodwill earned by his previous praise of the auction idea.

"There's nothing funny about this," declared Warburger earnestly. "I've created a situation that I know will get him and you're going to be the one to make it work. And let me tell you something else . . . something I never want you for a moment to forget. There's *more* in this than just catching Terrilli."

"What?" demanded Pendlebury, cutting the Director off at what appeared the beginning of a speech.

Warburger paused, frowning at the intrusion.

"Politics," he said. "If this goes as I intend, this Bureau is going to have Capitol Hill protection for years."

Pendlebury sat regarding the Director warily. The crotch of his trousers was drying, the cloth becoming like stiff cardboard.

"How's that?" said Pendlebury.

"We needed a front . . . something that Terrilli would never suspect. The exhibition that is to trap Terrilli is being staged in aid of a children's charity. And the organizer is Senator Kelvin Cosgrove."

"He's an asshole," said Pendlebury, aware of the Director's immediate wince and regretting the outburst.

"He's a powerful politician who stands a very good chance of becoming Attorney General. And this operation is going to get him the appointment," said Warburger.

"He's media happy," warned Pendlebury. "He'd blow it."

"No," argued Warburger. "Not this time. He knows the advantages will come when it's all over. He'll do nothing to foul it up. It's as important to him as it is to us."

"He'll not want any part in the actual operation?"

"Absolutely not," said Bowler. "He'll be kept fully briefed on what's happening, of course. But he wants no public acknowledgment for what happens until *after* Terrilli's arrest."

"Which he will get unstintingly," added Warburger.

"And for which the Bureau will receive his heartfelt gratitude and support throughout the duration of his office, if he's appointed," predicted Pendlebury.

"Exactly," confirmed the Director. "How's that for neatness?"

"Why me?" asked Pendlebury, more interested in his own safety than in flattering the Director. There would be at least a hundred other operatives at supervisor level whom he knew, quite realistically, Warburger and Bowler would prefer. He wondered if they'd tell him the truth or try to bullshit him.

"Because you're the one the computer came up with," said Bowler. "We cross-checked at your rank against any involvement whatsoever which might have made them known to Terrilli or his people. He's got an organization almost as efficient as ours and he's survived so long by properly using it. There's nothing you could have done for them to have a file on you. . . ."

Bowler trailed away and Warburger came in, as if they had rehearsed: ". . . and we've been impressed by your file. Very few failures."

"Thank you," said Pendlebury.

"And we don't want any failures on this," warned Warburger. "Get this right and we'll all be on guaranteed pensions."

"Or our widows will be," said Pendlebury pointedly.

"Precisely," said Warburger, careless of Pendlebury's reminder of who would be exposed to the danger. "Like I said, no mistakes."

"Terrilli's a don, right?" said Pendlebury. He hoped the honesty would continue.

"A favorite to become *capo di tutti capi*," confirmed Warburger. "And he's qualified to be the boss of bosses. He's certainly the best example of how organized crime has covered itself with squeaky-clean enterprises. Those front businesses of his gross a legitimate seventy million dollars a year."

"Why be crooked?" said Pendlebury, attempting some lightness.

Warburger misunderstood, snorting at the fat man's naïveté.

"Every week of every year, approximately ten boats leave ports in South America, predominantly Colombia, and each is carrying an average of six million dollars of dope. They get off the Grand Bahamian Banks or around Cuba and then peel off, one by one, doing a chicken run for the coast of Florida. Those that get past the coast guards are a bonus. They've all got radio equipment aboard that could monitor a shot to Mars. As soon as one gets arrested, those still waiting offshore know. And so when the coast guard boat goes in as an escort, those unarrested follow at a safe distance. While that one illicit cargo is being counted in Miami, the rest is being landed somewhere along the coast."

"That's about twenty-five billion a year!" said Pendlebury disbelievingly.

"And that's before it's adulterated for street use," agreed Warburger. "Terrilli's aircraft check the position of the coast guard vessels and he's got radio equipment around the coastline, all with some legitimate function, listening to all coast guard and customs radio traffic."

"Jesus!" said Pendlebury.

"And He'll be the only one I can't guarantee will be helping you," said Warburger, making his own heavy attempt at a joke.

"Do what?" prompted Pendlebury. "What sort of exhibition is it?"

The Director paused, looking down at the thick file before him. He had a satisfied smile on his face when he looked up.

"There's always a weakness," he said, refusing to be hurried. "With some it's sex. Others booze. Or drugs. Always something . . ."

The smile widened.

". . . Terrilli is so successful because he *hasn't* got any weaknesses. Not something that can be turned and used against him. But he's got a hobby. It took us a long time to discover it and even longer to establish how fanatical he is about it. But that's exactly what he is: fanatical."

"About what!" The Director's theatricality was annoying Pendlebury.

"Stamps," said Warburger simply. "In Palm Beach he's got a home that's built like and looks like a fortress. And somewhere inside, he's got a fantastic stamp collection."

Pendlebury frowned. "I don't appreciate how that gives us any edge."

"Neither did we, not at first. Not until we realized his addiction to it. We let some stamps be stolen and we put a trace on them, through dealer to dealer. And guess who was the eager buyer?"

"Terrilli."

Warburger nodded. "He's not interested in showing off, which is another reason why he's so high in the organization. The Mafia have always respected modesty. The stamps are entirely for his own enjoyment, something he can sit over and know no one else in the world possesses. And because no one else will ever see them, he can have as many stolen items as he likes, just so long as it goes on building up his collection."

"Why don't we tell the police, so they can get a warrant and bust him for what he's got so far?"

"We don't know how much of the local justice department he's got working for him," said Bowler. "And that's almost immaterial anyway. There'd be a leak, long before it got to the warrant stage. By the time anyone penetrated that funny castle, the collection would be as clean as my eleven-year-old son's. It's got to be independent of the local police."

"What's the bait?"

"Nearly all the collection that Tsar Nicholas of Russia had created, five years before his death. It was broken up years ago. But we've managed to get a lot of it back together and we've filled the gaps from a collection assembled by the man who organized the Tsar's folios. Terrilli will never be able to resist it," said Warburger.

Pendlebury looked doubtful. "Wouldn't someone as careful as Terrilli check how it suddenly came to be on show?"

"We don't think so," said Warburger. "It's his religion and people don't usually question their gods. And Cosgrove and his charity would withstand any scrutiny."

"What do I do?"

"Let it be stolen," said Warburger. "I don't want any half-assed security hero discovering locks taped open and imagining another Watergate. You're going in as a Pinkerton's man, with overall responsibility. It's got to look good . . . in fact, it's got to *be* good. Terrilli's people won't come in with panty hose over their heads and stolen cars at the curb, even if they don't suspect a setup. They'll check and they'll check and they'll check again and before they do anything, they'll want to be one hundred and one percent sure everything is kosher."

"I'll have no backup?"

"Not actually attached to the exhibition. Cosgrove will be in attendance at all times, for the public recognition afterward. But I promise he won't interfere. So you're by yourself. No matter how we tried to disguise it, they'd spot a squad if we put one in. But you'll have an army outside. The moment that collection or any part of it gets lifted you blow the whistle and they'll be with you, covering you every step of the way."

"And we hit Terrilli's house the moment it's inside?"

Warburger nodded. "We got Capone for income tax evasion and we'll get Terrilli for stealing stamps."

"What happens if you're wrong?" demanded Pendlebury suddenly.

"Wrong?"

"What happens if Terrilli doesn't make a move? Or does and for some reason we haven't considered, gets away with it?"

"If Terrilli does nothing," lectured Warburger patiently, "then a kid's charity gets a few thousand dollars it wouldn't otherwise have received. I don't accept that there's anything that we haven't considered, but if the stamps go and we lose them, then they're insured."

"There's always the unexpected," said Pendlebury professionally. "No matter how much planning or rehearsal, there's always something that threatens to screw it up."

As Pendlebury spoke, three and a half thousand miles away Charlie Muffin was walking into the City office of Rupert Willoughby.

He was such an unprepossessing man, thought the underwriter.

Charlie shook his head positively. "I'm not interested."

"Why not?"

"It's not a job . . . not a proper one, anyway. Something for a caretaker."

"The security of three million pounds' worth of stamps is hardly something for a caretaker," argued Willoughby.

"There'll be security," pointed out Charlie.

"Of course," accepted the underwriter. "We've insisted upon that, before agreeing to any sort of cover. But it's still an unusual situation. I'd feel happier if you were there."

"And it's Russian," reminded Charlie.

"Not anymore. The collections have been in Western ownership for years. What interest would they still have?"

Charlie shook his head again. "Never underestimate the Russian national pride. They'll be interested."

"Surely you don't expect them to put in observers."

"They might."

"But what harm would it do? You wrecked your own department and the American service, not the Russians."

Charlie smiled at the other man's innocence of the world in which he had existed—sometimes only just—all his life. He found it easy to envy Rupert Willoughby.

"I don't want *anyone* to find me," said Charlie.

"I think you're exaggerating the risk," accused Willoughby.

"Perhaps," admitted Charlie. The dangers weren't as great as he was attempting to make them, despite what had happened in Hong Kong. He frowned in sudden awareness. He was raising objections because he felt it was expected, not because he sincerely felt them.

"I'm asking you as a personal favor to me," said the underwriter, choosing the strongest lever to impose upon Charlie. "And because I know of your association with my father . . . how much he admired you."

"It'll be a waste of time," said Charlie, conscious of the weakness in his voice.

"I thought your complaint was that you had too much of that to waste anyway."

It would be activity, conceded Charlie. And he *was* bored. Anything occurring within America came under the jurisdiction of the FBI, not the Central Intelligence Agency. So the danger would be far less than it had been in Hong Kong.

"All I'm suggesting is a month in America, three weeks of that in the sunshine of Florida," encouraged the underwriter.

"What's Florida got apart from Disney World, oranges, and vacationing Jewish mothers worrying about their sons becoming doctors?" demanded Charlie.

"You never know," said Willoughby, relieved. Charlie was going to accept, Willoughby recognized. He was glad he had warned the organizers that he would be sending a representative.

CHAPTER 4

THE STOMACH tightening came at the passport check, even though Charlie knew the certificate with which it had been obtained was where the danger had existed and not now, with the document itself, which was as genuine as the visa that accompanied it. He wasn't unhappy at the apprehension. It showed he was properly cautious, which was how he was going to have to continue throughout the entire assignment. Properly cautious, despite his agreement with Willoughby that there was little risk. He'd been persuaded too easily, he realized belatedly. Why? Had it been boredom? The conceit about which Edith had constantly warned him? Or the closely connected flattery at being asked again for help by someone like Rupert Willoughby?

It had been eight years since the deception that cost the CIA its Director. If they discovered he was still alive, they would be as keen to get him now as they had been in those early years, when they pursued him throughout Europe. It would only take one mistake: like the error of going to Sir Archibald Willoughby's grave that they had observed so carefully, waiting for just such a slip. Charlie was uncertain if, during the past eight years, he had retained the expertise that had enabled him to survive so successfully in the past.

The immigration official flicked dutifully through the black-bound prohibited aliens' book by his left hand, stamped the passport, gave a quick, professional smile, and gestured him through to reclaim his baggage.

There was the usual delay, so it was a further hour before Charlie cleared the airport complex and settled back for the drive along the Van Wyck Expressway into Manhattan. The driver was a dour, taciturn man, which suited Charlie, who didn't want conversation anyway.

Although the exhibition was being staged at the Waldorf-Astoria, Willoughby's office had made him reservations at the Pierre. Charlie hurried through his registration, not feeling any

27

jet lag and anxious to examine the security precautions as soon as possible. He smiled, recognizing another link with his past. It had always been like this, once an assignment had begun. Sir Archibald had even worried about it, in the early days, concerned that in his eagerness to become involved, Charlie might miss something. He rarely had, though.

He telephoned from his room, so that the Pinkerton's official, Michael Heppert, was waiting for him when he arrived at the exhibition hall. Heppert was a slightly built, nervous man, eyes blinking rapidly behind the sort of thick-framed spectacles that opticians recommend as showing executive character. The man spoke in a constant hurry, starting each sentence with an intake of breath and hoping it would last with the outrush of words, and had the habit, which Charlie found mildly disconcerting, of reaching out and holding on to the person he was addressing, physically to hold their attention.

From the pride in the man's tour, it was obvious that Heppert had personally devised the security; he was like a teenager showing off a complicated model railway system the operation of which only he knew how to manage to avoid the engines derailing.

Charlie dated his suspicion of routine to his National Service, with war games staged to show the Russians just how prepared against attack the West was; men with red armbands running around straight-faced and calling their mates in green armbands the enemy. He conceded the basic purpose of such exercises, of course, training people how to move tanks and equipment and men about. But like a complicated dance which looked effective once you'd got the steps right, it worked because people learned a pattern and then always conformed to it. And the danger of conforming to routine or categories or patterns was that, like the dancing lessons or model railways, things always went from A to B to C in an undisturbed logic. Charlie couldn't dance and had never collected train numbers. And in the world in which he had lived for such a long time, men didn't wear armbands to identify themselves as the bad guys, any more than they obeyed rules so that everyone would know what everyone else was doing.

The rigidity of the security pattern for the stamp exhibition immediately disturbed him, long before he isolated something that didn't make sense. He waited for Heppert to remark upon it, but the man said nothing and so Charlie didn't openly ask why the video tape cameras that were to record everything that occurred in the exhibition had been installed in duplicate in such a manner as they had.

"Good?" queried Heppert at the end of the tour.

"Adequate," said Charlie.

"We hope more than that."

Charlie turned at the carefully modulated voice. The newcomer was a tall, carefully tailored and coiffured man, the white hair purposely worn long and with the upright yet slightly languid stance he guessed the man felt necessary for the patrician appearance for which he was obviously striving.

"Senator Kelvin Cosgrove," introduced Heppert with hurried servility. "Originator of the exhibition and chairman of the organizing committee . . ."

He turned to the politician.

". . . the representative of Lloyds of London," he said, completing the introduction.

"We've been expecting you," said Cosgrove with just the faintest trace of disappointment. Charlie withstood the senator's examination, feeling like an undernourished African arrival at the cotton plantation. At least the man managed to hold back from feeling his muscles or examining his teeth.

"Satisfied?" demanded the man. His voice clearly indicated Charlie's subservient role: someone who had to be tolerated but accorded only the minimum of attention.

"Seems all right," he said, conscious of Heppert's wince. The man would have ulcers, Charlie knew.

Cosgrove turned, and until he did so Charlie was unaware of another man, standing in the shadow of the doorway.

"Our insurers seem only moderately impressed," said Cosgrove condescendingly.

Heppert's customary unease seemed to increase as the third man moved further into the room.

"Our overall security controller," he said, continuing the introductions. "Mr. Jack Pendlebury."

"I haven't noticed any accreditation from you," said the man abruptly.

"No," agreed Charlie, refusing the attempt at intimidation. "Why don't you ask for it?"

Pendlebury's face stiffened and there was an almost im-

perceptible glance toward the politician, as if the man were
worried at being so openly confronted.

"May I see it?"

"Of course," said Charlie, the smile purposely wide.

Charlie offered his authority from Willoughby's firm,
watching as Pendlebury studied the papers. Pendlebury's hand
had the very slightest twitch and the skin around his eyes was
pinched. Not by the concentration of reading, but by pain,
Charlie guessed. He got the confirmation when Pendlebury
looked up at him and Charlie saw the red-veined eyes. The
man had a hangover.

"Passport," demanded Pendlebury.

Charlie recognized the man's attempt at recovery. He groped
through his pockets, appearing unable immediately to locate
it, and just when Cosgrove began moving impatiently, produced the document for Pendlebury to compare the picture it
contained with that affixed to Willoughby's authorized identity
card.

"There was a letter, sent in advance," reminded Charlie.
"To both you and the organizers."

"Yes," said Pendlebury.

"With a photograph," added Charlie.

Pendlebury felt into the rear pocket of his trousers and came
out with his hand bunched around a wad of papers. Some of
the letters and notes must have been weeks old, to judge from
the tattered, blackened edges. With what appeared surprise he
discovered a five-dollar bill, face losing its tenseness for the
first time, and then located the photograph he was seeking.

"Got it here," he said. Pendlebury waited, but when Charlie
said nothing, went on: "I guess you'll do. Seen the security?"

"A quick tour," said Charlie.

Pendlebury turned, including Cosgrove in the conversation.
"And you're happy?"

"I didn't say that," qualified Charlie. "It's impossible to
guarantee security for an exhibition held in a hotel."

He was aware of Heppert and the senator looking at him
sharply, as if he were being offensive, but Pendlebury smiled
again. It was a faint expression, as if the effort hurt.

"Right," agreed Pendlebury.

"It would need a clever man to steal anything from here,"
insisted Cosgrove defensively.

"That's what successful crooks are, clever," said Pendlebury, and Charlie warmed to the man, conscious that the senator was being patronized.

"At least it's only here for a week," said Charlie.

"But in Florida for three," said Pendlebury. "Lots of time for a clever man to make some detailed plans. We're going to have to watch ourselves."

"We've had enough rehearsals, both here and in Palm Beach," said Heppert. "In Florida we achieved complete security cover five minutes after a full-scale alert, when none of the guards were expecting it."

"That's right," said Pendlebury. "And everything went like a dream. Civil police backup came in ten minutes."

Charlie recognized that now Pendlebury was patronizing the other Pinkerton's man. Heppert didn't appear to realize it.

"Is there anything you'd like to discuss with me?" said Cosgrove to Charlie. The tone of voice indicated that the time allowed for Charlie's audience had expired.

"I don't think so," said Charlie. The senator was the sort of man who would like to be called "sir," Charlie knew, purposely avoiding the courtesy. He was fleetingly reminded of the men who had taken over the department from Willoughby's father and plotted his death. They'd been irritated by his lack of politeness, too.

"I'll be in Florida as well as here," said the man graciously. "Always available if you need me."

"Thank you," said Charlie. "I'll remember that."

The small group stood watching the senator stride regally away, and when Pendlebury turned back, Charlie saw he was smiling contemptuously. The man avoided any open criticism.

"Suppose we're going to be together for a while?" said Pendlebury, as if the awareness had only just come to him.

"Yes," said Charlie.

"So we should get to know each other?"

"Might be an idea."

Pendlebury looked across the foyer to the Sir Harry bar. "Drink?"

"Fine," accepted Charlie. For a man who looked as bad as Pendlebury to go so early to a bar indicated either an act of supreme courage or someone long accustomed to booze.

"Coming?" Pendlebury asked the other Pinkerton's man.

Heppert put his hand to his stomach, confirming Charlie's thought about ulcers.

"Bad stomach," he refused. "Maybe another time."

Pendlebury turned without attempting any persuasion, leading the way, and Charlie became completely aware of the other man's appearance. The trousers were quite shapeless and the jacket hung oddly backward off his shoulders, as if it were trying to escape the embarrassment. From behind, Pendlebury looked like a very old elephant on his way to wherever it is elephants go to die. As he passed the jewelers' window, Charlie caught sight of himself in the window reflection and saw there was a self-satisfied smirk on his face. He frowned, recognizing it as unjustified. He recognized something else, too. He could have been the second elephant in the line. It was easy to understand the disappointment of Senator Cosgrove, who would believe a man was as sharp as the crease in his trousers.

Pendlebury ignored the stools at the big center bar, choosing instead one of the side tables with the large armchairs. Because it was still before noon, the bar was comparatively empty and a girl came to them almost immediately.

"Vodka," ordered Pendlebury. "Large, just ice."

"Scotch," said Charlie. "With water.

"Read somewhere that vodka is good for avoiding hangovers," said Charlie. Even accepting Pendlebury's responsibility, the behavior at the initial meeting had surprised him. He wondered why Pendlebury found it necessary to be hostile to everyone.

"Don't put your faith in it," said Pendlebury with feeling.

"I don't. Any more than I do in rehearsing against robberies."

Charlie detected Pendlebury's instant interest and regretted the remark. It hinted at an expertise of which he didn't particularly want the other man to be aware and was therefore careless, like smiling in jewelers' windows. For the moment, he had decided to let them imagine he was content with the protection.

"Tells people where to go if anything happens," said Pendlebury, and Charlie was aware he was being encouraged.

"Yes," he agreed guardedly. "Useful for that."

The drinks came and Charlie waited, watching. Pendlebury took up his glass but didn't drink.

"Worried?" asked Charlie.

Pendlebury shrugged. "Like you said, you can't guarantee complete security in a hotel. Certainly not one this size, with so many people having the right of access."

He grinned at a sudden thought.

"I'd be more worried if I were you. Six million dollars is a lot of money to risk losing," he added.

"That's what insurance is, risk," said Charlie.

"Been at it long?"

Charlie felt the stomach tightening again. "Fair time," he said guardedly.

"Must be interesting."

It had to be the stock remark whenever two men sat in a bar and talked about their jobs. Yet from Pendlebury it seemed to have more point. Charlie wondered of whom the man reminded him.

"Something like yours," he said easily.

"Not really," dismissed Pendlebury. "Jesse James and his gang are dead."

"Why Florida?" demanded Charlie suddenly.

"Florida?"

"Why put on such an exhibition as this in Florida?" said Charlie. "I would have thought there were a hundred other cities, rather than Palm Beach, where these things would have had more appeal."

"You're probably right," agreed Pendlebury. "My job is to guard them, not say where they should go. Lot of money in Palm Beach. And people with time to spend it. I guess Cosgrove thought he'd get the best response there."

"What's Cosgrove like?"

Pendlebury shrugged. "Professional politician. Millionaire from his father's stock market expertise. Very ambitious. Wife about fifteen years younger, who is always in the magazines and social columns. . . ."

"Do you like him?"

"I haven't got to."

"So you don't?"

"His cologne is too strong."

Charlie smiled at the assessment. "Is the Breakers better than this?"

"About the same, security-wise," said Pendlebury. "Best

hotel in Palm Beach, site of all the exhibitions. We've installed extra electrical precautions, of course."

"Duplicated, like here?"

Charlie was looking intently at the other man, alert for his reaction. Pendlebury's mottled face remained unchanged.

"Common sense," he said. "A backup, in case one camera system malfunctions."

"Of course," said Charlie quickly. Seeming eager to cover his embarrassment at an apparently thoughtless question, he indicated the elaborately produced color catalog which he had carried from the exhibition room into the bar.

"Difficult to imagine these little squares of paper having such value, isn't it?" he said.

"Not really," said Pendlebury. He nodded toward the unseen exit from the hotel and Park Avenue beyond. "Take a cab to Eighty-second Street and you could probably find a Greek pisspot in the Metropolitan Museum of Art described as priceless."

Charlie saw that before starting it, Pendlebury had allowed a substantial quantity of ice to melt, diluting his drink. And that his own glass was empty. The American signaled refills from the attentive waitress.

"Cheers," he said, lifting his glass. It was the original, with all the melted ice.

"Cheers," responded Charlie. Perhaps the man was just a slow drinker. He looked again at the bloodshot eyes; then again, perhaps he was not.

The waitress lingered. "How do you want to pay?" she asked. She seemed to recognize Pendlebury.

"Charge it to the suite, like before . . ." he said, turning from the girl to Charlie.

". . . Got a suite here," he said needlessly. "It's very comfortable."

"Expensive, too."

"Yeah, that as well," agreed Pendlebury. He smiled, as if offering an intimacy. "Glad I'm not paying."

"I'm not keen on these publicity receptions that are announced on the program," said Charlie.

"Organizers consider them worthwhile."

"I don't."

"It would certainly provide the chance for anyone wanting to discover the layout," admitted Pendlebury.

"Perhaps we're being overcautious," said Charlie.

For several moments Pendlebury did not reply, studying Charlie. Then he said: "Which is better than being too casual."

"I'm never that," said Charlie.

"Nor am I," said Pendlebury, and Charlie believed him.

Giuseppe Terrilli's study was on the east of the castle, where the original chateau design had been modified to give a big-window view of the Atlantic. Normally he enjoyed the outlook, frequently swiveling in his chair to stare over it, while discussing some point with the two men who ran the nonpublic part of his operations and whom he knew to be informants to the inner council on everything that he did.

It was because of that awareness that today Terrilli ignored the sea, concentrating upon the figures before him, asking exactly the right questions and isolating exactly the right weaknesses, wanting to impress them with the efficiency that he knew had made him a near legend within the organization. They could never know how close he had come to making a ridiculous mistake. But he knew and the knowledge frightened him. It would have shown a weakness of which Giuseppe Terrilli had always felt he was incapable. For the first time in fifteen years, he had considered canceling the weekly review of the forthcoming shipments and of the distribution of that which had been landed during the preceding week, because he had feared he would be late in New York for a preview of the Romanov Collection.

"It's been a good fortnight," assessed Tony Santano. "Not one interception."

In an earlier era or a different location, Anthony Santano would have had the nickname "Big Tony," with his 6' 4" frame and build like a boxer. But Terrilli forbade the theatricality of New York; the organization there seemed to believe that Damon Runyon was still alive and eating nightly at Sardi's.

"Which means a twenty million three quarters profit," said the third man, John Patridge, a thin, bespectacled aesthetic scion of a New England family going back almost two centuries, a graduate from the Harvard Business School and with a genius for figures that would have earned him a fortune in

Wall Street had the organization not paid him more to keep their books in perfect order. He had been put into Florida by men never surprised at the fickleness of human behavior, to guard against any sudden omission by Terrilli to make full account of the activities for which the man was responsible. Wrongly to report one boat as being seized and placing its cargo on the streets in a private deal could mean a profit, after cutting it down, of $9,500,000, and that was a considerable amount of money, even in the cosmic amounts in which they dealt.

"It's going very well," said Terrilli. He was always careful never to appear too enthusiastic, because his was the planning and the forethought which made everything so successful, and thus enthusiasm might indicate conceit.

"Because it's so well organized," praised Patridge, always the more sycophantic of the two.

"If there's no other business," cut off Terrilli, "I have an appointment."

The accountant and Santano looked up, curious at the abruptness.

"I'm going to New York," added Terrilli.

"Business?" asked Santano, irritated that he had not been either warned or consulted.

"Yes," said Terrilli. "I'm going to look at some stamps, too. Be away for a couple of days."

The Terrilli Industries executive jet was making its arrival down the slip runway to the private section of La Guardia Airport by the time Charlie Muffin got back to his room at the Pierre Hotel in Manhattan. He was a little stiff-legged from the amount of whiskey he had consumed, but otherwise unaffected. He'd paced the third and fourth drinks, so that he and Pendlebury had been level-pegging, and in the end it was the American who had been suffering more. Charlie took off his jacket and then his shoes, lying back upon the bed, carefully moving his toes and examining the feet that seemed to have so much trouble being made comfortable. Pendlebury was a pissy-assed security man, nothing more, he told himself. Why was it, then, that he still felt unsure?

The telephone jarred into the room, making him jump and shattering the reflection.

"Guess who?" said a bright female voice, and for several moments Charlie lay with the telephone in his hand, trying to identify it.

"Who?" he said, defeated.

There was a mew of feigned disappointment.

"Clarissa," said the voice. "Clarissa Willoughby. I could hardly believe my luck when Rupert told me you'd be in New York at the same time."

"You're here?" said Charlie vacuously.

"Of course," she said. "And guess what?"

"What?" said Charlie. She'd love the quiz games with which American television was littered.

"We're staying at the same hotel. I'm just two floors above you. Isn't that terrific!"

"Terrific," agreed Charlie. He wondered if she'd detected the absence of enthusiasm. She would have ensured the hotel reservation, he guessed, realizing why he hadn't been able to stay at the Waldorf.

Suddenly Charlie's mind wasn't on the conversation with the underwriter's wife. He knew why Pendlebury made him uneasy, and the realization increased his uncertainty. Looking at Pendlebury had been like looking at a mirror image of himself.

"Why aren't you talking to me?" complained Clarissa.

"I just had a thought," said Charlie.

"Was it important?"

"I don't know," said Charlie. "I hope not."

CHAPTER 5

CHARLIE STOOD anonymous but carefully positioned against the wall of the exhibition room, reflecting how future anthropologists would categorize the animal functions displayed at twentieth-century cocktail parties and receptions.

The ritualistic behavior was always so similar, whatever the occasion. When he had still been held in esteem by the intelligence service, under the control of Sir Archibald Willoughby, Charlie attended British embassy receptions all over the world.

There had been Queen's birthdays and state independences and national holidays or presidents and premiers wanting to show off, and apart from some fancy uniforms, the occasional un-drinkable local drink, and perhaps a wider smattering of foreign languages, the opening night of the Romanov and Zarrins Col-lections was identical to any of them.

There was the usual crush around the canapés and pursuit of the champagne trays ("the feeding instinct") and a lot of bare female flesh being thrust beneath the appreciative eyes of the males, who, because they were only into their second glass of wine and therefore more inhibited than their ancestors, were feigning disinterest ("the mating instinct").

And then there was Pendlebury and Pendlebury's men and the hotel security people and a contingent from the New York City Police Department and himself. The hunting instinct, he supposed. Looking for the prey.

"Watch the watchers."

Charlie smiled at the recollection of the phrase. It had been one of the earliest dictums from Sir Archibald, who, despite never having operated in the field, knew more about trade craft than any man Charlie had ever encountered. And therefore someone whose advice Charlie respected, despite his dislike of rules.

Charlie decided that just as those embassy occasions could have overlapped upon this, so could something of his previous training. Pendlebury had told him of the police cooperation, which meant the man had been allowed access to the files showing anyone likely to attempt a robbery. So he stood against the wall, watching Pendlebury, who stood in the middle of the room, watching everyone who entered. Charlie saw that Pen-dlebury wasn't drinking. Neither was Charlie. And predictably, neither was he relying entirely upon a rule, even though it had been established by someone whom he had respected so highly. The stamps were displayed in enclosed glass cabinets arranged in a rectangle through the center of the room, and Charlie had positioned himself at the head, so that any activity that took place around the exhibits was as clear to him as any response that might come from Pendlebury.

Charlie estimated there were no more than a hundred people genuinely interested in the stamps. About twenty had produced their philatelic credentials and were now being personally escorted around the stands, each assigned one of Pendlebury's men, with permission to unlock the cases and examine the essays or frames more closely. And quite near him were grouped about five men whom Charlie had identified as White Russian émigrés. They had already made two circuits of the display cases, but in a manner different from the philatelists. They had looked reverently at the stamps, rarely talking to each other, in apparent awe of something which had once belonged to a man they revered. Charlie wondered why none of them was completely intact; two wore eye patches, one moved awkwardly, unbalanced by a missing left arm, and two limped, one obviously supported by a false leg. As Charlie watched, the men took champagne from a passing tray and seemed to assemble in a formal circle, as if an official toast were being drunk. Charlie decided he would have liked to talk to them; they looked as if they had been fucked about a lot, like he had.

The organizing committee, headed by Senator Cosgrove, was near the door. Tonight the man was accompanied by his wife. Sally, remembered Charlie, from the disdainful introduction he'd received thirty minutes earlier. He could easily understand why Clarissa Willoughby and Sally Cosgrove were friends. The American socialite butterflied from person to person and group to group, almost with a professional mannequin's awareness of any passing camera, bestowing greetings and gushing kisses. She'd seemed appalled at the possibility of Charlie appearing with her in any photograph, taking herself from his presence as soon as possible. It had pleased Charlie, for different reasons.

Charlie was aware of Pendlebury moving and became attentive, realizing the man was coming toward him. Pendlebury walked in such a way that the entrance was never obscured from his view; the man was very professional, Charlie decided.

"So far, so good," he said.

"Hardly expected a smash and grab, did you?" said Charlie.

"If this is the sort of interest they can expect, the charity should make a lot of money," predicted Pendlebury.

"The food and drink is free," reminded Charlie.

"Cynical bastard," said Pendlebury, amused. Throughout the conversation, he remained looking at the door.

"Never believed the Seven Dwarfs took Snow White in just to keep house, did you?" said Charlie.

"The senator's enjoying himself," said Pendlebury.

"So's his wife."

"Nice piece of ass," judged Pendlebury. "Used to be a cocktail waitress in Beverly Hills."

"That's what I like about America," said Charlie. "True democracy."

"Take an old-fashioned from her anytime," said Pendlebury

"Doubt if you'd get the offer," said Charlie.

"No," agreed Pendlebury regretfully. "You're probably right."

Momentarily, the American looked into the room, to where a security man was having difficulty closing a display case beside which a philatelist still stood. The lock finally clicked and Pendlebury sighed.

"That's a stupid idea," said Charlie. "The cases shouldn't be opened, in the middle of a function like this."

"Organizers probably felt it necessary."

"I don't," said Charlie. "I want it stopped."

"Organizers won't like it," warned Pendlebury. "Neither will the senator."

"They haven't got to."

There was a sudden flurry by the door and Charlie followed Pendlebury's look. Clarissa Willoughby was arriving, surrounded by a group of people. They all wore evening dress. The woman paused just inside the room, staring around. From a distance, Charlie decided she looked remarkably attractive. She still wore her hair in a bubbled style, which he didn't like, but she had discarded the feather-effect dresses. She wore a simple black tube, supported over her shoulder by just a single strap, the only jewelry a diamond pin on the opposite shoulder. She was big-busted, Charlie saw appreciatively. He'd always been a tit man.

Sally Cosgrove surged forward, arms outstretched, and there was much kissing and hugging, to the accompaniment of camera flashes.

Over the American woman's shoulder, Clarissa Willoughby saw him, and when she had detached herself from the greeting embrace, she waved. Charlie gestured back, wondering why he felt self-conscious.

"You *know* her?" said Pendlebury.

Charlie smiled at the astonishment in the other man's voice.

"Slightly."

"I'd like to know her a lot better than that," said Pendlebury.

"A lot of people do," guessed Charlie.

Led by the senator's wife, Clarissa and her group moved further into the room, making a pretense of interest in the exhibits.

Had Charlie not been following their progress, which brought his head around so that Pendlebury was directly in front of him, he might have missed the other man's reaction. As it was, Charlie was unsure whether there *had* been a change. He had expected a tightening within the man if there were any recognition, but instead Pendlebury seemed very slightly to relax. Charlie turned within seconds of discerning the American's attitude. There were four people in the doorway, apparently arriving separately. There was a masculine-looking woman, in a severe black pantsuit and carrying a long cigarette holder, an immaculately dressed, slightly graying man with a deep suntan, and a couple he presumed to be husband and wife who were immediately recognized by Cosgrove and some of the charity officials just inside the room and snatched further in for greeting.

"Recognize somebody?" demanded Charlie.

Pendlebury shook his head. "Wish I had."

Charlie looked back to the door. The four had moved into the room now and were lost in the crowd.

A waiter passed nearby and Pendlebury gestured with an expertise that came from long hours in barrooms.

"Champagne?" he invited. "French, not Californian."

"Gives me wind," rejected Charlie.

The American sipped his wine, looking directly at Charlie and smiling.

"One glass won't hurt," he said. He was looking beyond Charlie, to the display cases.

"The reception will be over soon," said Charlie. "I can wait."

"Afraid I shan't be able to join you tonight," apologized Pendlebury. "Got an appointment."

Charlie shrugged, not having expected the man's company. He heard familiar voices and turned toward Clarissa Willoughby. She was advancing slightly ahead of her party, smiling.

"Darling!" she cried. "I've been telling everyone what a simply fascinating man you are."

By her side, Sally Cosgrove stood uncertainly, recognizing in a sideways look the pantsuited woman who had been in the group at which Pendlebury appeared to react and waving, welcoming the excuse to leave Clarissa's presence while she spoke to the staff.

"Hello," said Charlie generally.

"Fran, John, Pandora, and Giles," recited Clarissa, sweeping her hand back but not looking at them. "And you've already met Sally. We're all going to the Four Seasons."

"Have fun," said Charlie.

"No, darling. You, too. I want you to come."

"Too busy," refused Charlie.

"Nonsense. It's all going to be over soon. You've no excuse."

Pendlebury had moved away and was watching the performance with an amused smile upon his face.

Clarissa shook her head.

"We're not leaving the room without you," she said in her little-girl-petulant voice. "I *insist*."

Charlie sighed. It had happened before, just like the funny way people looked at him. He'd never enjoyed it, not even the screwing bit, and that hadn't always been the eventual reward.

". . . and we'll call back to the hotel, so you can change," she said, looking down at him.

"I'll go as I am," said Charlie. "It's traditional for jesters to wear peculiar clothes."

There was an aircraft in permanent readiness for him at La Guardia, but Pendlebury was held by traffic on the Triboro Bridge, so it took him almost three hours to reach Washington. Warburger was too excited by what had happened to be annoyed at the delay.

"Well!" he said, repeating the demand of which Bowler had become sickened during the wait. "Well! Is it going to work or isn't it?"

"He came," admitted Pendlebury.

From his desk, the Director took up the copies of photographs which had been taken during the Romanov reception and wired down from New York, ahead of Pendlebury's arrival.

Pendlebury had brought the video film which they had just sat through in its entirety.

"He came!" repeated Warburger. "Just like I said he would. He *wants* it. I can almost *feel* the tingle in his hands, needing to touch them and know they're his."

Pendlebury accepted the offered still pictures. Every one showed Terrilli at some intense stance over a display case.

"That's all he did," said Pendlebury, as if confirmation were necessary. "Just spent an hour going from display to display, hardly ever looking up."

"He's a junkie and we've got the fix," insisted the Director.

"It certainly looks like it," conceded Bowler. "I never expected he would fly all the way from Florida. It clinches it, for me."

"What about the Englishman?" demanded Warburger.

"I think he's smart," said Pendlebury thoughtfully. "Appears not to be, but I think it's an act."

"Is he going to be a problem?" asked Bowler.

Pendlebury hesitated. Then he said: "Not if I handle it carefully enough."

"Don't make a mistake, will you?" said Warburger seriously.

"No," promised Pendlebury.

"If he becomes a nuisance, it could be resolved," said the Director.

"I know," said Pendlebury. "But there's no reason, not yet."

"Let's just keep our options open," said Bowler.

"I'll be careful," said Pendlebury.

"Be sure you are," said Warburger.

At least the meal and the wine had been very good, thought Charlie. He felt as if he were in one of those television advertisements promoting analgesics for teachers who get migraine attacks from the incessant chattering of children. Charlie decided he must be getting older than he had fully realized. Because there was no harm and because he knew he had a function to fulfill, to earn the dinner, Charlie had told them about the liner fire in Hong Kong and how he had been allowed to travel to Peking by the Chinese authorities for proof that it had been caused by the Hong Kong Chinese owner and not by communist agents. It had been easy to omit the part played by the fervent CIA man from whose death Charlie had stood aside, because to have intervened would have disclosed his true identity and have resumed the pursuit by both American and British intelligence services which had already cost the death of his wife.

The other men at the table had grown irritated at the account, jealous at the interest the women had shown to the story and convincing themselves it was exaggerated. Whenever they'd expressed disbelief, Clarissa, who knew little of the circumstances, had assured them as if she had been personally involved that Charlie was telling the absolute truth.

"Didn't I tell you he was absolutely *fantastic!*" she kept repeating.

Had he been a dog, Charlie thought, he'd have been expected to wag his tail. Perhaps he still would.

They had finished their meal when, his hand cupped as if proposing a Masonic handshake, the man whom Charlie had identified as Giles reached across the table toward him.

"Want some?" he invited.

Twice during the meal he and the girl with him, Fran, had snorted from the silver file of cocaine.

"No thanks," said Charlie.

"Frightened?" demanded the man, imagining a chance to deflate the obvious admiration of the women around the table.

"Yes," said Charlie. "It rots your nose."

"Smoking gives you lung cancer," came in the other man, John.

"I don't smoke, either," said Charlie.

"And screwing gives you the clap," said Fran, joining in the game.

"Life's a regular little minefield," agreed Charlie.

"Surely you do that!" said Clarissa, and Charlie became aware of the amused attention of everyone. Fran and the other girl, Pandora, must be twenty years younger than he was, Charlie thought. There was a vague embarrassment. And the recurring irritation he had first felt at the exhibition. At least Sally Cosgrove's refusal to come with them, pleading an official reception with her husband, had spared him her disdain.

"Only in a locked room, with the lights out," he said.

"That sounds dull," protested Pandora. "I never expected you to be dull."

"That's the trick," said Charlie, pushing his chair away from the table. "Never do what's expected of you."

"Where are you going?" demanded Clarissa.

"Back to the hotel," said Charlie.

"But we're going to meet Sally and the others . . . a club," she said.

"I'm not."

"I *want* you to."

It was an insistence from someone whose wishes were always obeyed. Everyone else at the table had grown quiet, Charlie realized.

He smiled down at her. "I've got to be up early in the morning. Business to discuss with your husband."

"I said I *want* you to stay!"

"Good night," said Charlie, extending the smile around the table before walking away. It would have been a grand exit had the loose rubber sole of his Hush Puppies not caught against the stair edge. If the restaurant manager had not saved him, Charlie would have fallen flat on his face.

"Cinderella is a girl's part, anyway," he apologized to the man.

CHAPTER 6

CONCEIT IS rarely regarded as a fault among the very rich and powerful. Indeed, it is often mistaken for the confidence which enables them to obtain their riches and position. And often it is the frailty which leads to their undoing. Giuseppe Terrilli knew about conceit and its dangers and he was therefore confident he would never become a victim of it, any more than he would ever become a victim of any human failing, which he recognized was a conceit in itself but still not a problem, because he acknowledged it and could guard against it.

All his life Terrilli had guarded against what he considered weakness. He had loved his wife absolutely and had seen no contradiction in his readiness to kill her if she had become attracted to someone else, not because of any sexual betrayal but because she might have revealed his secrets. He accepted he might have enjoyed the effect of alcohol or drugs, but disdained both because he knew they would weaken his self-control, and there had never been a moment, not since he was eight years old and had pushed his elder brother to his death from the top of their tenement building in New York's Little Italy and then held back from the instinct to look over the parapet, to see what had happened, knowing someone below might look up and identify him, when Terrilli had not known complete self-control.

With such self-awareness, Terrilli knew the risk of what he was contemplating; like the alcoholic, in brief moments of sobriety, accepts that gin is destroying his liver, or the heroin addict that each injection increases the possibility of an aneurysm to the brain. But unlike the man who declares the drink to be his last or the addict convinced the fix will be the final one before the cure, Terrilli was sure he could make it work. And the feeling was confidence, not conceit.

It just needed planning; the sort of planning he had put into establishing the narcotics operation as one of the most lucrative within the organization, grossing more than the countrywide prostitution or Las Vegas gambling.

It was from their criticism, rather than any police involvement, that Terrilli considered it important to protect himself. Which was why it had to be an outside operation, organized personally by himself and not something he could depute to Tony Santano. If he told Santano, then Santano would tell the organization. And then there would be a meeting of reasonable men, to convince him he was being unreasonable.

Terrilli was sure that Robert Chambine was the perfect choice for the robbery. For over two years, the man had been trying to transfer from New York to Florida, to become part of the family there. And for two years, Terrilli had held him off, waiting until Chambine could be put into a position to provide something. The exhibition was to be his chance and Chambine knew it. If he succeeded, then he would be made one of Terrilli's lieutenants. If he failed, Terrilli would have him killed.

"I'm grateful for the opportunity," Chambine said.

Terrilli had had a bar installed in the Waldorf-Astoria suite, but Chambine had seen the older man take just club soda and so he asked for the same, determined to impress in every way possible.

"It is to be a personal thing," said Terrilli. There was always the chance that Chambine would inform on him to the organization, to ingratiate himself.

"I understand," said Chambine.

"I would take it as an insult to myself if it were discussed."

"You can trust me," assured Chambine.

"I hope I can. How many people will you need?"

"I've got to see the size of the exhibition, but I wouldn't think more than six."

"Can you find them?"

"Of course."

"Discreet?"

"You have my guarantee. What is the security like?"

"Appears to be nothing more than normal."

"Sure you don't want it taken here?"

Terrilli shook his head. "Too soon. Everyone will be alert now. By the time the second week comes in Florida, they will have become complacent and sloppy."

"As soon as I've seen the stamps, tomorrow, I shall go to Palm Beach. I've already made a reservation at the Breakers."

Terrilli nodded his appreciation at the man's initiative. Chambine was a thickset, muscular man who had the habit of clenching and relaxing his hands when he was talking, as if squeezing a ball. He was unobtrusively dressed, which Terrilli liked, just as he liked the man's attitude, properly respectful without any servility. He wanted Chambine to succeed and not just because he was determined to have the Romanov Collection. Terrilli was growing increasingly uneasy at Santano's position. It would be good to have someone loyal alongside him.

"Contact will always come from me," he said.

"Of course."

"And I want everything brought to my house. Immediately."

Chambine frowned and Terrilli smiled at the surprise.

"No one would dream of suspecting me of any involvement," he explained. "I'm well regarded within the community."

"What am I to offer the others?"

"Fifty thousand each," said Terrilli immediately. He waited

for fresh surprise to show, but this time Chambine curbed it.

"That's a great deal of money," said Chambine.

"For that, I want the best."

"You'll get it."

"And you receive one hundred thousand," said Terrilli.

This time Chambine smiled. "You're very generous."

"I want the stamps."

"Consider them yours."

"Without any trouble," warned Terrilli. "I don't want over-confidence."

"My word."

"I'd like us to work together."

"I'd like that, too, Mr. Terrilli."

"We'll make it the Thursday of the second week. I'll have to warn my own security people, otherwise you won't be able to get into the grounds."

"That will give me more than sufficient time."

Terrilli stood up and the other man rose with him. "I don't like violence," said Terrilli.

"I'll see it's avoided."

"I don't mind if it's the only way . . . I'd just prefer a clean job, without any killing."

Terrilli walked to a desk against one wall, alongside which was his snakeskin briefcase. He took out several bundles of money, still in their bank wrappers.

"Fifty thousand on account and for advanced expenses for the people you'll take with you," he said. "I'd like you to count it."

Obediently Chambine did as he was told. Terrilli watched, without speaking.

"Fifty thousand," agreed Chambine finally.

He looked up. "Please don't think me presumptuous," he said. "But you shouldn't carry such amounts around, unless you have people with you."

"Why not?" demanded Terrilli curiously.

"Crime," said Chambine. "Despite what the police claim, there's still an amazing amount of it on the streets. It's not safe."

"People shouldn't put up with it," said Terrilli seriously.

* * *

Charlie didn't bother to undress, familiar with the rich-woman-amusing-herself routine and guessing she would come. There was a knock within an hour. Clarissa walked straight in when he opened the door, without greeting. When he turned, she was frowning at the room.

"It's not a suite," she said.

"No."

"I was expecting a suite."

"Sorry."

"Just as I was expecting courtesy tonight."

"I was courteous," said Charlie.

"You humiliated me, walking away like that."

"It's not really important, but the humiliation was yours. I don't do tricks to finger snapping."

"You mean you're not like my husband?"

"Have it whichever way you want."

"I intend to," she said, turning the expression.

Charlie walked further into the room, looking down upon the woman. Clarissa had seated herself on the bed, shoes thrown off. Perhaps her feet hurt, too, he thought.

"Why don't you go to bed?" he said sadly. Her eyes were fogged and he didn't think it was from alcohol.

"I want you."

He sighed, irritated by her. "I don't fuck to order, either."

"This time you do."

Charlie sat down in a chair, some way from the bed.

"Stop it, Clarissa," he said.

"Because unless you do, I shan't tell you."

"Tell me what?"

"Who is making inquiries about you."

"Who?" Charlie's concern was immediate.

"Nothing's for nothing."

"Who?"

"Later."

"Now!"

"No," she refused. "Earn it first."

He was always on his knees to someone, thought Charlie. And fifteen minutes later he literally was.

"That's very nice," she said. "I knew it would be nice. Here."

"What is it?"

"I brought you a toothpick from the restaurant."

CHAPTER 7

CHARLIE DECIDED it would be a mistake to overreact to Jack Pendlebury's investigation. He should continue to remain cautious. But not panic. The man was a security official, after all. And even without Clarissa's overloud praise at the exhibition, he would have done the same had he been in Jack Pendlebury's position. But, then, his training had been different; different, that is, unless Pendlebury was not who he claimed to be.

Charlie sat in the darkened projection room, delaying the start of the video film of the previous night's reception.

What can Pendlebury discover? he asked himself, lapsing into the unconscious habit of self-conversation when confronted with a problem. Very little, he thought. The assumed identity was quite genuine and would not be uncovered unless there was a deep examination of the birth certificate upon which he had obtained the passport. Were an inquiry made to London, then Willoughby would fully support him, just as Clarissa had when Pendlebury intercepted her as she entered the hotel the previous night. Pendlebury had looked tired and travel-weary, Clarissa said. Charlie closed his eyes, trying to recall what Pendlebury had said earlier in the evening. An appointment, Charlie remembered. But nothing about a journey. He smiled at a sudden thought. By Clarissa's reckoning, it had been past two o'clock in the morning when Pendlebury spoke to her. And the reception had ended promptly at six. If Pendlebury's appointment had been in Manhattan, that meant eight hours for the man to drink. Perhaps that was it; perhaps Clarissa, with her cocaine-numbed brain, had mistaken tiredness for booze and perhaps Pendlebury's sudden appearance at the hotel was nothing more than a drunken episode.

Still better to remain properly cautious, decided Charlie again, pressing the start button for the video film replay. Because Clarissa's interception wasn't the only curiosity. Or even the greatest. After the previous day's cocktail bar conversation with Pendlebury, Charlie had again checked the video mechanism, convinced he had not made a mistake during his tour with Heppert. And confirmed that he hadn't. The most likely malfunction of any electrical equipment had to be the power supply. Which made connecting both systems to the same source ridiculous, unless the purpose wasn't that which Pendlebury had so glibly offered. And now Charlie had reason to believe it wasn't. When he had asked for the film to be shown, he made the question casual, hardly more than an aside. And the technician had responded ingenuously, unaware of any point to the query. Despite the duplicated system, there was only one film available. So where was the other one? wondered Charlie.

Charlie had taken particular care to note where the surveillance cameras were during his introductory tour of the exhibition hall, because he considered photographs the most likely way of his being discovered. It was never possible to know all the people who might examine them, and it would only need someone with CIA associations and a long memory to identify him. He'd been lucky to avoid getting killed in the first vengeance hunt by the British and American services; it would be stupidity to expect escape a second time.

Charlie had the sequence of the previous night in his mind and was alert for his arrival. It had been difficult, because Charlie was aware of the two fixed cameras constantly trained upon the door and regarded it as the most exposed spot. He recognized the group of people behind which he had slotted himself and then, because he was intent for the first sighting, saw himself. Or rather, his left arm and part of his shoulder. He smiled, an expression part pride at how he'd managed it and part amusement at watching himself perform. The very point of entry had been the most dangerous, because everyone had paused, awaiting the announcement of their arrival. It was here that Charlie had raised the elaborate brochure, in apparent greeting to someone off-camera, and got past the surveillance showing no more than the vaguest outline of the back of his head and an almost perfect shot of Tsar Nicholas II, whose bearded face formed the frontispiece for the book.

He stopped the film, rewound it, and then watched a second time, trying to assess it impartially. There was no point in avoiding the cameras if the evasion were obvious; for a trained observer, that would create suspicion and therefore as much danger as a photograph itself. But Charlie *was* a trained observer; and he knew he'd managed it.

He sat back in the chair, contented; the greatest hurdle and he'd cleared it easily.

There were several shots of Pendlebury which Charlie began by regarding idly and then, increasingly, upon which he began to concentrate, one complete professional admiring another. Just as Charlie's surreptitious entry had been one of perfect concealment, so the observation the American was keeping was that of perfection. Despite his apparently aimless wandering throughout the room, Charlie saw there was never a moment when Pendlebury relaxed. And then came another realization and with it further curiosity.

He's not looking at the right thing, Charlie told himself, forward in his chair now.

To ensure he had not got a mistaken impression, Charlie rewound the film once more, to the very point where Pendlebury first appeared upon it, and then stared intently at the bulging, disheveled man. He watched for ten minutes and then stopped the reel, in mid-frame, and sat nodding to himself. He'd actually recognized it at the time and forgotten it.

Pendlebury's responsibility was to guard against the theft of the contents of the twelve display cases. But not once had he looked toward them. Which was neither natural nor logical. Certainly there had been security men in every aisle and another in personal attendance if a case had been opened, but there should have been a time when Pendlebury automatically checked the exhibits. But he'd only done so once, at the point where Charlie remembered criticizing the opening of the display cases. Apart from that isolated occasion, wherever he had walked, Pendlebury had always positioned himself with one view: the door.

"Why?" muttered Charlie and as he did so had the recollection of the incident when Pendlebury had appeared to identify somebody. He started the film again, smiling at the brief reappearance of his arm when Pendlebury had been talking to him, so that he had almost missed the swivel of the three cameras that could be turned from the control room.

Charlie reached out in readiness for the stop button when he saw they were approaching the moment when Pendlebury appeared to react. He halted it too early and then took it forward to the right frame in a series of jumps. Having got it, he replayed the film through at half speed, then rewound. A mannish woman, wearing trousers, the couple he guessed were married, and a suntanned man who clearly liked clothes and didn't care how much he spent on them. Charlie took the film back and forth several times, hoping for some recognition, and then gave up. He was about to ask the control room for freeze frames of the particular entry and then stopped, hand half out toward the linking telephone. He completely rewound the film, then spoke to the men operating the equipment for him, asking for still photographs of the sequences he selected. Then he went through at random, choosing four other episodes in addition to the entry that seemed to interest Pendlebury. Having disguised what he wanted, he ran the film on, alert for something else which he hoped would confirm his impression about Pendlebury's behavior.

It came immediately. After the entry of the particular group, the American had started looking at the display cases. And drinking.

The video ended within minutes. Charlie thanked the control room, then turned up the viewing room lights from the panel set into the arm of his chair.

Anything? Or nothing? Certainly Pendlebury was a paradox, an apparent professional who did unprofessional things. But by whose standards? His own, as a security firm controller? Or those of Charlie, who had been trained to the highest level of intelligence operative? And then there was the duplicate film about which the control room technicians were ignorant. Again, little more than odd, something for which there could be a perfectly logical explanation. Still wrong to overrespond; far better to wait.

"Surprise, surprise!"

Charlie turned, watching Pendlebury shamble into the room. Charlie saw the man hadn't changed his shirt from the previous day. There was spaghetti sauce on the collar.

"Why surprise?"

"Didn't think you'd fully appreciate the benefits of a film recording."

"England has come a long way," said Charlie. "Some of the better houses have got proper fireplaces, instead of holes in the roof."

"Find anything?" said Pendlebury. He was clearer-eyed than he had appeared at their first encounter. And there was no shake about his hands, either. So he hadn't been drunk when he accosted Clarissa Willoughby.

"I wasn't looking for anything in particular," lied Charlie. "Just thought I'd have another look at the faces."

"And?"

"Just faces."

Pendlebury stared at him. "Perhaps I'll have better luck."

"Is there anything to see?"

"Who knows?" said Pendlebury.

"The organizers have accepted my view and decided not to open the cases anymore," said Charlie.

"There are going to be some disappointed stamp collectors," said Pendlebury. "They'd been told they could examine as close as they liked."

"But there's going to be an insurance syndicate who is very happy," said Charlie.

Pendlebury looked at his watch.

"You didn't have time to get authority from London," he said, calculating the time difference between New York and London.

"No," agreed Charlie.

"You're empowered to make decisions like that by yourself?"

"Yes."

"You must be regarded very highly," said Pendlebury. "Or hold a special position in the company."

"Both," said Charlie. "Didn't Clarissa make that clear?"

"Clarissa?"

"The woman you bumped into in the foyer early this morning. Strange coincidence that, wasn't it? Particularly as you're staying at the Waldorf."

"Amazing," agreed Pendlebury, unembarrassed. "Attractive woman."

"The wife of the principal of my company," said Charlie.

"Told me she's thinking of coming down to Florida, as well."

Charlie frowned. Why had she told the American that?

"Got some friends at Lyford Key and wants to combine a visit," added Pendlebury.

"She hasn't mentioned it," said Charlie. "No reason why she should."

Pendlebury lowered himself into a viewing chair adjoining Charlie's.

"Going to watch it through a second time?" he asked.

"I don't think so."

"One of us might see something the other misses."

"We can compare later," said Charlie, rising.

"See you at the exhibition then." Pendlebury consulted his watch again. "They'll be ready now," he said.

"Ready?"

"The photographs you asked for. They were being developed as I came in."

Pendlebury was regarding him with his face absolutely blank. Charlie returned the look, without any expression.

"Thanks," said Charlie. He began walking toward the door, but Pendlebury called out, stopping him.

"You will tell me if there's anything I should know, won't you?"

"Of course," said Charlie. "Will you tell me?"

"Naturally," said the American. "We're working toward the same purpose, aren't we?"

"I hope so," said Charlie.

"Me, too," said Pendlebury. "I hope so very much."

The photographs had been developed, as Pendlebury promised. Charlie paused on the pavement outside, searching for a taxi. He had decided to try to identify the people with the social directors of either the Waldorf-Astoria or the Pierre Hotel. And if that failed, then approaching one of the society column photographers. It would probably take a long time and in the end be completely without point. But then again, it might not.

There was no possibility of his being criticized by anyone in the organization about his New York visit, but Giuseppe

Terrilli was a careful man and so he arranged two business meetings involving his shipping division while he was in the city. It meant staying over an extra day, but he did not go anywhere near the Romanov Collection again. He ordered his aircraft prepared for the morning of the third day and booked out of the Waldorf without even looking in the direction of the exhibition room.

He was smiling when he settled back into the back of the limousine for the ride to La Guardia. It was very much the look of a child who had probed the cupboards in November and discovered what it is going to receive on Christmas morning.

CHAPTER 8

WITH THE resources Charlie had once had at his disposal, it would not have taken more than a few hours to identify the people in the photograph. By himself, it took almost two days. But, then, he had had to create the diversion, expecting Pendlebury to check on the photographs he had obtained. For most of the first day he had sought the names of people on the other freeze frames, coming to those he wanted last.

The husband and wife team were first. The Waldorf social director recognized the man as a junior Canadian minister attached to the United Nations, which explained Cosgrove's greeting. The Waldorf man gave a lead to the masculine woman, too, and by the afternoon Charlie had her named as a fashion designer as interested in taking clothes off women as in putting them on. Charlie idly wondered in which capacity Sally Cosgrove knew her.

The suntanned man remained a problem, apparently known by no one. Charlie tried the New York *Times* photographic library, but was told it was not open to the public and then, in increasing desperation, looked up the philatelic magazines in the Yellow Pages and touted the picture—cut away now from the people who had stood momentarily at the door of the exhibition hall—around to every office listed. A photographer at the last thought he knew the man, but couldn't identify him by name. He believed him to be an industrialist, however.

With that slender lead, Charlie went to *The Wall Street Journal* and by noon of the second day knew the picture to be that of a millionaire named Giuseppe Terrilli.

Alone in his hotel room, Charlie spread the pictures and information he had been able to gather across his bed and stared down.

"Waste of time," he told himself, having gone from each picture and fact sheet and then repeated the process several times. A diplomat, freeloading off champagne and caviar; a lesbian, choosing the best social event of the night; and a rich man interested in stamps attending an unusual philatelic exhibition. Yet there *had* to be something. Charlie's instinct told him so and he placed great reliance upon instinct. It had been nothing more than that, eight years before, which had made him initially suspect he was being set up as a disposable sacrifice by the American and British intelligence services and he'd stood in a darkened East Berlin doorway and seen the car he should have been driving engulfed in flames and rifle fire.

And he felt it now. Something about the four people at whose pictures he was gazing down had brought a reaction from Pendlebury. And a peculiar one, too. Until their entry, the man hadn't drunk. As soon as they had come into the room, he'd taken a glass from a passing tray and hadn't stopped from then on. Until their arrival, he hadn't looked away from the door. Once they had passed through it, he had hardly looked in that direction again. He had relaxed, in fact. Another insoluble. Entrusted with the safety of stamps worth £3 million, why would a man relax when display cases were opening and closing like a cuckoo's mouth and the room jammed with people, creating the best conditions for a robbery?

And the relaxation had continued. Pendlebury hadn't neglected the job; he was far too professional for that. But there had been a sureness about him, as if he were confident the exhibition was safe. Yet at their first meeting, he had said a theft was always possible.

"If it's too quiet, make a noise."

Another dictum from Sir Archibald. But not as easily put into effect as it had once been. What could he do to put Pendlebury to the test and see if, for once, his instinct had failed?

Slowly he put the photograph into his briefcase, sighing as the answer came to him. Could she do it, without cocking it up? There would always be the risk, but he needed a third party and she was the only one available.

He picked up the telephone, hopefully dialing her suite number. He was at the point of replacing the receiver when Clarissa answered, thick with sleep.

"You all right?" he said.

She recognized his voice. "Perfect," she said. "Except that I always wake up with these strange urges."

"It's five o'clock in the afternoon."

"Afternoons are dreary. It's nights that are fun."

"I want to talk to you."

"Come up for breakfast."

Charlie hesitated; at least whores got paid for it, even the male ones.

"I don't like orange juice," he said. "Make it apple."

By the time he got to her rooms, Clarissa had combed her hair but she hadn't bothered about makeup. Despite the life she led, her face remained remarkably unlined. Charlie wondered if she had undergone much cosmetic surgery; certainly no one outside of a comic or beauty improvement surgery had breasts like that.

"I've just spoken to Rupert," she said. "I told him we were going to have breakfast together and he sends his love."

"Oh," said Charlie.

"He also asked if you were enjoying yourself and I said I didn't think so, not very much."

"Pendlebury told me you'd said you were going to Florida," said Charlie.

"I thought I might. I've friends on an island. Sally is going down."

"Will you go straight there?"

She grinned. "You got a better idea?"

There was a noise at the door leading into the sitting room and Charlie admitted the waiter. She'd ordered champagne, he saw, shaking his head at the artificiality of it all. He tipped the man and when he turned saw she had got out of bed. Her nightdress was completely diaphanous and she didn't bother with a wrap.

"Embarrassed?"

"No," he said.

"Shall I tell you a secret?"

"What?"

"I'm an exhibitionist."

"I would never have thought so," said Charlie. He uncorked the wine and poured it for her.

"Aren't you having any?"

"No."

He sipped his apple juice, watching her; she would have regaled her friends with what they had done together, Charlie guessed.

"Could you come to Palm Beach briefly?" he asked.

"Of course."

"Would you?"

"You propositioning me?" She was smiling, holding her wineglass between her hands and staring at him over the top. It was a very staged pose.

"I want you to do something for me."

"You make it sound very mysterious."

"It might be important. To Rupert, as well as me."

She moved the ice bucket so that he would have an uninterrupted view of her body.

"Do you think I'm spoiled?" she demanded unexpectedly.

Charlie hesitated, wondering what reply she wanted and not wanting to annoy her, until she'd done what he wanted.

"Utterly," he said at last.

"Do I irritate you?"

"Quite a lot."

She pulled a face, but Charlie knew he'd got it right. She wasn't offended.

"Yet you come to me for help."

"There isn't anyone else," said Charlie.

She laughed in genuine amusement. "Christ, you're odd," she said. "You really fascinate me."

She put her champagne glass down, pouring coffee instead.

"I went a bit over the top with that, didn't I?" she said.

"Just a bit," agreed Charlie.

"Now I've got indigestion." She belched very slightly.

"It's the bubbles," said Charlie.

The woman crumpled a croissant into crumbs without bothering to eat any of it.

"I'm supposed to be going out tonight," she said. "Same crowd, same places."

Charlie was curious at the boredom she injected into her voice.

She stared at him. "Know what I'd really like to do, instead?"

"What?"

"Go back to bed. With you. And spend the rest of the day there, watching television when we feel like it and not watching it when we don't."

He had expected to pay a price, remembered Charlie. And his feet *were* painful, after all the walking he'd done to identify the people in the photographs.

"Will you come to Palm Beach?" he demanded, wanting the bargain agreed.

"Yes," she promised.

"Do you want to call them, to say you won't be coming?"

She shook her head. "They won't really miss me."

"Not even Sally Cosgrove?"

"She'll manage. She doesn't like you very much."

"I know."

"Says you weren't very respectful to her husband."

"He wasn't very respectful to me."

"You're an inverted snob," she accused.

"Yes," agreed Charlie readily. "I probably am."

It had been an occasional complaint from Edith, remembered Charlie. Particularly after Sir Archibald had been removed and the new regime had taken over, demoting him from his special position within the department. He suspected she had regarded it as the jealousy of a grammar school boy for university graduates, but it really hadn't been. They had been bloody fools, all of them.

"I told her she was wrong," said Clarissa.

"Thanks a lot," said Charlie.

"Don't be flip," she said. "I don't want either of us to be flip, not tonight."

Was it a performance to fit the circumstances? wondered Charlie. Or genuine?

"I don't like being a cow to Rupert," she said suddenly. "I really don't."

"Why are you, then?"

She shrugged. "I don't seem able to help it. It's despicable, I know. But I really can't help it."

He'd known another woman, just like Clarissa. She'd been secretary to the ex-army general who'd replaced Sir Archibald. Like Clarissa, she'd screwed him for the novelty and he'd screwed her to find out what was going on behind his back. Then, like now, it had seemed a perfect equation. He hoped it worked as well with Clarissa as it had with the other girl.

"We could be missing a good program," she said, rising. She was already in bed, the television page of the *Daily News* in her hands, when he entered the adjoining room.

She cradled into his arms the moment he got into bed. He sat against the bedhead, supporting her.

"Tell me what you want me to do in Palm Beach."

"Later," said Charlie. He wondered how Pendlebury would react when Clarissa let drop that Charlie expected a robbery in Florida. If he were wrong about the American and Pendlebury panicked to the local police, he would look a complete idiot.

He took the newspaper from the woman.

"A Western, a quiz program, or a Clark Gable nostalgia film?" he said.

"Clark Gable nostalgia," she chose immediately.

"That doesn't start for another hour," he said.

"I know," she said.

"I'm not convinced that we're doing the right thing about this damned insurance man," said Warburger.

"Neither am I," added Bowler loyally.

"He's not done anything we can't handle so far," defended Pendlebury.

"He's got a freeze frame of Terrilli," reminded Warburger.

"And four other sets of photographs of different people," said Pendlebury. "The Terrilli photograph is no more important to him at the moment than those twelve other people."

"So why did he have them made?" demanded the Director. "Why Terrilli? Why any of them?"

"Because he's good, like I said," insisted Pendlebury. He was aware of the looks which passed between the Director and his deputy.

"You're not seeing this as some sort of personal challenge, are you?" demanded the Director.

"I would have hoped you knew me better than that," said Pendlebury.

"You've had a watch kept on him?" Bowler asked.

"Constantly," said Pendlebury.

"What's he done?"

"Gone around, trying to get the pictures identified."

"Nothing else?"

"Screwed the boss's wife."

"So are half the men in America," dismissed Warburger. "It's the other thing I'm worried about."

"Trust me," pleaded Pendlebury. "I know it's going to turn out all right."

"For a little longer," conceded Warburger. "I still might pull the rug from under him, despite what you say."

Bowler was escorting Pendlebury from the building when he suddenly stopped, reminded of something.

"Practice," he said.

"What?" asked Pendlebury.

"There was a memo on my desk yesterday. Apparently you're overdue for pistol practice."

"Surely you don't expect me to break away from what I'm doing, just to keep within the rules," said Pendlebury, whose ears always ached from the explosions, even though he wore ear mufflers.

"I suppose not," admitted Bowler, to whom regulations were important.

"You could grant me an exception," prompted Pendlebury.

"Just this once," agreed Bowler. "But there's no way you can be excused again. It's clearly stated."

"I know," said Pendlebury, relieved. "I know."

"Another thing," continued Bowler. "Your expenses are very high."

"It's a very important job," said Pendlebury. "And there are a lot of receipts."

"Don't get greedy," warned the Deputy Director.

CHAPTER 9

CHARLIE NEVER despised good luck, any more than he liked doubting instinct. Sometimes his good fortune had not been immediately clear, but at others it had shown itself as obviously as the hangover the morning after Hogmanay. His arrival in Florida was like several New Year celebrations rolled into one. It might never have happened had he flown to Miami, which had been his original intention. But Clarissa, who knew about such things because self-comfort was very dear to her, had asked him just before he'd left New York why he was bothering with an hour's car journey up the coast when there was a perfectly good airport at Palm Beach itself. And so he had flown there instead and as the aircraft circled for landing seen the name "TERRILLI" written on a hangar roof and then on several other buildings which he presumed were administrative and felt the sort of happiness that comes to a jigsaw aficionado when he finds the first bit that fits from a three-thousand-piece puzzle.

Having come to appreciate the advantage of Clarissa's accommodation in New York, Charlie had taken a suite at the Breakers. Without bothering to unpack, he settled at the sitting room coffee table and spread again the information and pictures he had obtained in New York, this time concentrating only upon Giuseppe Terrilli. His first reaction was one of annoyance, because the location of Terrilli's businesses in Florida had been mentioned in two of the newspaper cuttings he had photocopied in *The Wall Street Journal* office and he had missed the significance, which showed a carelessness of which he was not normally guilty.

"But is it the link?" he demanded of himself. If it was, then it was tenuous. There could be a dozen perfectly logical, understandable explanations why a man interested in stamps should choose to see the exhibition in New York, rather than wait for it to reach the city in which he lived. Nevertheless, it *was* a coincidence and like instinct, was always worth consideration. Reacting to his training, he reached sideways to a table upon which the telephone rested and took up the Palm Beach directory. The airport numbers were in heavier type and then came that of G. Terrilli, against an address off Ocean Boulevard. From the map he had already studied in the foyer, Charlie estimated Terrilli's home to be a five-minute fast walk from the hotel. He replaced the book, sighing contentedly: still a puzzle without even the edges completed, but surely he was beginning to recognize the colors.

At last he unpacked, gazing out as he did so at the cloudless sky and the people far below at the poolside and then, beyond, on the beach. Everything seemed bleached by the heat, so that the constantly tended and watered trees, lawns, and shrubbery stood out starkly green. Charlie turned back into the room, looking down at his comfortably spread shoes and shifting his toes so he could see the movement. It was going to mean a lot of walking, the pavements were going to be hot, and at the end his feet were going to hurt. Bugger it.

It took him longer than he had expected to reach South Lake Drive and he was already sweating when he got to the Chamber of Commerce building backing on to the golf course. The blue-rinsed lady welcomed a respite from a view of which she was bored and imbued with the proper civic pride launched into her prepared address about the benefits of the community. Charlie let her speak, intruding the odd question only when it became absolutely necessary and as he had with the photograph in New York clouded his inquiries with sufficient other queries to disguise any interest in Giuseppe Terrilli.

After an hour, in addition to what he had learned in New York about the man's business activities, Charlie knew him to be an archetypal Palm Beach resident, respected benefactor, admired philanthropist, a member of all the right organizations, and a stalwart pillar of the local society.

He thought the air conditioning was better at the Palm Beach *Daily News* and they gave him a chair in the newspaper library, where he spent three hours going back through ten years of bound copies, discovering the death of Terrilli's wife and studying intently the faded, grainy photographs of the mourners after the private funeral. In only two of the reports in all that time was there any reference to Terrilli's interest in stamps, and even then it was so oblique that Charlie would have overlooked it had he not been searching for it.

Back in his suite, Charlie ran cold water into the bath, took off his shoes, socks, and trousers, and sat on the bath edge, soaking his feet and trying to assess what he had discovered. Nothing, he decided after fifteen minutes. From the information he had been able to assemble, there was no reason why Giuseppe Terrilli shouldn't run for President of the United States or found a religion to rival Christianity.

Was he trying too hard? Had he spent so much time during the last eight years jumping at his own shadow that he'd lost the touch? Or was he just looking the wrong way?

He considered the question, answering it with another. Which alternative way was there to look?

"There are different ways of reaching the end from the same beginning."

Another piece of advice from Sir Archibald. So what had been the beginning? An unease about Jack Pendlebury and then Pendlebury's response to Terrilli. Since which time, he had been largely looking away from Pendlebury. Which was perhaps the mistake.

Charlie dressed and, because he knew it would be expected, went downstairs, contacted the security division of the hotel, and embarked upon a detailed tour of all the precautions that had been installed to protect the exhibition. Halfway through, the ubiquitous Heppert arrived, falling into step beside Charlie and repeating much of what the Breakers official had already said. Once again, the video was duplicated.

As he had in New York, Charlie ended by telling both he thought their precautions were adequate, aware once again of Heppert's disappointment. In an apparent afterthought, he invited the heavily bespectacled man into the coffee shop.

Charlie followed the American's aimless conversation for fifteen minutes before bringing the conversation to Pendlebury.

"Sound man," judged Charlie, inviting the other man's contradiction.

"First class," agreed Heppert immediately. "Came up with one or two things none of the rest of us had thought of."

"Been with your company long?"

Heppert shrugged. "Never met him before."

"Never met him?" Another piece of the puzzle, thought Charlie.

"I gather he's been attached to headquarters for some time, but I've never worked with him. He's highly regarded."

"Really?" encouraged Charlie.

"Seems to be allowed an awful lot of autonomy."

"Is that unusual?"

"Kind of. Our people normally like to be kept very closely in the picture."

Heppert put down his coffee cup so that he could consult his watch. It was a heavy digital affair, with a minuscule calculator built into one edge. It went with the executive spectacles.

"Should be here soon," said the man.

"Didn't he come down with everybody else?"

"Had to make a call at the Washington office."

Charlie estimated he had directed the conversation almost to the point where Heppert might become suspicious, so he allowed the talk to meander again. Charlie ordered more coffee, even though he wanted to leave, anxious that Heppert would never think back upon it and imagine some reason for the encounter.

It was late afternoon by the time Charlie got back to his suite. It took only minutes to get the telephone number of the Pinkerton's Washington office, and Charlie was connected before he had had time to ease off his shoes. He had to identify himself and his business and was finally connected to someone who confirmed Pendlebury's visit but apologized that the man had already left on his way south to Florida. He inquired if he could be of any help, but Charlie declined, promising to await Pendlebury's arrival.

Charlie replaced the receiver and lounged back in his chair. Everything checked, just as it should have. So perhaps he was wrong; his instinct hadn't always been right in the past. Just a very high average.

Pendlebury's call came within the hour, surprising him.

"You wanted me?" said the American with his customary curtness. "Washington office said you'd been on."

"They're efficient."

"That's the motto," said Pendlebury. "What do you want?"

"I wondered if you'd made it clear to the organizers that

there wasn't to be any display case opening here, any more than there was in New York."

"And you called Washington, just for that!"

"I wasn't sure how long you'd be there," said Charlie, aware of the man's suspicion. "If you'd intended staying over a couple of days, I was going to tell them myself."

There was the barest hesitation from the American. Then Pendlebury said: "I told them."

"Good," said Charlie. "What are you doing?"

"Unpacking."

"Shall we meet later on?"

"Fine," accepted Pendlebury. "I'll check the exhibition, then call you."

Charlie bathed and changed, awaiting Pendlebury, carefully rehearsing an approach that he hoped would be productive. There *had* been a curiosity in the man's voice about the Washington call, Charlie decided. So he would have to be cautious against doing anything to increase the attitude; he would have to be friendly, not intrusive. They met in the lobby and Pendlebury led the way to the Alcazar bar overlooking the ocean. Senator Cosgrove was already at a table with some people Charlie recognized from New York. Charlie nodded and the politician allowed a vague inclination of his head in response.

"Great view," said Charlie as they were seated.

Pendlebury grunted. "In most other bars at this time, there's a happy hour, with drinks at half price."

"You're on expenses," reminded Charlie. "Security as good as when you rehearsed it?"

"Yes," said Pendlebury. "It's fine."

"New York seemed to go well."

"Raised five thousand for the kids' charity," confirmed Pendlebury as the drinks arrived. "They're expecting to treble that here."

"You got any kids?" said Charlie, seeing the natural opening.

"Two," said Pendlebury. "Both in high school. You?"

"No," said Charlie. Edith had always been saddened by her infertility. Considering what had happened, it was fortunate that all the gynecological treatment had failed.

"Still time," said Pendlebury.

"My wife's dead," said Charlie. "An accident, about four years ago."

He reached into his pocket for the photograph he had selected. He offered it across the table and the American took it.

"Taken about five years ago," said Charlie. "We were on holiday in Switzerland."

The strain hadn't been showing too much on Edith's face then. They had only been running and hiding for about two years and he hadn't made the stupid mistake which had got him recognized by the British service, so the hunt hadn't started.

"Good-looking woman," said Pendlebury politely.

"You live in New York?" inquired Charlie. He was looking out over the Atlantic, a man politely keeping a casual conversation flowing.

"Long Island," said Pendlebury, searching around for the waitress. "Bastard commuting every day, but it's better than bringing up a family in Manhattan."

Charlie nodded, feeling again the sensation he had known seeing the word "TERRILLI" written on the hangar roof. If Pendlebury were attached to the New York office, why didn't Heppert know him? Producing the photograph had had a relaxing effect upon the other man, decided Charlie.

Pendlebury ordered more drinks, turning back to the table.

"Used to take me three hours getting in and out of London," agreed Charlie.

"About the same for me," said Pendlebury. "Sometimes I think I should get a small apartment in town and just commute at weekends."

"Get about much?" asked Charlie.

"Not a lot," said Pendlebury. "We've offices in most of the big towns. This sort of thing is unusual."

"Now I'm by myself, I welcome the chance to travel," said Charlie.

They both pulled back for the waitress to replace the glasses, and when she moved Charlie saw that Pendlebury was sorting through a billfold, selecting some photographs. Up in the suite he had wondered about the psychology of showing the other man a family picture but he had never expected Pendlebury to respond so readily.

"Here's the kids," said the American, offering a slightly out-of-focus Polaroid of two teenagers grimacing self-consciously into the camera, both trying to hide their teeth braces.

"And Betty," said Pendlebury.

The American's wife was a woman who would become fat within a year or two but at the moment was just keeping her figure with the aid of an all-in-one girdle and desperate diets every three months. Charlie smiled down at the portrait of the blond, shiny-faced woman, saw his bonus, and recorded it, handing the picture back before Pendlebury could become aware of any special attention and realize his error.

"Nice family," said Charlie politely. He made a show of swiveling in his seat, seeking something.

"What do you want?"

"Washroom."

"By the entrance," said the other man.

Charlie excused himself, hurrying to the toilet. He went straight into a cubicle, in case Pendlebury followed, hurrying a pen and paper from his pocket. The picture of Pendlebury's wife had shown her outside a typically American one-story home, with the garage forming one side. She had appeared to be making her way into the garage, because the doors were open and the camera had recorded perfectly the license plate. Charlie wrote it down, looking up reflectively. As well as the number, the license plate had listed the state. How was it, wondered Charlie, that Pendlebury lived in New York State and drove a Chevrolet Monte Carlo with Texas plates?

He returned to the table, to see Pendlebury had ordered again. The American was putting the pictures back into his wallet.

"Your wife's a pretty woman," said Charlie.

"Worries about her weight," confessed Pendlebury. "She's joined Weight Watchers."

"Changed since that picture, then?"

"Not much," said the American. "She's only been going to meetings for about two months. Crazy about candy, that's the trouble."

"You eating?" asked Charlie.

Pendlebury nodded with the eagerness of a man who had already studied the menu for which he wasn't paying.

"But later," he said. "I've arranged to see Heppert and the rest of the security team at seven, for a final run-through.

Senator Cosgrove is going to be there. Want to come?"

Charlie shook his head. "Better I don't see it, otherwise I might come to rely upon it."

"Probably a good idea," accepted Pendlebury.

Charlie decided against food, but for reasons different from Pendlebury. His telephone call to Houston took longer than he had anticipated. To the clerk in the state vehicle licensing department he explained that he had been involved in a traffic accident with a Chevrolet Monte Carlo, knew the owner's name was Pendlebury but had mislaid the address necessary for the insurance claim to be settled. It took a further ten minutes to locate the details from the license plate number, and once he had obtained the address, Charlie went back to directory information and established that Pendlebury was currently listed in the Houston telephone book.

It was quite dark by the time he had finished, but Charlie didn't bother with anything more than one side-table lamp. Pendlebury's lie about where he lived was the first tangible thing Charlie had from all the supposition and guesswork. But it was enough to satisfy him that his instinct hadn't failed. Not completely, anyway.

"What happened?" said Warburger.

"We'd established the routine that if anybody called Pinkerton's in Washington, where Jack was supposed to be going, they'd patch the call through to me. The Englishman came on about two this afternoon," said Bowler.

"What for?"

"He wouldn't tell me. I alerted Jack, who came back later to say the guy wanted to check about something concerning the opening of the damned display cases."

"What do you think?"

"An unnecessary risk, like I've said all along. I think we should dispose of him, rather than endanger everything."

"Might draw attention to the exhibition, which is just what we don't want to do," warned the Director. "Get any sort of activity around there and Terrilli won't come within a mile."

"It's not an easy decision, now it's gone this far," admitted Bowler. "I don't think we should have listened to Jack in the first place. We could have settled this in New York."

"Warn him," said Warburger. "Tell Pendlebury we're un-happy with it."

"One of the troubles with Jack," said the deputy, "is that he's a cocky little bastard . . . thinks he can handle everything."

CHAPTER 10

GIUSEPPE TERRILLI chose a downtown Miami Howard Johnson hotel for the meeting with Chambine, confident of the anonymity. He arrived early, but found Chambine waiting for him. Still club soda, the millionaire noted.

Chambine made to rise, respectfully, but Terrilli gestured him down, not wanting any indication of deference that might be remembered by a curious waiter. They delayed until one came and completed the order before talking. Terrilli saw the younger man had selected a table apart from others in the bar so they could not be overheard.

"Well?" demanded Terrilli.

"Fairly standard security," reported Chambine. "Electronic surveillance and the cases are wired, I suspect. A rotating staff of twenty uniformed people and some plainclothes. I don't think more than ten. Pinkerton's chief is a man called Pendle-bury. There is also an Englishman, representing the insurers."

"Anything unusual about them?"

Chambine shook his head. "Has-beens, both of them."

"What do you think?"

"It'll need the right planning," said Chambine. "But it won't be too much of a problem."

Terrilli smiled, pleased with the answer. Most people trying to please, as Chambine was, would have boasted that it would be easy and that would have shown worrying immaturity.

"Fixed the number of people you'll need?"

"Six, like I originally estimated."

"Got them?"

"All arranged," said Chambine. "Two from Vegas, one from Chicago, one from Philadelphia, and two from Los Angeles."

"Why the spread?"

"I didn't think it would be sensible to recruit all from the same city. It might have been noticed."

Chambine *was* good, decided Terrilli.

"What do they know?" he demanded.

"That they're getting fifty thousand for a heist, no questions asked."

"Organization men?"

"Every one. Just doing a little free-lancing."

"For whom?"

"Me," said Chambine. "I saw no point in involving you."

"You're very thoughtful."

"I've tried to be, Mr. Terrilli."

"I'm very grateful," said the older man. "And I intend to show it."

Chambine smiled, a hopeful expression. "I'd like another meeting, if it's possible, to discuss the final planning. But I'm a little concerned at the security at your house."

"It'll be arranged, on the night, don't worry," promised Terrilli. "You'll be expected."

"There won't be any trouble?" asked Chambine.

Terrilli smiled, knowing the meaning to the question.

"My people do as they're told. There's no cause for them to resent an outside operation."

"What about Mr. Santano?"

Terrilli let the other man know by the silence before he replied how near he was coming to impertinence.

"Santano will do as he is told, like everyone else. If you join my operation after everything is over, it'll be for the two of you to create a working relationship."

Aware he had gone far enough, Chambine said, "Unless you think otherwise, I intend to be the only person to remain on the island after the robbery. I'll bring the rest in and out the same night. It cuts down the risk of a chance arrest if the robbery is discovered earlier than I plan it to be."

"These guys got records?" demanded Terrilli instantly.

Chambine colored. "I've been as careful as I can. They're all minor things . . . juvenile stuff. . . ."

Terrilli took several moments to reply, apparently thinking. "In and out the same night," he agreed finally. "It won't matter how minor the convictions if they get arrested."

"If the worst were to happen, they could only identify me," reminded Chambine.

"And you could identify me."

"I wouldn't do that, Mr. Terrilli. Whatever happened, I'd never point the finger at you."

"You'd die," said Terrilli unemotionally. "Irrespective of any trouble it might or might not cause, you'd have to die."

"That's why I wouldn't do it," said Chambine, and Terrilli laughed, aloud, at the honesty.

"I think we are going to get on well," said Terrilli. "Very well."

"I thought our next meeting should be at least four days before we actually lift the stuff, to give me time to make alternative plans in case you don't like those I put forward."

"Agreed," said Terrilli immediately.

"I'm assembling everyone in Disney World," announced Chambine.

"Disney World!"

"Fifty thousand people a day, none knowing the other," pointed out Chambine. "It's got to be the perfect place."

"I suppose so," agreed Terrilli with obvious reluctance.

"You and I could always meet elsewhere, of course," offered Chambine, discerning the other man's attitude.

"No," accepted Terrilli after thought. "I like it. I really do. When are you bringing the other people in?"

"The two from the West Coast are arriving tomorrow. The others at daily intervals."

"Will you put them together immediately?"

"No," said Chambine. "It's always possible they may know each other, of course. Vegas isn't far from Los Angeles. But I won't establish the link until the weekend. There's no point until then. And six men hanging around might attract attention."

"Do you need any more money?" asked Terrilli, indicating the briefcase beside him.

"No thank you," said Chambine.

Terrilli lapsed into silence. Chambine sat attentively, not attempting to lead the conversation.

"I like very much your keeping me out of it," said Terrilli, breaking the pause. "On the night of the robbery, when it arrives at my house, I'll not meet any of them personally. I'll pay you off in a separate room and you can pay them, in turn. . . ."

Chambine nodded.

". . . It wouldn't take anyone long to discover who lived in the house, of course," went on Terrilli, thinking aloud. "But if no one actually sees me, then they can't prove anything."

"I think that's a wise safeguard," agreed Chambine.

Terrilli sat back in his chair, the movement indicating the discussion was over.

"I've rooms at the Contemporary Resort in Disney World," said Chambine. "Would Sunday be convenient for you?"

"Noon," agreed Terrilli, rising.

The two men shook hands and then Terrilli went out into the foyer, nodding to the doorman's questioning look about a taxi. He asked for the Omni complex on Biscayne Boulevard, paid before he left the car, and took the elevator as if going into the shopping complex. Instead he cut through to one of the linking entrances into the Omni Hotel, descending to the foyer, and within fifteen minutes was in another taxi, going uptown toward the Tuttle Causeway joining the mainland to Miami Beach. He paid the taxi off a block away from the Fontainebleau, finished the journey on foot, and entered the hotel through one of the side doors, near the golf course.

At the desk he inquired for messages, told them he was checking out, and sat waiting for his luggage to arrive. It came out of the service elevator at the same time as his chauffeur entered, looking for him. Without speaking, Terrilli indicated the cases, walking out ahead to the waiting car.

It was rare to find anyone as efficient as Chambine, Terrilli decided. The man would make an excellent lieutenant: better than Santano, who was becoming overambitious. He nodded to himself, reaching the decision. He would allow a proper amount of time, after the robbery, for Chambine to become fully acquainted with the operation. And then have Santano put away.

"Turn up the air conditioning," ordered Terrilli as the driver pulled out onto Collins Avenue. Walking to the Fontainebleau had made him sweat.

How long would it be until Chambine became ambitious? he asked himself. They all did, in the end. And had to be killed. Terrilli sighed. He had always considered it unfortunate, having to waste such talent. It was a pity a way could not be found to neuter their aspirations, like eunuchs were treated to become excellent caretakers in harems.

"Will we be stopping anywhere, Mr. Terrilli?" asked the driver.

"No," said Terrilli. "Straight home."

He'd decided to spend the afternoon with his stamps. When the Romanov Collection arrived, he would have to get more display cases and racks installed.

Whatever the permutation, there could only be one conclusion, decided Charlie. With it came the sweep of nausea similar to that he had known eight years before, in the Sussex churchyard in which Sir Archibald Willoughby was buried, when he realized he had probably been recognized and was only a pistol shot from disaster.

Pendlebury had unquestionably lied about working in New York. Yet Heppert considered him genuine. The man had practically dated the photograph of his overindulgent wife by talking of her two-month Weight Watcher membership. So Pendlebury couldn't be a criminal because he could not possibly have inveigled himself into such a position of seniority within a security organization in that time.

So he had to be there by consent. To whom would Pinkerton's consent to provide such a cover? A policeman, obviously. Yet the exhibition had opened in New York and was now in Florida. Not a local policeman, then. But federal. Why would the FBI want to attach a man to a stamp exhibition? And not just attach, Charlie corrected himself; put in overall security control?

It came together in a neat, logical sequence. But Charlie still felt the need for confirmation. He reached out for the telephone, accepting before attempting the test that it might not work.

Directory information gave him the Houston telephone number of the Federal Bureau of Investigation and he dialed it himself, so there would be no operator record of the call.

Had the professionalism not been so deeply ingrained, Charlie might have made the mistake of inquiring for Pendlebury the moment the number answered. But he didn't, aware that it would be at the switchboard where the man's cover would have been most protected against such an approach.

He asked instead for the station manager, refused to be put aside to an assistant, and when the man finally came on the line did not ask a question but stated a fact.

Jack Pendlebury had told him he would be out of town for a few weeks, Charlie said. But he had the information that Pendlebury had asked him to obtain and was anxious to know when the man would be returning.

"We're not sure," said the FBI manager. "Is there anything we can do to help?"

"No," refused Charlie, putting down the telephone. The man already had, more than he would ever know.

CHAPTER 11

PENDLEBURY'S VISIT to Washington had been scheduled anyway, to finalize the plans for the backup support with which he was to be provided in Palm Beach, but what had been discovered on the separate videotapes gave extra point to the interview with Warburger and Bowler. Every night, since the New York opening reception of the exhibition and now, in Florida, the duplicate tape had been flown to Washington, for both visual examination by recognition experts and then a scan from a computer programmed with the physiognomatic characteristics of every known Mafia associate on their files. Because of the speed at which it could be operated, it had been the computer which twice registered Robert Chambine. Upon reexamination, the visual experts had confirmed the identification.

The three men sat hunched forward in the viewing room, watching the latest film of Chambine touring the exhibition in Palm Beach, occasionally slowing the film better to establish an impression which occurred to any of them. Then they sat through the first film, as if it were important they recognized Chambine there, as well.

It was Warburger who put up the room lights, sighing back

against his chair and propping his feet against the back of that in front.

"Right again," he said. There was a self-satisfaction in his voice.

"We've run the tapes through until they're almost frayed at the edges," said Bowler. "Chambine is the only face that so far has any connection. Surely it's not going to be a one-man operation?"

"Couldn't be," said Pendlebury immediately. "The stamps aren't heavy, certainly. But they are difficult to handle. One man couldn't do it. It would take too long."

"Maybe he's a spotter," assessed Bowler.

"Or the man whom Terrilli has entrusted with organizing the job," suggested Warburger.

The Deputy Director went back to the file. "Only a soldier," he read aloud.

"Ambitious, you said," reminded Pendlebury. "What about surveillance?"

"We've initially moved in a twelve-strong team, three women included. No one to maintain observation on two consecutive days. We'll change the whole shift before the weekend."

Pendlebury nodded. "Any contact with Terrilli?"

"Not that we've picked up so far."

"Telephone monitor?"

"It'll be in place by tonight. Then he'll be sewn up tighter than a Thanksgiving Day turkey."

"Chambine has got to be the man," said Pendlebury, more to himself than the other men in the room. "It doesn't check out any other way."

"It's better than I ever expected," confessed Warburger.

"What's known?" asked Pendlebury, who had not had the advantage of previously seeing either film.

"Robert Chambine," recited Bowler, from the file before him. "Soldier attached to the New York family, minor conviction for loan sharking, suspicion of homicidal assault in 1975, released through lack of evidence, happily married, with two children, no known connection with Giuseppe Terrilli or any of the Florida people. Thought to be ambitious, as I said earlier."

"And not a stamp collector," said Pendlebury quietly.

"We played back every video taken at the Waldorf-Astoria," said Bowler. "We've only the sighting for him the night before the exhibition ended."

"Do I control the surveillance team on Chambine?" said Pendlebury.

Warburger nodded. "Pointless our trying to do it from here. It would lead to confusion. We're assigning a total of fifty people, just for him alone. That enables you to shift change, every two days."

"What's the rest?" asked the crumpled man.

Warburger stood up, going to a desk in the screening room and taking up a clipboard.

"Besides the people covering Chambine, we're allocating you another one hundred men. In addition, there'll be a communications section, answerable to you, plus three helicopters which we're placing at Miami, rather than at Palm Beach. Terrilli's air division is installed there and he might have some intelligence setup which could get suspicious of the sudden arrival of three helicopters, even though the company owning them has no traceable association with us."

"I don't want any army like that on the island," warned Pendlebury. "There's no way it could go undetected."

"We accept that," said Bowler. "But at all times during the day and night I think we should have a moving group of maybe twenty to thirty people within five or ten minutes of the hotel."

For several moments Pendlebury didn't speak, considering the planning. Then he said: "Controlled by the communications unit?"

"Right," said Warburger. "Who in turn would transmit whatever orders you gave. Give you instant mobility."

"Should work," said Pendlebury.

"In addition to your immediate team, I'm moving thirty men to Miami and another thirty to Fort Pierce, for extra support if you should need it."

"Lot of men," said Pendlebury reflectively.

"The first time we met, I told you I meant this to work," said Warburger vehemently. "Now we know we've got him hooked, I'm even more goddamned determined."

"Where are we putting those not on shift?"

"Howard Johnson hotels and Holiday Inns at Lantana, Lake

Worth, and Boynton Beach. Even off duty, they'll be tuned to the communications division, so they're on instant call."

"What about the sea?" said Pendlebury. "There's a lot of water to get lost in."

"We haven't forgotten that," said Warburger. "We've got two cutters, each containing six men apparently on an extended fishing trip, moving in and out of Jupiter. . . ."

The Director saw Pendlebury move to speak, but held up his hands, stopping him.

"I know Terrilli has got a sea division and I know our guys are amateurs. I don't see them bringing off any sea interception if it becomes necessary. They are there as first defense. If it becomes obvious there's a need for sea expertise, we'll call in the coast guard."

"We've put a lot of work into this," said Bowler.

"I believe you," said Pendlebury.

"So what have we overlooked?" asked the Director.

Pendlebury considered the question, seeking the flaw. Then he said: "I can't think of anything."

Warburger smiled at the assessment. "There isn't *anything* we haven't thought of," he said.

"And there's been luck," said Pendlebury, uncaring of offense. "Chambine's appearance after that of Terrilli was something we could never have expected. Or hoped for."

"Chambine is going to be the key," accepted Warburger.

"How closely have you briefed those watching him?"

"I personally instructed them," said Warburger.

"How are things going with Senator Cosgrove?" asked Bowler.

"Good enough," said Pendlebury.

"He's not demanding too much involvement?"

"Not yet," said Pendlebury. "But I kind of imagine he wants to be around when it happens."

"He won't get in the way," promised Warburger again. "He'll be present at the press conference, of course."

"Press conference?" said Pendlebury.

"I thought we'd stage one, in Palm Beach, after the arrests," said the Director. "Might even come down myself."

Bowler saw Pendlebury wince. The man tried to disguise the expression by looking down and slightly moving his wrist, so he could see his watch.

"Anything more?" said Bowler.

"I don't think so," said Pendlebury. "I'd like to get back. And I don't think there's any point in my coming here again, not until after it's all over."

"What about the Englishman?" remembered Warburger suddenly.

"Nothing," said Pendlebury. "It's going fine."

The Director leaned forward, to give emphasis to what he was going to say. "Now that the pattern is establishing itself, I think we have wasted a lot of time over that man."

"I don't fully agree . . ." started Pendlebury, but Warburger talked over him. ". . . he creates an uncertainty. And I don't like uncertainties. I went along with you this far, but I want you now to take a positive directive. At the slightest indication of any difficulty, you're to have him removed."

"It would be a shame to frighten away Terrilli or his people," tried Pendlebury.

"And an even greater shame to lose them," argued the Director. "The damned man can do nothing but get in the way."

As Warburger spoke, Charlie Muffin was emerging from the Senate Records Office not two miles from where the three FBI men had been in conference.

It had been easier than he expected, but then Charlie was unused to the Freedom of Information Act or the efficiency of American library systems and computer records. Giuseppe Terrilli's name had not been linked with organized crime since the Democratic administration's investigations under Bobby Kennedy. And even then, it had involved situations that existed much earlier. In 1958 a Giuseppe Terrilli was named as a link between crime in America and the gambling syndicates in Havana, before their expulsion by Fidel Castro. There was then a gap of four years, when the name of Terrilli appeared again, this time in connection with the refusal of a gambling license for one of the Las Vegas hotels later discovered to be wholly Mafia-controlled. After that, nothing.

Not on Terrilli, at least. But by going back as far as he had, Charlie had come across another name and it had intrigued him as much as what he had learned about the Mafia associate.

It would never have shown up but for the excellent cross-referencing available in the records office and only then because he had probed so deeply into the Bobby Kennedy investigation.

Kelvin Cosgrove had never been involved in any Terrilli probe. But he had been associated with others and appeared to have established himself so highly that there had been speculation of his being appointed Attorney General after Bobby Kennedy's assassination.

It could still be a coincidence, Charlie thought, waving down a passing taxi to take him to Dulles Airport. But increasingly, he was disregarding the anomalies upon which he kept stumbling as coincidence.

CHAPTER 12

THE INITIAL planning meeting of Terrilli's men who wanted to steal the stamps and the FBI group who wanted them to do it took place within two days and 150 miles of each other.

That called by Chambine occurred first. So determined was the New Yorker to impress Terrilli and be invited to join the Florida operation that he had taken even greater care over the selection of those who would help him than he had indicated to Terrilli during their Miami meeting. Finding men with minimal criminal records had been the first essential, but it naturally followed that they were therefore people of above average ability to have evaded detection for so long. All were past thirty, men who no longer considered machismo was kept in the crotch of their jockey shorts. Four were married and outwardly lived respectable, responsible lives in affluent suburbs of the cities in which they lived. One, David Bertrano, was honorary secretary of his local PTA.

It was Bertrano whom Chambine had deputed to have the suite, choosing him for no other reason than it was from Chicago that he took his first recruit and that was where Bertrano operated.

The purpose was to provide a comfortable meeting spot when they met as a group, which everyone else understood, so there was no jealousy at this apparent favoritism.

Bertrano had had coffee and sandwiches provided before anyone arrived at the Contemporary Resort in Disney World.

There was a bar in the corner, but no one asked for booze when they had assembled and Chambine noticed it, content that he had obtained professionals. Leonard Saxby and Peter Boella came from Las Vegas, Umberto Petrilli from Philadelphia, and Walter Bulz and Harry Beldini from Los Angeles.

Even though it wasn't his suite, Chambine took the role of host, formally introducing the group to each other. The responses were polite but equally formal.

"No doubt you'd recognized each other before today?" said Chambine.

"Nearly everyone," conceded Bertrano. Realizing the reason for the question, he added: "There's been no contact."

"I'm glad."

"It's obviously something big," said Saxby. "Nobody's laying out fifty grand for nothing. We didn't want to do anything to foul it up."

"It is big," admitted Chambine. "There's a particular need for what we're going to take."

"What is it?" asked Bertrano.

"Stamps," said Chambine. He waited for the surprise to register, but there was no reaction from anyone, and once again Chambine congratulated himself upon the selection.

"What sort of stamps?" asked Boella.

"A very special collection," said Chambine. "Used to belong to the Russian Tsar."

"We're not to know who wants them?" said Beldini.

"No," said Chambine, intent on the response to the refusal. Once again the group remained impassive.

"Is it on show?" asked Bulz.

"Palm Beach," said Chambine. "The exhibition opened three days ago."

"So you know the security," said Petrilli, investing the organizer with the same expertise as the rest of them.

"Rotating staff of twenty uniformed people. Ten plainclothes, as far as I can establish. Display cases possibly wired and ten swivel cameras and two fixed mountings," said Chambine.

"What about the person in charge?"

"A stumblebum named Pendlebury. No problem. And there's some kind of Englishman attached to the insurance company. No problem there, either."

"Staff at night?" asked Saxby.

"Three-man night shift. No one actually on duty in the hall; they make half-hourly checks."

"But the cameras will be kept on?" said Petrilli.

"Of course," said Chambine.

"How do we overcome that?" said Saxby. "Block the supply?"

"No," said Chambine immediately. "It's wired so that if there's any interruption to the power, a battery-operated alarm sounds. . . ."

From a briefcase, he took plans and drawings he had made during the time he was at the Breakers. While he laid them out, Boella, unasked, poured coffee, while the others huddled around and behind Chambine.

". . . Here," he began, indicating a camera at the top of the drawing, "is the biggest risk. It's one of the fixed cameras and it's equipped with a fisheye lens, giving it cover of almost all the chamber. That's the one we hit first. . . ."

". . . How?" demanded Saxby.

"Simply by going in with twelve cloth covers, which we shall tape over each lens."

Saxby laughed at the simplicity, but Bertrano said: "It would still be impossible to avoid some of us being photographed, even for only a few minutes."

Chambine nodded. "That's why this first camera is important. It's the most dangerous."

He indicated Bulz and Beldini.

"You two will go in first. You'll wear black track suits and black hoods. . . ."

He pointed to eight red crosses on the plan.

". . . Those are the permanent lights. I want those shrouded as soon as you enter. That cuts down the photographic quality enormously. . . . You"—he pointed to Bulz—"will do that. While you"—he nodded to Beldini—"will go first for this fixed camera, then crisscross the floor, covering first the camera to the left, then the camera to the right. . . ."

He turned back to Bulz.

". . . As soon as you've shrouded all the lights, you hit this other fixed camera at the end of the room. That's not a fisheye, so we can afford to wait. . . ."

He sat back from the plan, looking to the two men from Los Angeles.

"I've got exact measurements of the room," he said. "And measurements, although obviously they're only estimates, of the camera and lighting equipment placed around the room. I've rented a warehouse in Orlando and had duplicate equipment delivered there yesterday. After this meeting, I want you to take these plans and build a facsimile of the camera protection. And then practice. I want to come here three days from now and see you two extinguish those lights and cameras in under five minutes. . . ."

He stopped, waiting for their comments and hoping no one would attempt a joke at the proposal. The six other men stayed serious.

"Anyone see any problems?" he demanded. It was a test he felt necessary.

"It won't work," said Bertrano. "The room is bound to have smoke censors, as part of the normal fire precautions. And if we have cloth over the lights for longer than a few moments, they'll smolder and set off the alarms."

"Right!" said Chambine, smiling. "The timing is three minutes to get the cameras covered, then another two to remove all the cloths. We'll need the light anyway to see what we're doing."

"Is the exhibition at the Breakers?" said Petrilli.

Chambine nodded.

"Big hotel, with a full night staff," continued the man from Philadelphia. "Getting out isn't going to be easy."

Chambine went back to his plans, drumming his pencil against the drawing of the exhibition hall uncluttered by any markings of lights or surveillance equipment. Only shown were the positions of the display cases and the windows.

"Here . . ." he said, encircling two windows at the top corner, ". . . are the two windows overlooking the parking lot. There's just a veranda and a section of lawn in the way. The windows are wired, obviously, but we can bypass that. The ground lights are a problem. . . ."

He gestured to Saxby and Boella.

". . . You two will never actually enter the hall. I want you both outside, behaving like ordinary visitors. You'll be there to warn us of any sudden attention that might come from out-

side. But before that, you douse these . . ."—he produced another drawing, showing the outside lighting—". . . but you
won't put out the section near the exhibition hall first. I want
it to look like isolated fusing. And I want to create a diversion.
I want some by the pool and near the drive to go initially. And
then those which might worry us . . ."

He paused, to impress them with the importance of what
he was going to say.

". . . getting the timing right for the lights is as important
as the practice that you're all going to do in the warehouse.
If one light goes out at the wrong time . . . or doesn't go out
at all . . . then there's no way we'll get away with it."

"Do we do it from the actual fuse box?" asked Saxby.

Chambine shook his head. "We'd never be able to guarantee
getting to the boxes on time. And it's impossible to find out
without actually testing which fuses operate which set of lights.
We'll have to cut the ground cables. It won't matter when they
discover what's happened. By that time the collection will be
gone anyway."

"We won't be able to practice that," said Boella.

"I know," said Chambine. "It means you and Saxby coming
to the hotel before the robbery. I would like to have avoided
that, but there's no alternative."

He looked at the others in the room.

"They'll be the only ones," he warned. "I don't want any
chance recognition . . . any indications of us being a group."

"What'll we do?" asked Saxby.

"Make no contact whatsoever with me," said Chambine.
"Just appear to be ordinary visitors. Use the bars, the pool if
you want. Even the golf course. But give yourselves the
opportunity to isolate the cables leading to the lights I've
marked and work out how they're best cut. I want a complete
plan prepared before I return to the warehouse to see the rehearsal with the cameras."

The two men nodded.

"Palm Beach is an island," pointed out Bertrano. "What's
to stop the bridges being sealed once the light cables are discovered cut?"

"Time," said Chambine confidently. "Before the true cause
of the ground light failure is discovered, we will have delivered
the collection and you will have been paid off. Even if you

were stopped—and it's a million to one chance—then any search of your car would show nothing."

"The stuff's not leaving Palm Beach?" queried Bertrano.

"No," confirmed Chambine. "It'll be in our possession for less than thirty minutes."

Bertrano smiled. "Doesn't look like being too difficult a job," he said.

"Don't think like that!" snapped Chambine. "Start thinking it's easy and you'll relax, and when you relax, something will go wrong."

"I didn't mean..." Bertrano tried to protest, but the New Yorker refused him.

"I'm not interested in what you meant. You're all being paid a lot of money for something that has got to go without a hitch. I don't want anyone celebrating or relaxing or thinking it's easy until you're all back home and the fifty grand is in your safe-deposit boxes."

"I'm sorry," said Bertrano.

"It's all right," forgave Chambine. He was not unhappy at the episode. It had provided a way of stressing the importance of what they were attempting.

"What if we *are* interrupted?" demanded Saxby quietly.

Chambine sipped coffee, glad at having arrived at another point.

"You've got guns?" he asked.

Saxby, Boella, and Petrilli nodded.

"Ours are in the left luggage at the airport," said Saxby.

"...And mine's at the Greyhound station," added Petrilli.

"I'd prefer no violence," said Chambine. "Only if it can't be avoided.... It'll foul up the escape and bring any police in far quicker...."

He hesitated, caught by a sudden thought.

"...And if we do get away with it," he said, "I want those guns dumped immediately we clear the hotel. I don't want anyone seized for something as stupid as having a weapon on them, when there's no other reason for suspicion...."

"What about a diversion bigger than a few blacked-out lights?" suggested Bertrano, trying to recover from their dispute.

Chambine shook his head positively. "A few fused lights is a hotel maintenance problem, until it's discovered otherwise.

I don't want anything dramatic that's going to attract the attention of the police."

There were various movements among those sitting before him, as they accepted the logic. Chambine studied them, deciding to emphasize the warning.

"There's no way that later you will be associated with this job," he began. "But I don't want it coming back from your ends. No big spending . . . anything ridiculous that might attract the attention of people in cities where you live. . . ."

The men started making gestures of assent, but Chambine continued, "If this comes off, as I intend it to, there's no reason why there shouldn't be others, for the same fee. Maybe even higher."

It was unlikely, he knew. But as outwardly respectable as they might appear, the men around him all possessed the essential ingredient of criminality: greed. The promise of further money would do more to instill in them the caution he wanted than any direct threat.

"I think we're all adult enough to avoid that," said Bertrano, speaking for the others.

"I'm sure you are," said Chambine. "It was just something that needed saying."

From his pocket, Chambine took a key with an address label attached. He handed it across to Bulz and said: "That's to the warehouse. I want it perfect in three days, okay?"

"Guaranteed," said Bulz.

Chambine turned to Saxby and Boella.

"I don't want to know when you're coming to the Breakers. All I want is something that won't fail outlined to me when I come to see the other preparations."

The men from Las Vegas moved their heads in agreement, but said nothing.

"That's it, then," announced Chambine, standing. "I'll see you all in Orlando."

"Going straight back?" asked Bertrano.

"Why?"

Bertrano looked at his watch. "The fireworks display starts in half an hour," he said. "First over the Magic Kingdom and then out there on the lake."

"It's spectacular," confirmed Boella. "You should stay and watch it."

"No time," refused Chambine. "You enjoy it."

Chambine moved quickly away from the identifying suite, descending one floor by the stairway before moving toward the elevator. Within minutes he was in the lobby, through which ran the monorail train that completely encircles Disney World. He was alert to people boarding with him for the journey to the main gate but saw no one paying any particular attention to him. As the pneumatic doors hissed closed, one of Pendlebury's men rose from behind his copy of *Time* magazine to telephone the pay phone near the main exit, to warn the man waiting there that Chambine was on his way.

It was because of the complete success of the surveillance operation that Pendlebury called his meeting within forty-eight hours. It meant more work than it had for Chambine. The FBI man could not assemble all the agents over whom he had control, because of the risk of attracting attention with so many, and so he had to journey from as far south as Miami right up through the coastline to Lantana, Lake Worth, Boynton Beach, and Fort Pierce. From each he selected a man to be in charge of the groups assembled there, conscious of the need to delegate responsibility, to ensure quickness of movement. With this smaller group, all of supervisor grade, he held a final conference, after the others, moving to the mainland and taking rooms at the Howard Johnson hotel at Okeechobee Boulevard in West Palm Beach.

"I'll make no apologies for repeating what you've heard before," Pendlebury began. "More than anyone else on this operation, you people have got to know what you're doing and do it right. If any one of you fouls up, then the whole thing will fail."

Behind him was a blackboard, upon which were thumb-tacked photographs of the six men with whom Chambine had had his meeting. The FBI supervisor took up a pointer, announcing the identity of each man as he isolated each picture.

He turned back into the room. "Every one with a positive connection with organized crime," he declared. "Yet brought from widely separate parts of the country. I think that shows a very careful selection of people."

"What are they doing at the moment?" asked a man called Harris, who had been appointed controller of the backup group in Miami.

"Nothing except being ordinary vacationers," said Pendlebury. "We've got twenty men watching them, rotating every two days to avoid any recognition."

"Are they remaining in a group?"

The question came from Roger Gilbert, who was in charge of the Lake Worth squad and as such would be immediately involved when the collection was stolen.

Pendlebury shook his head. "There was only the one occasion, when they gathered in the suite to which we followed Chambine and from which we were able to recognize the whole team. Since then, they've behaved like strangers to each other."

"What about that warehouse in Orlando to which we've followed Saxby and Boella?"

"I might try electronic monitoring, although the size and acoustics might defeat us. I'm not risking an entry," said Pendlebury positively. "It's a good bet they're using it for some kind of rehearsal, so there would be no point in our risking discovery by trying to get inside."

"There's one thing that worries me," said Harris.

"What?" said Pendlebury.

"The amount of manpower involved in this. It's practically an army."

"The size is necessary to *avoid* detection," stressed Pendlebury. "It means we can constantly alter shifts. Disney World is ideal; there are far too many people moving around for anyone to get suspicious."

"I hope you're right," said Harris doubtfully.

"What's the word on Terrilli?" asked Al Simpson, who headed the Boynton Beach team.

"Nothing," said Pendlebury. "We've managed to attach a telephone monitor to the outside supply line, but all there has been is calls connected with legitimate businesses. And certainly no contact with Chambine. Now we're all placed, there's no way we will miss any meetings that might occur."

"What about the suite at the Contemporary Resort?" said Gilbert. "They're keeping it on, which surely means more meetings."

"Much better than with Terrilli," said Pendlebury. "We've got microphones into every telephone receiver, so the whole place is live. There's no way anyone can even go to the john without our knowing about it."

"So we'll know in advance when they're going to move?" said Simpson.

"I hope so."

"I think it looks good," said Gilbert confidently. "We're more on top of this than we have been on any of the other auctions. I don't see how it can go wrong."

"We've been lucky," said Pendlebury cautiously. "I never thought it would work out like this when the job began."

"What's the feeling in Washington?" asked Simpson.

Pendlebury thought about the question. "Optimism," he said finally. Feeling a proviso necessary, he added: "They're a little concerned at the danger of overconfidence."

"I don't see how it can go wrong," repeated Gilbert. "We can control the play, whatever happens."

"I'd welcome a little more uncertainty," admitted Pendlebury. "I don't want any complacency."

"How's the exhibition going?" asked Harris suddenly.

"Great," said Pendlebury. "Made about eight thousand already."

"Everyone is going to come out of this happy," forecast Gilbert.

"I'll drink to that when it's all over," said Pendlebury.

The Cadillac bringing Clarissa Willoughby from the airport pulled up in front of the Breakers at about the time Pendlebury was bringing his conference to an end, fifteen miles away.

Charlie had taken a suite for her adjoining his own. He thought there was a reserve about her greeting, but dismissed it, telling her to come to his room as soon as she had unpacked. There was a knock on the linking door within fifteen minutes.

"An English tea," announced Charlie, sweeping his hand out to the table that had been laid in the sitting room. "Even cucumber sandwiches in brown bread."

"Lovely," she said and meant it. Freed from New York and the role she believed she had to play, Clarissa had lost her brittleness. She wore jeans, a silk shirt, very little makeup, and looked beautiful.

Attentively Charlie served her tea, aware of her attention.

"Sally and the others have already gone down to Lyford Key," she said.

"Oh," said Charlie.

"I was glad being able to stop off here."

"I'm glad you were able to come," said Charlie. There was an odd formality about the conversation, he thought.

"I've got some friends here," she said. "They've got a mansion right on the sea."

"Going to contact them?"

"I don't think so."

"Why not?"

"I came down to be with you. How long can I stay?"

He turned, to look fully at her, surprised at both the question and her attitude. And then he confronted the thought. If what he suspected was happening, then it might be physically dangerous for her to remain.

"Not long," he said.

"Why not?"

"There might be some danger."

"I wouldn't get in the way."

"You might not be able to avoid it," said Charlie.

"I feel comfortable with you," said the girl, and Charlie thought again at the hestitation of their greeting in the foyer. Was it a new game? he wondered. He would prefer that to the other alternative.

"I want you to tell Pendlebury something for me," said Charlie, hurrying the conversation beyond the embarrassing pause. "But I want it done very carefully. It's to sound as if you've let something slip . . . as if you're unaware you've told him."

Now she frowned, as if she suspected him of mocking her.

"Is this serious?" she said. "It sounds slightly ridiculous."

"I know it does," admitted Charlie. "But believe me, it's very serious."

He came to sit opposite her, reaching out to take her hands into his own and staring directly into her face.

"It's not a joke, Clarissa. I think there's a risk . . . to the firm, to Rupert . . . of losing three million pounds."

"Good God!" She laughed nervously. "You *must* be joking!"

"I'm not," insisted Charlie.

". . . Well . . . why not tell the police?" groped the woman.

"I don't think it would help," predicted Charlie.

"Now, that *is* ridiculous!"

"I know it seems that way. But it's not."

"I don't understand," protested the woman.

"I can't fully explain it, not yet anyway. If I did, it might spoil what I want you to do."

"What?"

"I want you to let Pendlebury learn, apparently by accident, that I think there's going to be an attempt to steal the Romanov Collection."

"What!" exclaimed the woman.

"And that would cost the firm three million pounds," reminded Charlie again.

"You *must* tell the police," said Clarissa.

"I don't think it would stop it happening," said Charlie patiently. "I believe the thing is being officially organized. Even if the police don't know about it, then I'm sure their awkward involvement could be prevented."

Clarissa frowned, confused by the conversation.

"Will Pendlebury and his people stop it?" she demanded.

"No. I'm pretty sure of that, too."

She looked up at him, caught by a sudden thought. "I've got friends involved in the organization. Kelvin and Sally. They must be warned."

"No," said Charlie desperately. Perhaps asking the woman's assistance had been a mistake.

"You can't think . . ." protested Clarissa.

"Not Sally, no," agreed Charlie. "But I suspect the senator is aware of what's going on . . . some of it, at least. . . ."

"I wish I hadn't agreed to help you," she blurted hurriedly. "I don't understand and it frightens me."

"I'm sorry," said Charlie, immediately recognizing the expression of regret as automatic. Unable accurately to predict what Pendlebury's reaction might be, there could be a danger, involving Clarissa as he had. It was hardly the way to repay the friendship that Willoughby had shown him. Any more than going to bed with the man's wife, however willing she might be.

CHAPTER 13

CHARLIE MUFFIN stood at the window of his suite, staring unseeingly out over the Atlantic, assembling in his mind what he already knew and trying to decide what further action to take.

An anticrime politician was fronting a £3 million exhibition, which, after a cosmetic display in New York, had been moved to the unlikely venue of Palm Beach. Less than three hundred yards away lived a man with previously established links with organized crime. Giuseppe Terrilli's hobby was stamp collecting. And Jack Pendlebury was an FBI operative infiltrated—obviously knowingly—into control of security.

"A setup," judged Charlie, in private conversation. So what could he do? Certainly more than he was attempting with Clarissa Willoughby. At best that could only prompt some ill-considered response from Pendlebury, which would do little more than confirm what he'd already established. What then? There could be no open confrontation. That might lead to a personal investigation that would disclose he had not always been an insurance company official but was, in fact, a former intelligence officer supposed to be dead.

Let it happen?

That was the logical way—the only way—to avoid any personal risk. Just let it happen and trust that whatever the FBI hoped to achieve would result, eventually, in the recovery of the stamps, which Charlie had little doubt they would not oppose being stolen. He sighed, shaking his head and turning away from the ocean view.

Until Sir Archibald Willoughby had been replaced by former soldiers who had introduced into the service ex-public school limp-wrists, Charlie Muffin had established himself as the premier operative within the department. Even under someone as independent and innovative as Sir Archibald, however, there had still been a degree of bureaucracy with which they had had to conform, and part of it had been the yearly psychiatric and psychological examinations for his continued suitability. And because he had always later burgled the filing cabinets of the personnel officer, to find out what his assessment had been, Charlie knew that every time there had been a report upon his peculiar inability to avoid open confrontation.

"Tenacity syndrome" was one of the more pompous attempts to describe it which had taken his fancy. Vindictiveness had been another judgment, which Charlie had thought unnecessarily critical. He didn't regard it as either tenacity or vindictiveness. He had just always resented anything that made him look a prick. And that was what would be happening if he didn't interfere. Pendlebury and whoever else was involved would be pissing themselves with laughter, imagining they were financially protected if anything went wrong. And Charlie had been part of sufficient foolproof schemes to know how easily they all got cocked up and ended in disaster.

And for the syndicate of which Willoughby was the head to be responsible for a £3 million settlement would *be* a disaster.

What's the answer, Charlie? he demanded of himself.

It came with the suddenness and clarity of all good ideas, and Charlie sniggered at the perfect simplicity of it. What was it he'd said that day in Willoughby's office—"Never underestimate the Russian national pride." So he wouldn't. Who better to safeguard what had once been Russian than the Russians themselves?

Unwilling for there to be any connection between the call and the hotel where he might be discovered staying, Charlie went to the lobby and changed ten dollars into coin at the cashier's desk and then drove across Lake Worth to the mainland, traveling without any intended direction. Merely because there was a signpost to Riviera Beach, he turned northward, slowing when he entered the township and managing to park within twenty yards of a drugstore. He ensured that the door was tightly closed behind him when he entered the telephone booth and got the Washington number of the Russian embassy from information within minutes. As he was about to make the call he hesitated, stopped by another thought. He would have to use the name, he decided. Otherwise there was a risk of the warning being ignored as a crank call.

The Washington connection was immediate. The switchboard operator was a woman, but her intonation was mannish.

"The Second Secretary," insisted Charlie. "I'm calling on behalf of Comrade General Valery Kalenin."

He put a curtness into his voice, a challenge against any argument.

There was a lull of uncertainty on the line.

"Put me through to the Second Secretary," repeated Charlie.

The line went blank and then another voice, obviously a man's this time, said: "Who is this?"

Ignoring the question, Charlie said: "An attempt is to be made to steal the Romanov Collection, currently on display in Palm Beach, in Florida."

"Who is this?" demanded the voice again.

"Ensure the information reaches Comrade General Valery Kalenin," said Charlie, replacing the receiver.

He returned to the car, going back south along the coast road. It had been seven years, he reflected. Near eight, in fact. Would Kalenin still be the operational head of the KGB? Charlie had liked the squat, burly Russian during their meetings in Vienna and Prague, when he had determined the retribution against those who had tried to have him killed.

"You'll regret doing it afterward," Kalenin had warned when there was still time for the whole thing to be called off.

"They were willing to let me die," Charlie had argued. "I shan't be sorry."

But he had been wrong, he admitted to himself, turning the rent-a-car back across the bridge toward Palm Beach. There had rarely been a day when he and Edith were on the run when he hadn't remembered what the KGB chief had said. And after Edith had died, during the time when the British and the Americans had come so close to catching him, that regret changed to abject remorse. If it hadn't been for Willoughby, Charlie sometimes wondered if it would not have eventually become suicidal.

Reminded of Willoughby's friendship, Charlie thought again of what he had asked Clarissa to do. By the time anything happened, she would be miles away, at Lyford Key, he decided. His mind refused the assurance. No matter what the justification, it was no way to repay Willoughby's help. He continued the reflection, snorting at his own hypocrisy. If he were completely honest, he would admit to being a willing bed partner, too.

"You're a shit, Charlie," he told himself as he parked the car outside the hotel. "A proper shit."

He heard movement through the open linking door of their apartments as soon as he entered his own rooms. At the sound of his door closing, she came through, smiling at him. She had been swimming. Her wet hair was coiled back with a band and she still wore the bathing wrap in which she had come from the pool. Without makeup, she looked very young.

"Wonderful news," she said eagerly.

"What?"

"I met that man, Pendlebury. He was in the bar by the pool and spoke to me. We chatted and then he asked me where you were and I said working because you were worried and when he asked why I said because you thought there might be an attempt on the collection... isn't that fabulous...?"

Her words tumbled out in her excitement, which gradually faltered at the look on his face.

"What is it, darling?" she said.

"Nothing," said Charlie. "I was just reminded of something that occurred to me coming back in the car."

She came further into the room, putting out her arms to hold him. "That's what you wanted, wasn't it?"

"Yes," he said. "That's what I wanted."

"You don't sound pleased."

Knowing her need for reassurance, he pulled her close and kissed her forehead.

"Thank you," he said. "I'm very pleased."

She clung to him and Charlie stood, staring out over her head to the view at which he had been looking when the idea about the Russians had come to him, three hours earlier.

Survival—his own, personal, unhindered safety—had always been the motivating force in Charlie's life. He had conceded it, to himself, very early in his operational career and then defended it, later, when others had recognized the trait and criticized the lengths he was prepared to go. There had, of course, been the proper awareness and a proper regret that people sometimes had to suffer, but Charlie had rarely been troubled by any lasting conscience, perhaps because usually people he was using were in the same profession and would not have been concerned doing the same to him.

But suddenly it wasn't easy anymore. He pulled her away

from him, kissing her lightly on the forehead. He didn't think he was going very much to enjoy living with the sort of conscience he was feeling now.

Jack Pendlebury sat unmoving in a chair in his sitting room, two floors below Charlie Muffin, considering what the woman had told him. He decided that Clarissa Willoughby was stupid. And that therefore the information had been volunteered unwittingly.

He was connected to Warburger within minutes, and as soon as he told the Director the reason for the call, Warburger brought Bowler on the line in a conference call.

"Kill him," said Warburger immediately.

"But at the proper time," argued Pendlebury, content with the idea that had come to him.

"That's now," insisted Bowler.

"No," said Pendlebury. "My way we get an indictment for murder against Terrilli."

CHAPTER 14

GENERAL VALERY Kalenin was a short, square-bodied Georgian considered unique within the Kremlin and therefore regarded by some with awe, by others with suspicion, and by nearly everyone with respect. He had come unscathed through the Stalin era, even during the purges of the intelligence departments which had followed Lavrenti Beria's fall from favor and survived, too, the apparent liberalization under Krushchev, which in reality had been nothing of the sort. He had achieved this not by sycophancy, even in Stalin's time when the attitude was considered essential, because he regarded sycophancy as inevitably the surest way to disaster. It had even happened to as adept a toady as Beria.

Kalenin had done it by absolute and utter dedication to his job, thus creating an efficiency unparalleled in any other department of Soviet government, and because the majority of

Soviet government is clogged by bureaucracy, this increased his prestige.

That he was able to show such dedication was possible because of the unusual sort of person that Kalenin was. A bachelor with a brilliant, calculating mind, he had absolutely no social ability, and because of some psychological quirk, which he accepted without regret because he didn't know what he was missing, he had no sexual inclination, either male or female. The lack of interest was usually obvious to both, which deepened the attitude in which he was regarded because men in Kalenin's position invariably used their power for personal indulgences. Beria had actually created a squad of men to kidnap pubescent virgins off the streets of Moscow.

With virtually nothing to distract him apart from his absorption in the history of tank warfare, in which he was an acknowledged expert, Kalenin's entire existence was devoted to the Komitet Gosudarstvennoy Bezopasnosti, and actually within the KGB he was a revered figure. He worked sixteen hours a day in their headquarters in Dzerzhinsky Square, a gray-stone building which before the revolution had belonged to the All-Russian Insurance Company, or in any of the capitals of the Warsaw Pact, of which he was overall intelligence commander, no matter what lip service was made to the pretense of separate, national identity. Any surplus time was spent organizing solitary war games with his toy tanks on the kitchen floor of his apartment in Kutuzovsky Prospekt and it was during this relaxation that he occasionally regretted the absence of friends. Even though he was scrupulously fair, never cheating with the dice, it was always difficult to perform as leader of both sides.

Normally, something as minuscule as an anonymous telephone call to a foreign embassy would not have been forwarded for his personal attention, because Kalenin regarded delegation as an essential part of efficiency. But it was not normal for anonymous telephone callers to refer by name to the head of the KGB, because as with sex, Kalenin was absolutely disinterested in any fame or notoriety, actually going to extensive lengths to conceal his identity throughout the Eastern bloc and taking absolute care that it was not known in the West.

The report was made initially from the American Capital by telex, and within twenty-four hours Kalenin had demanded a full account. Because the call had lasted barely thirty seconds, there wasn't much of it. In addition, the KGB resident in Washington had included a full report of the Romanov exhibition, even attaching some newspaper reviews of its display in New York.

Kalenin's office in Dzerzhinsky Square reflected the man, a starkly bare, functional room, with a disregarded view of other offices and chancelleries within the Kremlin complex, and two days after Charlie Muffin's contact, Kalenin sat there, quite alone, the completed file before him.

The time was long past when the government of Russia dismissed as bourgeois irrelevance the legacies of Tsarism. The treasures of the Armory in Moscow and the Hermitage in Leningrad were actually offered as a tourist attraction. The attitude was different, of course, for anything that had been taken from the country in the immediate confusion after 1917. But not very different. Because his survival depended upon such awareness, Kalenin knew there would be irritation within the Presidium if anything were to happen to the Romanov Collection. What was Russian remained Russian, wherever it was. That knowledge would have been sufficient to initiate a reaction, but the risk to a collection of stamps was not Kalenin's predominant concern as he sat reflectively in his sterile room. He was far more interested in the identity of a pay-phone user in the American state of Florida who knew his name. For that reason there was one part of the Washington report upon which Kalenin had sought clarification, and he pulled the addendum toward him now. An English voice, the initial report had said. The additional information was that the expression had meant to convey there was no intonation of any foreign language. Either English or American, then. But because of the location, more likely American. A CIA trap, to trick him into some reaction that might get Russians involved and enable a political embarrassment? A possibility, Kalenin supposed. But it was a very clumsy effort; too clumsy to be the strongest likelihood.

What, then? Kalenin posed again the question that had occupied his mind for the past forty-eight hours and again could not offer himself an answer. The burly man sighed, closing the folder. He would have to discover the solution, he knew; that was how he had existed for so long at the echelon he occupied. Even though he doubted entrapment, Kalenin knew he would have to guard against it. But because the operation was in Florida, he had already determined a way to achieve that. And in such a fashion that if the CIA were involved, whatever scheme they had evolved would explode in their faces. A man who constantly planned ahead, Kalenin had had flown to Moscow fifty CIA-trained Cubans within twenty-four hours of their seizure after the abortive Bay of Pigs invasion during the Kennedy administration. It had only taken three months of imprisonment to turn them. Twenty would be put into Florida, to protect the exhibition. And if the CIA sprang a trap, they'd find they had caught their own men; Kalenin was sure that through the news media he covertly controlled he would be able to expose their capture and their history within hours of it having occurred.

The selection of the man who would attempt to discover the identity of the mystery caller, rather than protect the exhibition, was something that required deeper consideration. There *was* a man, an operative who had been installed with a deep cover in the California city of San Diego and allowed to establish an outwardly respectable job and life, both of which would have defied any investigation, no matter how detailed. Kalenin hesitated from activating him, unwilling to expend such an investment. But as head of the KGB, his identity was officially defined as a state secret. So it followed that the knowledge of it and use from American pay phones could be officially described as endangering state security.

Kalenin reopened the file before him, seeking a date. He would have liked to brief the man personally, but with only twelve days remaining before the end of the exhibition in Florida did not consider he had sufficient time to withdraw him to Moscow and then return him to America. It would have to be a briefing from remote control.

Kalenin depressed the button on his office intercom, then sat looking toward the door but with his eyes pitched over it, counting from the second hand of the clock mounted there the time it took the secretary to reply. It was a man who entered, one minute and forty-five seconds later. Kalenin preferred male to female secretaries, simply because over a long period he had found them more efficient. He nodded on this occasion, impressed with the speed of the response.

Kalenin accepted the second file, opened it, and stared down at the photograph of an open-faced, smiling man, his hair cropped into a college crew cut. "Yale" was inscribed across the front of his sweat shirt.

Result of a one-night union beside a park bench twenty-eight years earlier between a falsely hopeful factory worker and a drunken seaman in the Lithuanian port of Klaipeda, Anatoli Nosenko had been plucked from the orphanage at the age of four and taken first to a special house inland at Kaunas and then, after a medical examination had proved his fitness and his Western rather than Slavic appearance judged acceptable, taken across country to the special school in the Moscow hills. At the age of five, when most Western children enter kindergarten, to scrawl with crayons, shape Plasticine, and grope with their letters, Anatoli commenced daily eight-hour training to enable him to become a deep penetration agent within the United States of America. Within a week of his arrival, he was ascribed the name John Williamson and never again referred to by his Russian identity. His instructors, who themselves had been specially schooled in language laboratories, spoke to him only in American-accented English, and he listened to taped American radio programs and watched videotape recordings of American television. He was taught baseball and allowed to favor a particular team and follow their fortunes from the league standings during the season. He ate hamburgers and knew they came from McDonald's, preferred his Kentucky fried chicken straight and not in barbecue batter, and found peanut butter and jelly sandwiches too sweet. He thought root beer tasted like medicine and always chose diet cola. At the age of fifteen, coupled with his continued Americanization and education, there began additional instruction in radio communications and intelligence gathering. When he was seventeen, Williamson, whose educational qualifications were at least three years ahead of any comparable American teenager because of the unremitting, concentrated tuition, underwent six months of final preparation, during which his role was made clear to him. He was to be introduced into America and allowed to create a completely normal existence, giving no thought whatsoever to the Soviet Union until the time when he received the message activating him for the work for which he had been so exhaustively prepared. That message might arrive within a year, five years, ten years, or maybe—

although unlikely, in view of the effort and expenditure—never.

It was because of that training and expenditure that Kalenin deeply debated the utilization of such a man. It took him a further thirty minutes, once again weighing all the alternatives, before making the commitment. The preparation of the briefing, to be sent on the coded diplomatic wire to the Washington embassy and forwarded from there in such a way that the sender would have no idea of the recipient or purpose of the message, took Kalenin a further seven hours and it was almost midnight before he again looked up to the clock over the door.

He leaned back, stretching, decided that the El-Alamein campaign which he had intended to re-create on the floor of his apartment that night would have to be postponed.

The initial message, merely alerting Williamson that he was being activated, arrived five hours later in the bachelor apartment with the view of the port in which he worked as a freight clerk in a shipping firm. Obedient to his training, his first response was to initiate the cover story to protect himself against any curiosity for what, to those who knew him, would be regarded as unusual. In preparation for such an alert, Williamson had let it be known that he had family in the East and got a week's leave of absence on the grounds of his father's impending death, after a long and painful illness, in Washington.

By ten o'clock in the morning he had packed, canceled all deliveries, and set out for the poste restante mailbox where he knew his complete instructions would be awaiting him.

It was exactly nine years, eight months, and nine days from the Wednesday morning when he had arrived, on a students' ticket on the Paris-Dallas flight, and then boarded the Greyhound bus for San Diego. He was very excited. The package was waiting and he put it immediately and unopened into an inner pocket of his jacket and walked until he found an unoccupied park bench before unsealing it. He sat for thirty minutes, committing his instructions to memory, then found a washroom in a nearby motel where he shredded the paper and flushed it, piece by piece, down a toilet. There were some other things in the package, which he put into his pocket.

By noon he was at the airport, with a ticket secured for the three o'clock flight to Miami. There had never been a day when a part of him had not remained tense, in readiness for this moment. Many times he had tried to conjecture the sort of mission for which he would be roused and never imagined it would be anything like this. Knowing the importance of General Valery Kalenin, he was aware, too, of the confidence in which he was held.

The type of mission had not been the only surprise. The conclusion of the briefing remained with him, more indelibly than the rest. He had been trained for such an eventuality and schooled to perform the function, but had always wondered how he would react if he were told to kill a man.

And that was what the message had insisted, most explicitly. He was to discover the person who knew the KGB chief's identity, learn how it had come about, and then, to prevent any further dissemination, kill whoever had that knowledge.

The flight was on time and the plane half empty, so the seat next to Williamson was unoccupied, enabling him to put his bags there and provide more foot room.

He sighed. It was good to be working properly, after so long. He wondered if he would be able to get it done and return to San Diego within the week. In only one thing had he veered from the intense training he had received in Moscow. He had never been able truly to appreciate either American baseball or football, so the advent into the United States of European soccer had delighted him. He rarely missed a match of the Los Angeles Aztecs, and their next game, somewhat ironically, was against the Tampa Bay Rowdies. He didn't want to miss it.

CHAPTER 15

JACK PENDLEBURY felt no hesitation bringing one of his squads into Palm Beach because they were not to be employed in any way connected with the exhibition and he was therefore confident they would not be detected by whatever check Guiseppe Terrilli might make.

Within an hour of his poolside conversation with Clarissa Willoughby, the American had withdrawn Roger Gilbert from Lake Worth and appointed him controller of the surveillance operation on Charlie Muffin, with responsibility for thirty men. It took Gilbert a further two hours to get his people into position, identify their subject, and establish a rota system under which each group operated with a safety margin of duty every third day.

Charlie located the surveillance almost as soon as it was imposed. Relief came with the identification, because since Clarissa's supposed indiscretion Charlie had been tensed for some response and would have been more alarmed had there not been one.

Charlie was sure that his training and past experience still gave him an advantage. It enabled him to think like Pendlebury, which was of primary importance. And now he was aware of being watched, it meant he could, without Pendlebury suspecting it, influence the man's responses.

"A clever animal, knowing it is being pursued, can always lead its hunters to disaster."

That had been another of Sir Archibald's catchphrases and Charlie had used it before when an operation had temporarily slipped out of control.

He left the Breakers, pausing at the end of the drive to check his watch, and then began pacing along South County Road, a man establishing a time schedule. At Bethesda, Pendleton Avenue, and then Barton Avenue he consulted his watch again, then turned left, to bring himself out to Ocean Boulevard. At the entrance to the private road to Terrilli's house, he hesitated, looking once more at his watch, continued on for about a hundred yards, and then retraced his steps. As he passed the private road, he allowed another pause and glanced in toward the unseen, castellated mansion. Despite the heat, which made him sweat, Charlie returned to the Breakers at the same brisk pace. Twice during the journey he checked the time.

Inside the hotel, he queued at the cashier's for change, then entered one of the public telephone booths, from which it would be impossible for anyone later to establish from the hotel switchboard to whom he made contact. Shuddering slightly as the air conditioning cooled the perspiration on him, Charlie went through a fifteen-minute charade of making long-distance calls, in fact dialing for the time, the weather information, the small advertisement department of the Palm Beach *Daily News* to ask about small-ad rates and the airport to inquire about services to Miami, New Orleans, and New York.

He composed a satisfied expression upon his face before leaving the booth and went immediately to the Alcazar, where he had arranged to meet Clarissa.

She was already waiting. She wore a crisp white dress, with little jewelry, hardly any makeup, and her hair was tied back in the way he had told her he liked.

He waved exuberantly at her, kissed her cheek as he got to the table, and then gestured extravangantly at a waiter, announcing as he looked back to the woman: "We'll celebrate."

"What?" she asked, frowning slightly at Charlie's performance.

"It's a game," he said more quietly. "I'm trying to worry people."

"Do I need to know the rules?"

"No. Just follow along," said Charlie. Once, he thought, she would have turned the remark into some sort of sexual innuendo. Her attitude was a pleasant improvement.

"Where have you been?" she asked.

Raising his voice, Charlie said: "Taking an important walk."

Clarissa grimaced through the window toward the sun-whitened sand.

"It's too damned hot for walking," she said.

"Not for the sort of walking I did," said Charlie.

"You seem very pleased with yourself."

"People seem to be responding in the way I want."

"When am I going to know the secret?"

"As soon as I do," said Charlie seriously and more softly.

"More puzzles?"

"But we've got a lot more of the pieces fitted together than we had a few days ago."

"Has Pendlebury approached you yet?"

"Not yet."

"Isn't that odd?" said Clarissa. "Surely as the man in charge of security, he should have contacted you immediately, after what I told him."

"Yes," agreed Charlie. "That's what he should have done. But he isn't thinking properly."

He raised his drink to the woman and said, loudly again, "To the success of the operation."

She drank, disguising her bewilderment.

In a corner of the room but with a better view of the ocean, Robert Chambine sat unaware of the couple, Coca-Cola before him and a copy of the Miami *Herald* discarded beside it. He was looking toward the door when Leonard Saxby and Peter Boella entered. There was not the slightest indication of any recognition between them. The two men went immediately to the bar, gossiping about that morning's golf score.

"I had a call from Lyford Key this morning," announced Clarissa. "They want to know when I'm going down."

She had been looking away from him, but now she stared directly into his face.

"How much longer would you like me to stay?" she said.

There was none of the imperious demand that had been in her voice in New York. And she didn't speak in italics anymore, Charlie realized. She'd performed the function for which he had asked her to come to Palm Beach. But was proving additionally useful for this charade.

Charlie suddenly became aware of the intensity of her expression, and his mind was thrown, with frightening clarity, to his earlier thoughts in the hotel suite and then through the years to an argument he had had with Edith, soon after they had gone on the run and he had explained fully to her what he had done and the people he had deceived to make it possible.

"... There's a cruelty about you, Charlie," she had accused. "A cruelty that sees nothing wrong in using anyone, even me...."

He'd denied it, of course. And four years later stared down at the pulped body of the only woman he would ever love but upon whom he had constantly cheated and known he'd never lose the guilt of using her.

"I'd stay if you want me to," said Clarissa. She hesitated, a smile trying hopefully at the edges of her mouth. Then she added: "I'd like to, really..."

"No," he stopped positively. "It's better you go."

"... Please..." she tried, but Charlie shook his head at her again.

"I told you it would be dangerous," he said. "And it might."

"You're just saying that... an excuse," she said.

"I'm not," said Charlie sincerely. "I promised Rupert there wouldn't be any danger."

"Hardly kept your promise, did you?" she demanded, turning the words back upon him and reminding him of the other guilt.

Charlie frowned, nervous of the direction of the conversation.

"Let's not be stupid, Clarissa."

"Never that," she said. "The society firefly, that's me."

It was her first attempt at brittleness for a long time and it failed and they both knew it.

He moved to speak, but she burst out ahead of him. "Don't tell me how much older you are than me."

"I am."

"That's a cop-out," she said. "Like married men always try to end an affair by saying their responsibility to their children is too great."

"I wasn't going to talk about age," said Charlie.

"What, then?"

"You'd become bored . . . honestly you would."

"I wouldn't," she said defiantly.

"It's like . . ." He stopped, searching for the expression. ". . . like a holiday romance," he resumed badly. "There wouldn't be any novelty left, back in England."

"I wasn't regarding it as a novelty."

"Think about it," he said. "That's all it is, really."

To cover the sigh, he brought the glass to his lips. The conversation had disconcerted him. Mixed with the surprise was an irritation; it was creating a situation he didn't want, taking his mind from Pendlebury and Terrilli and the Russian stamps.

Behind him and therefore unseen, Saxby and Boella finished their drinks and left the Alcazar, wandering out into the parking lot alongside the exhibition room with the apparent need to check something in their golf equipment in the trunk of their car.

"I don't find it easy to beg," she said.

"Then don't."

"I don't want to go away from here."

"I want you to."

"It's normally me who dictates the end to these sort of things," she said.

"I'm not discarding you," attempted Charlie. "I'm asking

you to go down to Lyford Key because it might be safer for you there than here."

"You'll see me when we get back to London?"

"As a friend," he qualified.

She laughed, trying to make it a sneering sound. "What's the difference between screwing a man's wife three thousand miles from home rather than two miles away?"

"None, I suppose," admitted Charlie honestly. "It just seems different, somehow."

"I think you're a bastard," she said.

To remind her that it had been she who initiated the seduction would qualify him for the description, Charlie decided.

"Yes," he said. "I am."

She made as if to rise, abruptly, but then relaxed against the table.

"I'm sorry I've been a nuisance," she said.

"You're not."

"An embarrassment, then."

"Nor that, either."

"Could there *really* be danger?"

"Yes," he said. "Quite easily."

"And you could get hurt?"

Charlie thought about the question. "I've usually managed to avoid it," he said.

"But you *could?*"

"I suppose so. That's why I don't want you to say anything of this to Sally. It mustn't get back to Cosgrove."

"Please be careful," she said.

"I'm always that," promised Charlie.

"I've a car coming for me at eight," said the woman. Seeing Charlie's expression, she said: "I didn't think you'd want me to stay. And I could have always canceled it."

"Of course," he said.

"It's only twelve-thirty."

"Do you want lunch?" he invited.

"No."

"Another drink?"

"No. I want to say good-bye properly."

He rose, to help her from her chair. She didn't stand immediately, instead remaining where she was and gazing up at him.

"It's strange," she said. "If anyone had told me a month ago that this was going to happen, I'd have said they were mad."

"Novelty," repeated Charlie.

"I wonder how long it will take to wear off?" she said, rising at last.

Pendlebury regarded the arrival of Saxby and Boella as marginally more important. He immediately allocated more men to the two known criminals, ignoring Warburger's fears about detection because he felt the sudden situation justified the risk. When he learned about their checks on the lighting cables, he nodded happily, confident the operation was going exactly as he intended and that he was in complete control.

The initial surprise at the Englishman's visit to Terrilli's home did not last long. It meant he had identified the video picture, that's all. It still needn't alter the timing of the man's death.

Pendlebury left his room and shambled to the elevator, head sunk against his chest in concentration. He'd delayed too long openly to confront the man about his suspicions of robbery, Pendlebury decided. He would have to behave as if he attached no importance to what the woman had said.

He was still deeply in thought when he emerged at ground level, so that the presence of one of his people near the desk momentarily startled him.

"Any news of the insurance guy?" he said.

"Spent three hours with the woman," said the agent. "She's just left and he's gone back to his rooms; probably needs the rest. Must be quite a performer."

"Yes," said Pendlebury. "I think he is."

John Williamson planned his attempted entry into the exhibition chamber very carefully, knowing there was only five minutes before it closed. The security men were in a bunch, even those in plain clothes, so the Russian managed to achieve an almost group photograph with the Minnox camera concealed within the specially hollow book he carried beneath his arm. He allowed himself to be halted and smiled apologetically at his stupidity at expecting to view the stamps so late, glancing around and isolating the security cameras while he was talking to an attendant. There would be time enough later, he assured the man. He was staying for several days.

He was turning when the elevator opened to his right and he saw the unkempt figure of another of the security men whom he'd identified from his observation of the exhibition earlier in the evening. From the deference, someone in authority, Williamson had judged.

As Charlie Muffin strolled casually across the lobby, Williamson managed three exposures on his camera, two full face and one profile. With luck, he thought, he might get the other man who had gone upstairs about thirty minutes earlier: another person of authority, the man had decided. And similarly scruffy. If he didn't manage it that night, there was always the following day.

For the moment, Williamson considered the Cubans more important. He was impressed with them and intended telling Moscow. Despite being provided with a complete description, it had taken him several hours to identify them all. He seated himself casually in one of the lobby chairs, less than fifteen feet from Manuel Ramírez, whom he knew to be the leader from the information he had been provided with in San Diego. The Cuban was a middle-aged, thickly built man, his hair already whitening at the temples. He appeared quite at ease in the luxury of an American hotel; had Williamson not been a trained observer, it would have been impossible to detect the attention that Ramírez was paying to the exhibition, even though it was now closed for the night. Williamson continued his gaze around the lobby. Ramírez had perfectly assigned his people, ensuring that every possible entry was in sight. Because he had come only minutes earlier from the parking area, Williamson knew there were two more men outside, with the garden windows covered.

He looked back to Ramírez, feeling a brief moment of pity for the man who imagined the operation his passport back to America. Quickly he stifled the feeling, surprised at its appearance. It made unarguable sense to expose them, if the need arose, so that the CIA would be embarrassed.

He rose, moving toward the restaurant. All he had done so far, he conceded to himself, was establish the procedures which were basic at the commencement of any operation. It was time he concentrated on the purpose of his mission, isolating the man who knew General Kalenin.

The maître d'hôtel greeted him at the entrance to the dining room, hesitated in search for a single seat, and then led him to within three tables of where Charlie Muffin was also sitting, alone.

CHAPTER 16

ROBERT CHAMBINE, who had two children at a $2,000-a-year school in Scarsdale, stood unobtrusively at the edge of the warehouse, intently watching the group go through their rehearsal and thinking of the end-of-term plays through which he and his wife always sat, proud at their daughters' participation.

Chambine was surprised at the analogy, because really there wasn't very much similarity. These six weren't playacting and it showed. They had improved upon the equipment he provided and, using the plans and measures, had created a workable reconstruction of the exhibition room at the Breakers. Polystyrene blocks represented the walls, with gaps for windows and doors. Each camera and spotlight had been fixed to a photographic extension pole, set at precisely the height and position at which Bulz and Beldini would have to work.

The innovation at which Chambine was particularly impressed was the Polaroid cameras, of which he had not thought. They had bought four, and while Bulz and Beldini came in through the side door and went through their practice, covering first lights and then lenses, the other men positioned themselves by four of the cameras and took photographs as rapidly as they could. It fell far short of what the videotape would record, but it had enabled the two men who would be going first into the room to realize and therefore guard against the points of maximum exposure.

Throughout the polystyrene was threaded red and yellow cord, indicating the wired alarms, and these had actually been connected to battery-operated bells which rang if, during any part of the rehearsal, anyone disturbed either a window or door alarm or stepped on one of the pressure pads that Chambine had guessed at and therefore marked around the display cases.

As much thought had gone into the cases as with everything else. The entry through the side door was practiced so that a lengthy bypass lead, with alligator clips at either end, could be simply clamped into place to maintain the circuit and the intervening alarm wire cut, enabling the door to be opened with a gap of about two feet.

Chambine initially frowned at the other leads with which Bertrano entered the practice area, after Bulz and Beldini had immobilized the cameras, unable to think of a purpose either for them or for the expandable steel rods the man carried in his other hand. And then he smiled at the expertise. The rods were extended and then slipped beneath the cases, with Bertrano and Petrilli at either end. At Bertrano's nod, they lifted, but only slightly. Chambine saw they had anticipated that the case legs would be wired, to trigger an alarm the moment there was any extended movement. With the case about three inches from the ground, Bulz and Beldini went on their knees and clipped more bypass leads into place, linking them with the alarms on the adjoining case so that at all times the circuit would remain intact.

"Good," applauded Chambine, moving further into the warehouse when the rehearsal was over. "Very good indeed."

The performance had gone far more smoothly than he had ever hoped it would.

"Our first attempt timed out at forty-five minutes," said Bertrano. "The last three runs have all come out around twenty."

"The camera covering averages out at about four minutes," added Bulz. "We can lose about another minute, but it increases the risk of exposure before a camera. Even though we'll be masked, we figure it isn't worth it."

"I agree," said Chambine. "Four minutes is fine."

"Can you imagine any other alarms we haven't thought of?" asked Bertrano.

Chambine shook his head. "Nothing," he said. He turned to Saxby and Boella.

"What about the outside lights?"

"Better than we expected," said Saxby. "Every fourth lighting pedestal has a small junction box. Idea must be to *reduce* the possibility of a full-scale blackout. All we'll have to do is to make our selection and take out the entry cables with wire cutters."

"Have you worked out a pattern?" demanded Chambine.

Boella produced a drawing. It was quite detailed, showing the area off South County Road and Breakers Row, with the hotel golf course sketched in. The lights were designated in green and those they intended extinguishing were crossed through in black.

"Swimming pool and beach area first," set out Saxby, indicating the initial targets. "That'll create a diversion. Then some in the gardens, but still away from the exhibition area. Those around there and the parking lot will be the last."

Chambine moved his head, as satisfied with this as he had been with the other preparations.

"We thought about midnight," said Bertrano. "By that time those still around will be sufficiently drunk and the hotel staff will be tired."

Chambine stood nodding.

"At midnight," took up Saxby, "we hit the lights by the pool . . ."

". . . and we go in through the side door, immediately after the security checks by the guards," said Bertrano.

"We paced out the distance," said Saxby. "Four times, in fact. Allowing three minutes for any eventuality we haven't considered, we'll be outside the exhibition hall, with all the lights out, in fifteen minutes."

"And by that time," said Bertrano, "we will have all the cases except the last two freed from whatever wiring there might be and positioned near the parking lot window."

"Which is fifteen minutes ahead of the next security patrol," remembered Chambine.

"We want to talk about that," said Bertrano. "One thing which could stretch our timing is how long it will take us to load the cases into the cars. Even if there is no interruption, I can't see us clearing the parking lot before twelve twenty-five. That's only five minutes before the inspection. It's hardly long enough."

"Wouldn't it be better if we waited and took the guards out?" asked Boella, obviously the spokesman for the proposal.

"It would take maybe half an hour . . . perhaps longer, to discover what had happened to them. That would give us much more time . . . we'd be clear of the island."

Chambine made a reluctant movement with his head. "I said I didn't want violence if it could be avoided," he reminded them.

"We're not sure if it's safe to avoid it," pressed Bertrano.

"If we are out of the parking lot by twelve twenty-five, then we will have disposed of the cases by twelve-forty," said Chambine. "By twelve-fifty you'll be paid off and on your way. If the alarm is raised promptly at twelve-thirty, I can't imagine the police getting themselves organized in twenty minutes, can you?"

"And what happens if we don't get away from the parking lot by twelve twenty-five?" asked Boella stubbornly.

For several moments, Chambine did not reply. Then he said: "I agree it's a problem."

"So how do we resolve it?" asked Bertrano.

Chambine sighed, reaching the decision. "I shall be outside in the parking lot, with Saxby and Boella," he said, addressing them as a group. "I'll be responsible for time checking that part of the operation. If it becomes clear that we're not going to be able to get away . . . completely away . . . a few moments before twelve twenty-five, then we'll stay and hit the security people as soon as they enter the room. . . ."

There were relieved smiles from the men in front of him.

". . . I'm agreeing to it because it is obviously the sensible thing to do," he went on. "But if I can, I'll avoid it. . . ."

He looked particularly at Saxby, Boella, and Petrilli.

"Don't forget what I said about those guns," he warned them. "If we get away without trouble, I want them dumped. I'm not having something as sweet as this screwed up by an unlicensed-weapon arrest."

Saxby and Boella nodded and Petrilli said: "Sure, I won't forget."

"I mean it," stressed Chambine.

"Okay!" said Saxby.

Chambine hesitated at the challenge in Saxby's voice and then decided to let it pass. Instead he looked at Bertrano. "I'd like the suite, for a meeting."

"Sure," agreed the man from Chicago.

Chambine extended the conversation, to include them all.

"And I'd appreciate your all being away from the hotel, from noon to maybe four o'clock."

Saxby grinned. "So he's a shy guy."

"Yes," said Chambine. "He's a shy man. And for fifty thousand apiece, he buys his right to stay that way."

"Nobody minds," said Bertrano.

"I'll be here before noon," said Chambine. "At exactly midday, I'll telephone the Papeete Bay Veranda at the Polynesian Village hotel. I want to know you're all there."

Chambine waited for any objection to this open doubt that one of them might remain, to discover who the financier was.

"We said we'd be away from the hotel," reminded Bertrano quietly.

"And I said he buys the right to remain anonymous," said Chambine. He waited, but no one appeared to want to take the conversation further.

"I think this is going to work," said Chambine, wanting to reduce the feeling that had arisen between them. "I want to thank you all for what you've done."

"We are as determined for this to succeed as you are," said Bertrano.

Chambine nodded. "We'll not meet again, as a group, until Thursday. I'll be in the foyer, ready for you to arrive...."

He looked at Bertrano. "... As soon as you enter, I'll leave, to be in the parking lot when Saxby and Boella start taking out the lights. I will have earlier in the day put the station wagon and backup car into position immediately outside the exhibition room...."

"What about cars after the payoff?" interrupted Petrilli.

"I'll be responsible for that, too," assured Chambine. "There's a parking meter area, overlooking the sea on Ocean Boulevard. There'll be rent-a-cars parked there. I'll give you the keys and numbers at the same time as the money. I'd like you all to make plane reservations to get out of Florida as soon as you can on Wednesday morning. Probably be safer to fly from Miami."

There were assorted gestures of agreement from the men before him.

Chambine waved his hand toward the practice area. "And I want all this stuff dumped. And I mean dumped. I don't want anybody trying to hock any of the cameras or lights and being remembered if there's any police check. Just discard it. Understood?"

"Understood," said Saxby.

"It's going to work," repeated Chambine enthusiastically. "It's going to work beautifully."

He went out of the side door of the warehouse, to which five of Pendlebury's surveillance squad had followed him from Palm Beach and at which one man would remain, later to retrieve the listening device that had been planted after the observers attached to the group at the Contemporary Resort had trailed them to the building, the day they had begun rehearsing and upon which every practice had been monitored.

Within three hours of Chambine's encounter with the men who were going to carry out the robbery, the recording was on its way, by car, to the FBI controller at the Breakers.

General Valery Kalenin had one friend, and the contrast between them made that association inexplicable to the few who knew about it. Alexei Berenkov ranked among the most successful agents ever infiltrated into the West. A flamboyant extrovert of a man, he had remained undetected for nearly fifteen years and behind the facade of a wine importer's business in the City of London developed a network that had penetrated the NATO headquarters in Brussels and the Cabinets of two British administrations.

His capture had been a setback to Kalenin's service. But because of their friendship, remote though it had been all those years, the seizure had distressed Kalenin even more than it would have done to have lost any other operative of Berenkov's caliber. It was that feeling which had made him cast aside his customary caution and agree so readily to the operation, about eight years earlier, in which the heads of the American and British intelligence services had been trapped by an aggrieved British agent; they had provided Kalenin with guaranteed hostages that he had used to get Berenkov repatriated from the British jail in which he had been serving a forty-year sentence.

Since Berenkov's return, the habit had developed for them to meet at least once a week, alternating between Kalenin's spartan apartment and Berenkov's home, where the man's wife always prepared the Georgian meals she knew Kalenin enjoyed.

This week it was Berenkov's turn to visit Kutuzovsky Prospekt. They had eaten well but less elaborately than at Berenkov's house and sat now over coffee and the remains of the French wine upon which Kalenin knew his friend had become a connoisseur during his time in the West and which he preferred to Russian products. Berenkov kindled a Havana cigar and sat back contentedly, thrusting his legs out before him.

"It's a good life," he said. "I consider myself a lucky man."

Since his repatriation, Berenkov had been assigned to the spy college on the outskirts of Moscow and established himself as one of the better lecturers. The cowed nervousness that he had had immediately upon his return had completely disappeared now, and only the complete whiteness of his hair remained from his period of imprisonment.

"I've a slight concern," said Kalenin, who often used their meetings to talk through any problems that might be particularly troubling him.

"What?" asked Berenkov, his attention still on the cigar.

"Seems I've been identified," said Kalenin shortly.

"Identified?" Berenkov came up from the cigar, immediately attentive.

"It really is most bizarre," said the KGB chief. "There was an anonymous telephone call to the Washington embassy, warning of a robbery of some Tsarist stamp collection. And the caller identified me by name."

"The CIA would know, of course," said Berenkov thoughtfully.

"That's what makes me suspicious," said Kalenin. "It could be some peculiar operation to discredit us."

"You must respond, though," said Berenkov.

"I have," said Kalenin. "I didn't want to do it, but I finally decided to awaken a sleeper."

"It was justified," said Berenkov at once. "You had to find out. What's the man say?"

Kalenin looked at his watch. "His initial report is due in the Washington diplomatic bag by tomorrow morning. I gather he's got some photographs of people involved with protecting the collection, but not very much more."

"Not an easy assignment," sympathized Berenkov, aware that his friend would have left instructions to be contacted, so

that he could return to the Kremlin as soon as the information
arrived.

"No," agreed the general. "What would you have done?"

Berenkov did not reply immediately. Then he said, "Probably disclosed myself, in the hope of whoever it was responding
and identifying themselves. But to whom could our man disclose himself?"

"That's the trouble," agreed Kalenin. "There isn't anybody."

"What about the robbery?"

"I've put some other people in, to watch that," said Kalenin
dismissively. "There appears no reason at the moment to think
anything is likely to happen."

"Could be a difficult one," said Berenkov.

"Yes," said Kalenin. "That's what worries me."

CHAPTER 17

HAD THE training of the Russian called Williamson commenced when he was an adult—or in his early teens, even—
he might have quickly despaired at the difficulty of what he
had been asked to do. But by beginning his instruction from
such an early age, the Russians had been able to mold his
mental resilience as well as his intellect, so that while he might
appreciate the difficulty of an assignment, the thought of regarding it as impossible would never have occurred to him.
The lead would have to come from the exhibition, Williamson
decided. And so it was from that and from the people connected
with it in positions of authority that he would have to work.

Thoroughly to acquaint himself with the layout and design
of any area of operation had been one of his earliest lessons,
so he had located the staff laundry even before embarking upon
the photographs of everyone involved in the security.

He was helped not only by the size of the Breakers but by
the number of staff employed to guarantee the guests' comfort.
Little more than an hour's observation convinced him that such
was the volume of people using the facility that one uniform

would not be missed. He only needed a waiter's jacket anyway and by midmorning of the day after his arrival had succeeded in stealing one and carrying it unobserved to his room.

He ordered a cold lunch from room service, intently studying the waiter who served it within thirty minutes, to ensure he would make no mistake with his disguise. He waited five minutes after the waiter's departure and even then discreetly checked the corridor before emerging, cloth over his arm and jacket an almost perfect fit, the tray balanced without difficulty on his crooked arm. Because Charlie's suite was the nearer, he went there first. He rang the bell twice and then shouted "room service" through the closed door before fumbling apparently with a passkey but which was, in fact, a steel picklock to enter the room.

Once inside, he worked with the speed of the professional he was. He kept the tray in his hand, to provide an excuse and an apology for a misunderstood order in case the man was still inside, but having checked throughout he put it down, moving first to the doors. Beneath that leading out into the corridor, he jammed two rubber wedges, against any surprised discovery, then from their containers took the minute devices which had accompanied his instructions from Moscow.

They were the latest devised by the KGB, transistorized pinheads that secured inside a telephone receiver, turning it into an open microphone for any discussion which might take place within the room as well as relaying any conversation upon the instrument itself. Magnetized, they were so small they adhered actually within one of the perforations in the mouthpiece and would have needed an expert technician with laboratory facilities to discover.

Williamson was emerging into the corridor within four minutes, shaking his head for the benefit of any casual observer and studying the written order to find out where he had made his mistake.

The service elevator took him to the floor upon which Pendlebury had his rooms. Williamson's face twisted with distaste at the condition inside, but didn't pause in what he had come to do. Better acquainted now with the suites, Williamson was in the corridor, again doing his bewildered but mistaken waiter head shaking, within three minutes. His arm was aching by the time he got back to his own room, still carrying the tray.

To check the installations, he used his own telephone to call both sets of rooms, hearing the ringing loudly upon his monitoring equipment. Satisfied, he connected what appeared to be an elaborate radio and tape cassette player to two receiving spools, coupled to the devices in each room, so that anything that occurred in either would be recorded.

By the end of the first day, from Pendlebury's apartment, he had learned enough to satisfy him that the anonymous caller to the Washington embassy was telling the truth and to realize, as well, that the intended robbery was government inspired if not planned. By eight o'clock he had airfreighted to Washington complete reports from the eavesdropping of both rooms, with a particular request for the voices on the tapes to be scientifically tested for voice prints against the recording they held of the unknown man who had given them the warning. He also asked for any information on a man called Giuseppe Terrilli, whose name had featured on the tape from Pendlebury's sitting room.

Because, for a man of Williamson's expertise, it was a logical, almost natural thing to do, he did what Charlie Muffin had done a few days earlier and looked up the name in the telephone book. And by nine o'clock had reconnoitered the Terrilli mansion, acquainted himself with the degree of protection installed around the building, and returned to the Breakers very contented with his day's work. He still hadn't abandoned hope of getting back to the West Coast in time for the Aztecs' game.

CHAPTER 18

GIUSEPPE TERRILLI sat forward in his chair, gazing down at some spot by his feet. The occasional nod, hopefully of approval, was the only movement from the man as Chambine outlined the preparations they had made and talked of the rehearsals in the Orlando warehouse.

Because he remained anxious to impress, Chambine took

a long time, but Terrilli gave no sign of impatience. When Chambine finished, the older man remained sitting in the same attitude of concentration. Chambine waited, on the edge of his seat, wondering what the response would be. He hoped he was managing to conceal his nervousness.

At last Terrilli looked up and Chambine relaxed very slightly at the smile.

"You've thought it out very well," he said. "And appear to have chosen the people well, too."

"Thank you, Mr. Terrilli."

"There seems little likelihood of failure."

"I don't think there will be."

"The only problem I can foresee is the timing between the visits of the security guards."

Chambine had omitted that morning's discussion in the warehouse, knowing the other man's attitude to violence. Now he said: "Some of the others are worried, too."

"If it has to happen, it happens," said Terrilli shortly.

"I've made plans if it becomes necessary to silence them."

Terrilli smiled again. "I'm sure you have."

"But only in emergencies," added Chambine.

"I'd like you with me permanently," said Terrilli. "How would you feel about that?"

"I'd like it very much."

"I'll do it properly," promised Terrilli. "Formally ask your people in New York, so there will be no offense."

"It would be better to leave amicably."

"Of course. What about your family?"

"I've a house to sell, in Scarsdale. And children to move from school. No problem."

"New York is always regarded to be the place where the power lies, in our organization," reminded Terrilli. "Why do you want out?"

Chambine smiled, happy at the relationship which appeared to be developing between them.

"Because I'm not convinced that the tradition will last forever," he said.

Terrilli nodded at the flattery. "Who knows?" he said. "What will you do after the robbery?"

"Finish my vacation," said Chambine. "To leave immediately after might create suspicion."

"Tell me something," said Terrilli, believing he had lulled the other man sufficiently. "What would you say if, having joined me officially, someone from another part of the organization invited you to do the sort of thing you're doing for me now?"

"Refuse," said Chambine, immediately aware the older man wanted the assurance of loyalty. He hesitated, knowing Terrilli required more and assembling the words so the man would be satisfied.

"I didn't set this up for the hundred thousand," he said, talking quietly and looking directly at Terrilli. "I did it because I knew it to be a test of my ability. I'm not interested in freelancing. I'm interested in joining you."

"Do you regard yourself as ambitious, then?"

"Properly so," said Chambine cautiously. "You'd never have any cause to doubt my support, Mr. Terrilli."

"I'm glad of the guarantee," said the other man. "There had better be no contact between us after the hand-over; the investigation around the hotel will be intense and I don't want any connection."

"I understand."

"I'll be in New York in three weeks. We'll meet then and finalize the arrangements."

"I'll look forward to it. Should I wait until your visit before making any positive plans?"

"Yes," said Terrilli. "It's proper that I should be the person to tell your people. You could always put your house on the market, of course."

Terrilli rose and put out his hand. Chambine stood and took it.

"Until Thursday night," said Terrilli.

"There'll be no problems."

"I know."

Terrilli, who was quite unaware that he had been under surveillance from the moment he left his castle home at Palm Beach, even to the extent of his helicopter being followed by another maintaining radar location from Palm Beach airport to Orlando, was careful about his departure from the hotel, pausing several times to check, suddenly, for anyone who might be watching. Knowing he would have been conspicuous in his normal conservative suit in a vacation resort, he had dressed in sports jacket, slacks, and loafers and merged unobtrusively with the people who boarded the monorail to take him back to the Disney World exit. The giggling teenage girls who sat two seats away, fooling with their Mickey Mouse caps, were both Pendlebury's watchers.

Removed temporarily from the constant attention of his aides, Terrilli felt vaguely uncomfortable boarding the open-sided tram that toured the parking lots. He had written his parking spot on the back of his entry voucher receipt, conscious of how easy it would be to get lost.

The driver had kept the air conditioning running and Terrilli got gratefully into the back of the Rolls that had been driven up in advance to collect him from Orlando airport. It was midafternoon and the traffic was moderate, so it did not take them long to go through the landscaped parks and rejoin Interstate 4. Within an hour, Terrilli was at the private section of Orlando airport, boarding his helicopter.

He had convened his weekly meeting with Santano and Patridge for five o'clock and arrived back fifteen minutes early. It gave him the opportunity to change from his sports clothes, in which he had become positively discomforted, back into a business suit.

The lieutenant and the accountant were on time, as was customary. Terrilli sat at his ocean-view desk and the other men took their accustomed seats. Patridge fussily fitted his glasses into place, took his accounts from his briefcase, and after handing duplicate copies to Terrilli and Santano carefully began taking them through the figures.

"Three interceptions?" cut across Terrilli.

"It was a bad week," agreed Santano.

"It's too many," insisted Terrilli, refusing the man's dismissal.

Santano shifted uneasily and Patridge remained gazing down at his figures.

"The boat captains were new," Santano attempted to explain. "They bunched up, which they'd been told not to do. And didn't allow sufficient time for the lead boat to make the chicken run."

"It's too many," repeated Terrilli, his voice disarmingly soft and conversational. "If the captains are inexperienced, we don't employ them. This puts us down..." Terrilli paused, going back to the papers before him. ". . . Something like eight million dollars."

"I'm sorry," said Santano.

"So am I sorry," said Terrilli. "I'm sorry and other people are going to be sorry and everyone is going to ask why it happened. Maybe even spread the sorrow."

"Perhaps I should go down to Colombia, to tighten up the recruitment of ships?" suggested Santano.

"If the alternative is to lose eight million dollars a week, then I think you should," said Terrilli.

"Four vessels *did* get through," said Patridge, trying to balance the problem. "That's nine and a half million on what they were carrying."

Terrilli turned to him, his voice remaining hard.

"Are you satisfied with just a fifty-five percent profit?" he demanded. "I'm certainly not."

"It's the first time it's happened," said Santano.

"It should never have happened at all!" shouted Terrilli unexpectedly, and both men jumped, startled by the change in the older man's voice. "One ship, we budget for. Two is an occasional but still acceptable risk. Three is ridiculous. There'll be a demand for explanations . . . and they'll want better answers than the problem of employing inexperienced people. . . ."

"I could do down to Columbia first thing tomorrow," offered Santano.

Terrilli's pause was almost unnoticeable. "No," he said. "I want you here for Thursday. Call the airport and have them put an aircraft on standby for you on Friday morning."

Terrilli wondered about Santano's reaction to learning that he had put a personal matter above the interests of the organization. The man looked curiously across the desk at him but said nothing.

Terrilli nodded for Patridge to continue and the man went back to his papers. The accountant had received the estimated crop yield from Colombia's La Guajiri peninsula, and from it he predicted a 30 percent increase over the previous year's profits. It provided the opportunity for Terrilli to remark that profitability depended upon lack of interception, but he held back from the sarcasm, knowing that Santano was curious at being delayed until Friday and unwilling to alienate the man further than he had already done.

When Patridge had finished, Terrilli turned to Santano and said: "Anything?"

The lieutenant shook his head.

"Thank you both," said Terrilli shortly. There were times when he invited them to stay on, for a drink and even occasionally dinner, but from his demeanor it was obvious to both of them that this was not going to be such a night. They were at the door when Terrilli called out:

"I want to talk to you alone, Tony."

The man came back into the room and the accountant lingered uncertainly near the door.

"It'll take a while," said Terrilli.

"I'll say good night then," said Patridge, going out and closing the door carefully behind him.

"I'm sorry about the interceptions," began Santano immediately, imagining that was the reason for his being held back.

"It mustn't happen again," said Terrilli, not wanting to talk at once about the robbery.

"I'll get positive guarantees about employment in Colombia," promised Santano eagerly. "We've had a good run lately and obviously our people there are getting careless. . . ."

"If it's carelessness, then it must be stopped," insisted Terrilli. "We've made examples in the past. It's time we made some more. If they've got to be taught the hard way, it's really their fault."

"I'll see to it," said Santano. "Sure you don't want me to go down tomorrow?"

"There's a reason for you to stay," said Terrilli. "I want you here on Thursday night, to organize something."

"What?"

"I want the gates opened, the alarms turned off, and the guards warned to expect a group of people, arriving in a hurry, sometime between twelve-fifteen and twelve-forty-five."

"What's happening?" demanded Santano. Because he had known the man for so long, Terrilli was aware of the changed attitude. Soon it would become resentment.

"Something is being delivered," said Terrilli.

"By outside people?"

"It was safer," said Terrilli. "If anything goes wrong, there's no association with us. And I couldn't risk that, right on our doorstep."

"What is it?"

"The Russian stamp collection."

"A personal thing," identified Santano immediately.

The speed of the man's reaction showed that his loyalty was first to the organization and then to him, recognized Terrilli. It would be well to get Chambine alongside as soon as possible.

"Yes," agreed Terrilli. "A personal thing."

"I don't like the idea of outside people," said Santano, coming as near as he dared to criticism.

Again Terrilli judged the man's concern to be the danger to their setup, rather than for any possible personal difficulty.

"I've chosen them carefully," said Terrilli. "They're good men."

"Shouldn't I run a check, just to make sure? There's still four full days."

"I told you," reminded Terrilli. "I don't want anything to be associated with us."

"But they must *know!*"

"One does, that's all."

"So all he's got to do is talk if he gets picked up."

"I don't think he will."

"It's difficult to assess what a man will do, offered the choice between twenty years or a deal."

"He knows I'd have him killed, whatever protection was promised."

"Let's hope he remembers," said Santano.

"There are two vehicles," said Terrilli. From his wallet he took the numbers of the rented cars that Chambine had given him earlier in Disney World. "Once they're in, close the gates. But have people standing by. They're leaving again immediately after the payoff. No one will remain here longer than fifteen minutes."

"If there's a chase, the law will be led straight to us," said Santano.

"I'm confident there won't be."

"We can't be sure."

"This is how I want it to be," said Terrilli, refusing the argument. Santano was right, he accepted.

"All right," said the younger man tightly.

"I want everyone ready," emphasized Terrilli. "No mistakes."

"There won't be," promised Santano.

Terrilli decided he had been wise to wait until now before telling Santano what was to happen. There was insufficient time for the organization to make any effective protest. But one would be made, he was sure.

"No method of identification, apart from the car numbers?" queried Santano.

"That'll be all that's necessary."

Santano rose, moving toward the door again.

"Make sure everyone knows," repeated Terrilli, not appreciating the opening he was giving the other man.

"Everyone will know," undertook Santano heavily.

Charlie Muffin knew that if they had reacted to his telephone call, the Russians had to be in place by now. Which meant he had to identify them. Idly, through most of the day, he had moved about the exhibition and its immediate vicinity, aware of the pointlessness but trying to mark them anyway. He had suspected no one, which could be either good—if they were that expert—or bad, if Moscow hadn't bothered to respond. He planned the test carefully, knowing there would not be another chance of disguising it. By one o'clock in the morning, the hotel was becoming deserted, only a few late-night drinkers and a noisy party remaining in the Alcazar. He had needed Pendlebury with him, because in the man's company those watching him would be less alert. Pendlebury had maintained a reserve, even though he had drunk sufficiently for Charlie to have expected him to relax. Charlie left his barstool at one-fifteen, heading toward the toilet. In his jacket pocket, the knife he had taken from his breakfast table and which he was still unsure would be strong enough for the purpose bumped against his side. At the door to the washroom, he suddenly veered away, hurrying now toward the parking lot. He had already chosen the window into the exhibition room, one that was further away from the lights.

The window edge was rimmed, which made it difficult to slip the blade between it and the sill, and twice Charlie slipped, once almost cutting his hand. Satisfied at last there was sufficient leverage, he paused, breathing heavily to prepare himself for the run that was to follow, then twisted and jerked the knife upward.

The blade snapped, with sufficient force to sting his hand, but the window opened enough to trigger the alarm. It burst out, a discordantly strident note.

Charlie managed to regain the foyer seconds after Pendlebury had lumbered, startled, from the bar. Charlie stood just inside the entrance, alert to everything. The uniformed security men came running from their cubbyhole, holster flaps unbuttoned, gazing wildly around and making for the main entrance into the hall. Those whom Charlie had already isolated from their surveillance of him and about five whom he had not flustered into the foyer, making their identification as FBI operatives easy by looking to Pendlebury for guidance.

Which left about fifteen other people, just ahead of the curiosity seekers who were filling the reception area. Foreign, judged Charlie immediately. But certainly not Slavic. More Latin, from their coloring. And one man who didn't fit the pattern or appear to be part of the group. Very fair and American-looking. Someone who had been in the lobby by chance, decided Charlie, looking away from Williamson.

The Russian made no response to Charlie's scrutiny. An hour before he had had confirmation from Washington, from their voice-print test, that it was Charlie on the tape and he was now considering how to kill the man, obedient to his instructions. It wouldn't be very difficult, he had decided.

At Pendlebury's urging, the security men unlocked the main doors into the room and flooded it with light. As they were about to enter, another of Pendlebury's people came in from the parking lot, the handle of the broken knife in his hand. As Pendlebury seized it, remaining near the entrance, Charlie wandered up and said quietly, "It took eight minutes."

Pendlebury frowned up at him.

"From the moment the alarm sounded to the time the security men went in. It was eight minutes," said Charlie.

"Did you stage this?" demanded Pendlebury, face whitening with the beginning of rage. There was none of the drunkenness which Charlie had suspected earlier in the bar.

"Hardly good enough, eight minutes," said Charlie. "Thieves could be halfway to Miami by now."

Heppert hurried up to Pendlebury. Charlie could see pajama bottoms leaking from beneath the man's trousers.

"Nothing gone," reported the Pinkerton's man. "Knife snapped as the window was being forced."

"I'm waiting for an answer," Pendlebury said to Charlie.

"Yes," admitted Charlie. "I wanted to see how efficient things really were. I'm not impressed."

"And I'm not impressed by fucking playacting."

"It wasn't playacting," said Charlie. "It was a valid security exercise that I've got every right to make. So don't fuck and rage at me; you should be shouting at people asleep on the job."

From outside came the sound of sirens and then the glare of their revolving lights as the local police tires howled into the parking lot.

"And their arrival took twenty-two minutes," said Charlie, offering the American sight of his watch for confirmation. "I'd been assured it would only take ten."

"What the hell do you think you're doing?" said Pendlebury, still angry but more controlled now.

"My job," replied Charlie. "What the hell do you think you're doing?"

It had taken all his self-control to remain in the cocktail lounge the moment the alarm sounded, waiting instead for the protection of the small crowd that took several minutes to form, but Chambine managed it. He stayed on the edge and therefore concealed, watching the conversation between Pendlebury and Charlie and the local police. News that it was a false alarm quickly spread through the people in the foyer, who began drifting back to the other rooms. Chambine remained where he was, actually able to see into the hall when the window was checked for permanent damage before being refastened and the doors relocked by the uniformed guards.

It was another five minutes before one passed near enough for Chambine to address him without it appearing obvious.

"What was it?" he asked casually.

"Some sort of test," said the man. "Frightened the shit out of me."

"Me, too," said Chambine honestly.

CHAPTER 19

FOR THREE hours after his inconclusive and latterly, with Pendlebury, rowdy attempt to discover if the Russians had responded to his Washington call, Charlie had tried to evolve a further, confirming check. He was unhappy with the only idea that occurred to him, but couldn't think of another, so he decided to try it anyway. If it proved nothing, then he was the only person inconvenienced. The alarm call awoke him gritty-eyed and disoriented and immediately convinced the proposal was more stupid now than it had been barely four hours earlier. But he was awake now, so sod it.

It was not yet dawn, although there was a faint yellow tinge from where the sun would rise. Without its hardness, both the sky and sea were smudged gray. Charlie dressed quickly, without bothering to wash or shave, and although he knew he'd be buggered at the end, ignored the elevator and descended the eighteen floors by the stairway. He was panting by the time he reached the first floor and remained for several minutes inside the stairwell, recovering his breath, before finally going down to the ground level. He managed the doors with the minimum of noise and then strode, purposefully now, across the lobby toward the exit. The night staff were still behind the desk in the reception area and several porters clustered in the bell captain's annex. One of the uniformed guards for the exhibition had just finished his half-hourly check and nodded to Charlie, who responded, looking beyond the man to where the seats were.

Three of the men whom he had identified with his phony alarm the night before were still sitting there, trying their best to appear dawn-party people who would not go to bed.

As he went through the exit into the parking lot, attempting to give the impression of someone embarking upon an early morning constitutional walk, Charlie was reminded of his earlier impression. Definitely Latin. It would provide excellent

cover, in a state as Spanish-oriented as Florida, exactly the sort
of precaution that Kalenin would consider.

Remembering his own surveillance, Charlie went briskly
north along South County Road, past the private road entrance,
and then turned left into Royal Poinciana Way. Once he turned,
trying to catch sight of those whom he expected to be following,
but saw no one. At the next junction he turned south, down
Cocoanut Row, and then completed the square into Cocoanut
Walk to take him back to the Breakers. By the time he approached the hotel the sun was up and there was already the
slight, breathless warmth indicating that it would be a hot day.
As he went through the parking lot, he saw two more of the
men he'd isolated in the lobby the previous night. The three
he had seen earlier had left the reception area.

"The guard has changed," he told himself.

Charlie took the elevator back to his suite. He showered
away the early morning perspiration and then gratefully clam-
bered back into bed. His feet and legs throbbed from the unaccustomed exercise and he sat with his back to the headboard,
trying to massage some relief into them.

He could still be mistaken about the people whom he believed the Russians had put in, Charlie knew. But the instinct
upon which he placed so much reliance told him he wasn't.
He let his mind run over what he had established so far, trying
to complete an understandable picture. He sighed, transferring
his attention from his right leg to his foot. He had all the parts,
he decided, but still he didn't know where to put them in the
puzzle. Which meant the most important thing was still absent.

You still aren't in control, Charlie, he warned himself. And
then the other idea came and Charlie smiled, recognizing it as
infinitely better than the one which had sent him jogging around
Palm Beach streets before it was even light.

Within ten minutes he was connected to Willoughby in
London. The underwriter listened without interruption as Charlie outlined his proposal, waiting until the man had finished
before putting forward his argument.

"It would never work," said Willoughby. "Not if they
wanted to challenge it in court."

"I don't expect them to," said Charlie. "I just want to cause
more upset, to see which way people will jump."

"Were these assurances about the time it would take security people and civil police to attend an emergency written down?" asked Willoughby.

"No," said Charlie. "They were verbal undertakings, given by a man called Heppert. He's a Pinkerton's employee."

"Then it certainly wouldn't be sufficient," insisted the underwriter. "Our insurance is with the organizers, not with the security firm. And verbal agreements are always the most difficult to prove, anyway."

"But the policy demands proper security. And we are claiming that it isn't proper."

"What do you want me to do?"

"Three things," said Charlie. "First advise Pinkerton's you are considering withdrawing cover, because of what transpired when your employee staged a simple test last night. Send exactly the same warning to the organizers. And then—and this is the most important—issue a press release as soon as possible. I want this picked up as quickly and as widely as we can manage."

"Our lawyers would never endorse it," persisted Willoughby.

"They might, if something *did* happen to the exhibition," disputed Charlie. "And I'm not concerned if we have to back down in two or three days. The effect for which I'm hoping will have taken place by then or it never will."

"Are you *sure* this is necessary, to protect the cover?"

"I wouldn't have bothered calling you if I weren't."

"It could expose the company to a certain amount of ridicule," said Willoughby reluctantly.

"What's more important, minor ridicule or three million pounds?" said Charlie.

"I'll do it if it's the only way."

"It is. Don't forget the press release, to the American news agencies. That's most important."

Charlie eased himself down into the bed. He still had time to sleep, before any response. And all that bloody walking had made him very tired.

General Valery Kalenin was such a self-contained man that there had been very few occasions in his life when he had ever been dumbfounded. But had he been asked, which he never was, he would have readily admitted to open-mouthed surprise as he had sat in the bare office surroundings, started working his way through the photographs that Williamson had provided, and arrived within minutes on one of a man he knew so well.

Kalenin had never been completely satisfied that Charlie Muffin had perished in the mysterious, midair explosion of the American Air Force plane which it had taken him six months to discover had been returning at least fifty CIA men to Washington after the London vengeance hunt in which Charlie's wife had died. The charred passport and items of personal belongings discovered in the wreckage had invited belief, of course. But for someone who knew Charlie as well as Kalenin did, it also invited the thought that the material had been planted aboard the plane destroyed in retribution for what had happened to the woman.

Charlie Muffin had been a rare man, remembered the KGB chief. He did not think he had ever encountered anyone so professional. Nor so vindictive to personal challenge. Kalenin had often thought back with surprise how shortsighted had been those people who took over the British department in which Charlie had been such a success and then judged him dispensable. Not only was the decision a waste of an agent whom Kalenin had often wished he had the like within his own department. It had also guaranteed the inevitable reaction from Charlie.

Abruptly Kalenin remembered his dinner guest of the previous evening. Because of Charlie, it had been possible to return Berenkov to Russia within three years of his sentence. The man knew it, because Charlie had initially been so involved in his capture and with his later interrogation that an odd respect had developed between the two men.

In the early months of his return to the Soviet Union, Berenkov had frequently asked for news of Charlie, guessing at the hunted existence the man had created for himself and wanting to know his success at survival. It would be pleasant, being able to give Berenkov the information for which he had so often been anxious.

The thought of Charlie's personal safety reminded Kalenin of the operation he had initiated. He lounged back in his chair, contemplating the effect of his knowledge. He wanted to know a great deal more, he decided. A very great deal more. And certainly the last thing he now desired was Charlie Muffin assassinated. Deciding that the urgency demanded telephone rather than cable communication, he reached out toward the instrument to connect him, via repeater stations that would disguise the true origin of the call, to the American Capital, hoping as he did so that he was not too late to prevent Williamson carrying out the instruction to kill whoever it was who had his identity. He stopped, smiling, with his hand above the telephone. There was little risk of that, he reassured himself. Charlie was a survivor.

CHAPTER 20

THERE WAS a dichotomy between Pendlebury's appearance and habits and the way he regulated his work life. As uncaring and casual as he was about himself and as distrustful as he was of restricting regulations, he nevertheless organized every assignment with painstaking care and neat efficiency and so it was with this, the biggest thing in which he had ever been involved.

Aware from the electronic eavesdropping of every detail of Chambine's robbery, Pendlebury had devised an operation which covered and then nullified every stage of it and made the failure of Terrilli's entrapment virtually impossible.

Pendlebury thought of it as a ripple effect, in reverse, so arranged that as Chambine's men passed through a series of checkpoints, the bands drew together behind them, finally creating around the Breakers and Terrilli's mansion a noose from which it would be impossible to escape.

Because he knew the robbery was scheduled for Thursday, he sensibly had not bothered to utilize the vast force at his disposal, maintaining instead the necessary but reduced surveillance teams and resting the remainder until the actual moment they would be needed.

He had assumed they would make the journey from Disney World to Palm Beach by road during Thursday, but just in case arranged to have a helicopter available at Orlando, should they charter a small aircraft. The watchers at the Contemporary Resort would trigger the whole operation, with their notification to the communications unit that the six men were on their way. Between Disney World and Palm Beach, Pendlebury proposed to establish twelve radio-controlled cars from which he was confident he would be able to maintain absolute but undetected observation. The immediate surveillance vehicles were to be staffed by agents from Lantana and Lake Worth contingents at the signal from Disney World. Pendlebury had arranged for the units in Miami, Boynton Beach, and Fort Pierce to close down toward Palm Beach, concentrating his force at the spot where it was needed. By the time Chambine's men crossed the Flagler Memorial Bridge, Pendlebury intended to have 150 men within a five-mile radius, awaiting instructions, with two helicopters in the air, guaranteeing aerial observation. The cutters based at Jupiter were to be activated the moment the men left Orlando, giving them sufficient time to move around and position themselves within sight and radio contact of the Breakers and the mansion.

He had reviewed the arrangements several times, even asking Warburger and Bowler for constructive criticism, and decided, even before their unqualified approval, that he had evolved a perfect scheme.

A believer that attention to detail was the keynote to success, he was yet again examining every section of it when Heppert, who ironically heard the news on the same local radio station that alerted Giuseppe Terrilli, just a mile away, knocked anxiously at Pendlebury's door and, immediately he was admitted, blurted out that the English insurers were withdrawing cover because they were unsure of the security arrangements.

"Shit!" said Pendlebury with a vehemence that startled the Pinkerton's man.

"Yes," agreed Heppert, misunderstanding the other man's outburst. "I think it's most uncalled for, too."

Concerned he would be affected by any apportionment of blame, Heppert added: "I only meant the figures I gave to be rough estimates. I never supposed they would be taken literally."

"The bastard," said Pendlebury, driving his fist against his thigh in frustration. "The rotten, awkward bastard. It's the first time I haven't anticipated him."

Heppert frowned both at the remark and at the extent of Pendlebury's annoyance.

"I presume you'll call head office," said Heppert, unwilling to take the responsibility. "We'll have to get guidance."

"Yes . . . yes, of course," said Pendlebury, as if the idea hadn't occurred to him.

"The exhibition organizers have asked for a conference," reported Heppert. "They've asked the Englishman to attend, as well."

"Give me an hour," demanded Pendlebury, looking at his watch. "Say two o'clock."

He was reaching for the telephone when it rang anyway and Warburger came immediately on the line.

"What the hell's happening?" demanded the Director.

Pendlebury cupped his hand over the receiver, looking at Heppert. "Two o'clock," he repeated, dismissing the man.

Pendlebury remained unspeaking until Heppert had closed the door, then said into the mouthpiece, "He did something I hadn't expected. Staged some damned-fool test last night, then claimed security was lax. I presume he complained to London."

"I've checked," confirmed Warburger. "The announcement came from there. Can they remove cover, just like that?"

"I suppose so," said Pendlebury. "That's not what is immediately concerning me. The organizing committee are demanding a conference, so they're obviously frightened. God knows what Terrilli's reaction will be."

"He might abandon it, you mean?"

"He could," said Pendlebury as a fresh wave of exasperation engulfed him. "Will Cosgrove be able to hold out against any premature closure?"

"I don't know," admitted Warburger. "He's already called me, direct. He wants a private briefing, from you personally."

"What shall I tell him?"

"Everything."

Pendlebury paused, surprised at the man's reply. "Even the idea of getting Terrilli indicted for the Englishman's death."

"He wants involvement. Let him have it."

"I'd rather not."

"It's an order," snapped Warburger. "And give the rest of the organizing committee any sort of assurance they need. Tell them we'll put in more guards . . . anything. I'll fix it with Pinkerton's here."

Pendlebury replaced the telephone and sat back, trying to

calm himself and to think the complication through. That's all
it was, he tried to reassure himself; merely a complication.
They were still more than in control of the situation, whatever
Terrilli instructed his people to do. As he poured himself the
first drink of the day, Pendlebury realized his hand was shaking,
rattling the bottle top against the glass edge. The effect of this
morning's news rather than the alcohol of the previous night,
he knew. The telephone rang again fifteen minutes later, while
he was cleaning his teeth of any trace of alcohol before his
meeting with the exhibition organizers. He recognized the voice
of the communications chief.

"Terrilli's made a call," reported the man. "About ten minutes ago. To Chambine at the hotel."

"What did he say?" demanded Pendlebury urgently.

"It was to arrange a meeting."

"Do we have it covered?"

The man paused, anticipating the question. "It's the beach,"
he said unhappily. "There's no way we could monitor it."

"Damn!" said Pendlebury, the word hissing through his
clenched teeth. "The son-of-a-bitch has fucked everything up."

"Terrilli?" asked the communications man curiously.

"No," said Pendlebury, irritated. "Forget it. Now listen. Get
on to the Contemporary Resort. Tell those listening there I
want to know every word that's said, in every room in which
we've installed devices. We might stand a chance of picking
up whatever they talk about there: Chambine is almost certain
to make contact. Now get off the line; I've other calls to make."

Pendlebury hurried Roger Gilbert to his room, outlining
within minutes what Charlie had done.

"Is it serious?" demanded the man.

"It is if Terrilli cancels everything. And that's what he might
be meeting Chambine to discuss."

"What do you want?"

"Six of you, on the beach in five minutes," said Pendlebury.
"Stripped and apparently enjoying yourselves. You obviously
won't be able to get near enough to hear what's going on,
particularly if Chambine goes to Terrilli's private strip. But
I'm betting that Terrilli will come to the hotel area, where there
are more people and therefore protection. As soon as it's over,
I want you all back here, giving me as full an account as it's
possible to assemble. Understood?"

"What about the Englishman?"

"We've enough men to cover him," said Pendlebury. "He'll be at a meeting with me most of the time."

"It'll mean using yesterday's people," warned the man.

"Then be careful," said Pendlebury. After Gilbert had left the room, Pendlebury remained half crouched in a sitting room chair, reviewing what he had done. He had become complacent, he realized critically. Everything had conformed so easily to his expectations that he had overlooked the unexpected and now he was having to move too fast. And speed unsettled Pendlebury. He liked to consider problems leisurely, imagining a move and then supposing his opponent's counter to it, like chess. He looked toward the vodka bottle, decided against it, and went down to the exhibition room.

Cosgrove was just inside the door of the side chamber. Heppert and the chief of the uniformed guards stood slightly apart and the Englishman was alone, near the linking door into the main hall. Charlie Muffin smiled at Pendlebury's approach, guessing from the look on the man's face that the threat of withdrawal had had the disruptive effect he had hoped.

"This is monstrous," said Cosgrove in his politician's voice.

Pendlebury ignored the organizing chairman, halting just in front of Charlie.

"What the hell are you doing?" he demanded.

"You keep asking me that," complained Charlie. "I thought I'd made that clear last night. I'm trying to protect the exhibition. That's what I came here for."

"You've put the fear of God up everyone."

"The time it took people to react to an alarm bell last night put the fear of God up me," said Charlie. "It should have had the same effect on you."

"I said this is monstrous," repeated Cosgrove, forcing his way into the conversation. "Do we have proper cover here or don't we?"

"At the moment, you don't," said Charlie. It pleased him to deflate the pompous man, particularly as he knew from Clarissa of the earlier annoyance.

"My firm have asked me to say how sorry they are for any inconvenience," said Pendlebury.

"There's already been a committee meeting," reported Cosgrove. "They don't see how they could possibly continue without the proper insurance protection. I argued against cancellation, but the feeling was that the risk is incalculable."

"We are willing to draft here immediately as many extra people as you consider necessary," assured Pendlebury.

Again the white-haired man regarded Charlie. "What is necessary for security doesn't really seem to be my prerogative," he said.

"No," said Charlie. "It's mine. You were not here for the test I made last night, but had you been I'm sure you would have been appalled. It took eight minutes to open the exhibition doors, even to discover if anything had been touched. And a full twenty minutes for the local police to arrive."

"I was here within minutes," Pendlebury attempted defensively.

"Outside," qualified Charlie. "By yourself for another five and with no idea of what might have been going on behind those locked doors."

"Shall we sit down," invited Cosgrove, indicating a semicircle of chairs that had been arranged.

Charlie had expected Pendlebury to be irritated. But not as annoyed as he obviously was.

"How many extra men would you consider necessary for your firm to continue the insurance?" Cosgrove asked Charlie, once they had settled at the table.

"It's not a question of numbers," said Charlie. "It's a matter of efficiency."

"We could increase the amount of patrols, perhaps to every fifteen minutes," offered Pendlebury.

Charlie sat gazing at the man, aware of his desperation and curious at it.

"Well?" demanded the chairman of Charlie.

"We would also like an improvement upon the nighttime checks," said Charlie. "At the moment the guards merely look through the windows. I want the doors opened and the cases examined."

"Agreed," said Pendlebury tightly.

"A number of display case keys were available in New York," reminded Charlie. "I want them fully accounted for."

"They will be," conceded Pendlebury.

Cosgrove shifted hopefully. "So we're in agreement?" he said, smiling.

"No," refused Charlie. "The announcement about cover was made from London. Obviously I must consult with them first, to see if all their doubts are resolved."

"Where does that leave us!" demanded the man, allowing his open annoyance to show for the first time.

"With limited cover and the understanding that we would dispute our liability were anything to happen to the exhibition until we have formally issued an addendum to the policy, guaranteeing the points agreed here."

"It would take days for a document to arrive here," protested Cosgrove. "I think I should warn you that we are taking legal advice about this. If our lawyers advise it, we will consider issuing a writ against your company, demanding the continued protection."

"I expected you to take the proper advice," said Charlie, unconcerned. "As far as the document is concerned, it was my intention to have it telexed from London, here to the hotel."

Cosgrove smiled briefly. "That would be acceptable, certainly," he said.

"How long will it take to get a reaction from London?" asked Pendlebury.

Charlie looked at his watch. "It's seven-thirty at night there now," he said. "I can speak to my principal at home, but I doubt very much that we could manage it today . . . I don't even know about tomorrow. There are members of a syndicate to consult."

"But this is preposterous!" repeated Cosgrove. "We couldn't continue, faced with this uncertainty."

"What would you do?" demanded Pendlebury.

Cosgrove shrugged. "At the meeting this morning there was talk of curtailing the exhibition."

Charlie had been watching Pendlebury as the other American spoke, so he saw the open concern on the FBI man's face.

"We could have extra staff here by tomorrow," said Pendlebury.

"It's not my agreement that's necessary; it's the insurers," said Cosgrove.

"The whole thing could be settled within three days," lured Charlie. "Four at the outside."

"I don't think we would be prepared to run the risk for that length of time," responded Cosgrove.

"No," said Pendlebury, unaware of the trap Charlie had set. "It must be resolved before then. Two would be the longest we could consider waiting."

Charlie kept from his face any expression of satisfaction at Pendlebury's slip. Two days was acceptable; four was not. So whatever was going to happen was scheduled for either Wednesday or Thursday. The meeting was proving far more productive than Charlie had hoped.

"You're not prepared to confirm full cover, with the promises that have been made here today?" Cosgrove demanded of Charlie.

"No."

"But you will contact your principal immediately?"

"Yes."

"And warn your London office what I said about lawyers?" added Cosgrove.

"Of course," said Charlie.

"Until we've restored the insurance, we'll restrict opening," decided Cosgrove. "We'll delay until eleven in the morning. And close earlier than nine. Five, I think."

"That should make it easier for you properly to organize your security," Charlie said to Pendlebury.

"I never regarded it as disorganized before," said the American.

"It was, though, wasn't it?" said Charlie.

Anticipating there would be reporters and cameramen outside the room, Charlie lingered, unwilling to be photographed. The journalists descended upon the recognizable figure of Cosgrove, and Charlie moved quickly around the crush, hurrying back to his rooms. He kept the telephone to his ear, after booking the call, listening to the connection being made to London and trying to identify any other sound which would indicate a tap on his line. Willoughby answered immediately. Fairly confident there was no monitor, Charlie outlined to the underwriter what had happened and what he suspected.

"Wednesday or Thursday is only a guess?" said Willoughby.

"I think I'm right," said Charlie.

"What do you want me to do?"

"Nothing," said Charlie. "Just keep the whole thing in the air."

"I'll have to put it to the company lawyers tomorrow. If it's judged that we're introducing frivolous objections, I would be contravening Lloyds regulations. The American lawyers might claim that."

"I don't care what arguments go on," said Charlie. "Just as long as nothing is resolved. When have you ever known lawyers give an opinion in hours rather than days?"

"Never," admitted the underwriter.

"Exactly," said Charlie. "As long as we're known to be doing the proper things, we can't be accused of breaking any regulations."

"Have you thought you could be wrong about all this?" asked Willoughby suddenly.

The question momentarily halted Charlie. Despite his apparent success in tilting Pendlebury off balance, Charlie still had a vague feeling there was something he had missed.

"No," he said. "I'm not wrong."

Charlie replaced the receiver from his call to Willoughby at about the same time as Pendlebury, two floors below, ended his conversation with Warburger, in Washington. Pendlebury went to the window of his room, worrying at the panic he'd detected in the Director's voice and staring down at the specks on the beach far below, knowing it was ridiculous but trying to see Terrilli and Chambine and his surveillance team. An impending disaster, Warburger had called it. An exaggeration, Pendlebury thought. But from their meeting that morning, not much of one.

Pendlebury had been right in guessing that Terrilli would choose the hotel section of the beach. Despite owning it, Terrilli had rarely been down to his private seafront. He crunched awkwardly over it now, unhappy at the surroundings. He found it easy to relax by the side of his pool, assured of people in attendance and with cleanliness guaranteed, but the sand irritated him, getting into his shoes and making it uncomfortable to walk, and although the beaches had been swept that morning, there was still the occasional palm frond or scrap of paper which he found messy. He crossed the barrier designating his own property, and among more people his distaste increased. There seemed to be a lot of shouting and children were screaming and he knew that when they all went home they'd leave the place like a garbage dump. Disdainfully he lowered himself to the sand, as far away from any other people as he could find, and while he waited for Chambine he took off his tennis shoes and tried to clean the grit from between his toes. He looked up when the sun was temporarily shaded from him but showed no response to the man for whom he was waiting. Chambine didn't stop immediately. Instead he spread a beach mat several feet away, stripped off his toweling top, and lay out, not looking at Terrilli.

"You hear the news?" demanded the older man.

"Not the first announcement," admitted Chambine. "But I picked up after the meeting that was held in the hotel this morning."

"What was the result?"

"Inconclusive. There are going to be greater security measures taken. But the insurers still seem unhappy."

"What about cancellation?"

"Not yet . . . but it seems likely."

"So we can't wait until Thursday?"

"I don't think so."

"Will that be a problem for you?"

"I shouldn't think so," said Chambine. "They seemed ready when I went to the warehouse."

"Could it be tonight?"

Chambine didn't reply immediately. "Yes," he said, after thought.

"I think it would be best, before they get any extra men organized and in place."

"Of course."

"I don't like having to make the change."

"Neither do I."

"But I don't think there's a choice."

"No," agreed Chambine. "I don't think there is."

"You'd better leave first," suggested Terrilli. "You've things to organize."

"Your people will be expecting us?"

"I'll see to it. We'll keep to the original timing."

Chambine got up slowly, dusted off his mat, and rolled it up.

"See you tonight," he said, still bending so the conversation would be hidden from anyone.

"I'll be waiting," promised Terrilli.

He remained for the minimum amount of time on the beach,

then rose gratefully and returned to his house. He went straight to the changing cabin alongside the pool, stripped off his sand-gritted clothes, and left them for collection later. Terrilli looked up at Santano's approach.

"There's been a change," said Terrilli. "Warn everyone who needs to know. It's going to be tonight."

Two miles away, a relieved Jack Pendlebury learned the same thing from his communications unit monitoring all the telephone calls into the Contemporary Resort Hotel in Disney World. Pendlebury smiled across at Roger Gilbert, who had just given a depressing report of their quite unsuccessful attempt to discover the purpose of Chambine's beach meeting with Terrilli.

"It's going to be all right," said Pendlebury, uncaring at the emotion evident in his voice. "They haven't called it off; they've brought it forward. It's tonight."

Gilbert half stood, imagining the need to respond in a hurry, but Pendlebury waved him down, content he was in charge of the situation once more.

"Everyone is in the right place," he said. "There's no hurry. It'll all go just as we planned."

"What about the Englishman?" queried Gilbert.

"Kill him," said Pendlebury positively. "Kill him and dump him in the exhibition room. And then let's see Terrilli get out of that."

Pendlebury had argued with Warburger and Bowler that it was possible. And now he was going to prove it; he was going to get a murder indictment against Terrilli, as well as one of robbery.

Williamson knew he would have to get Moscow's agree-ment, but he could not foresee any objections. Having learned from his monitoring of Pendlebury's rooms of the Americans' intention to assassinate Charlie, Williamson intended merely to remain on the sidelines, to ensure they carried it out satis-factorily. And then, virtually free from any possibility of in-volvement, return to California.

Williamson accepted he had been exceptionally lucky. But Moscow wouldn't know that. As far as they were concerned, he had responded brilliantly to a difficult assignment.

Because he was anticipating congratulations, he was not

surprised at the summons from the Washington embassy, telling him to cross from Palm Beach to the mainland, to establish contact from a pay phone. Williamson actually passed Charlie Muffin, as he left the hotel, and drove over the Flagler Bridge without the hindrance he had expected from the traffic. The number he called was not any of those attributed to the embassy and therefore free from any interception.

Williamson's superb training, which as much as luck was responsible for what he had achieved in so short a time, again prevented his expressing the slightest surprise at the succinct instructions he was given.

Under no circumstances was he to carry out his original instructions to kill Charlie Muffin. Rather, he was to do everything to protect the man from any harm.

CHAPTER 21

WILLIAMSON'S INSTRUCTORS had never sought to eradicate fear, because Russian psychologists at the training academy considered a man not properly frightened incapable of proper caution. And so while he had still been talking to Washington, the man had recognized the danger that the alteration created and felt the first wash of apprehension.

But it was not, as those psychologists might have expected, at the thought of injury or even death, concerned though he would be when the moment came. Williamson's initial reaction came from an uncertainty that had grown with every week he had spent in America and which, try as he had, he had been unable to dispel.

To protect Charlie Muffin, he would have to involve the Cubans. Which meant becoming known to them. And once that disclosure was made, he knew he would constantly risk exposure.

It was not the actual capture of which Williamson was afraid, but what would follow. The inviolable rule of his service—the insurance under which every Russian agent worked—was that eventually an exchange would be arranged and he would be repatriated to Russia.

And he knew he didn't want to go back.

The feeling did not come from any disloyalty or lack of patriotism but from the excellence of his preparation. While his allegiance remained unquestionably to Russia, Williamson *was* an American. He genuinely liked the California sunshine and twenty-four-hour drugstores and being able to pick up a telephone and get a meal delivered within an hour.

His education had shielded him from the harsher aspects of Soviet life, but he knew they existed. He didn't want a shared apartment or the Bolshoi or bone-numbing Moscow winters or restaurant waits of four hours for a nearly inedible meal. That was why, still in the mainland telephone booth, he had decided to brief only the leader of the Cubans and try to avoid any meeting with the entire group. Because he knew Ramírez would accept unquestioningly his identity from Washington, saving him the time-wasting necessity of establishing proof of who he really was, Williamson had ordered the Cuban leader contacted first by the embassy and then instructed to come to his room at the Breakers. The tentative sound came at the door and Williamson admitted the man, checking the corridor behind as he did so.

"No one has seen me," assured Ramírez. "I checked."

Williamson turned back into the room, extending his hand. Ramírez took it, unsmiling.

"I thought I was working alone, without a controller," said the Cuban. There was no resentment in his voice, just curiosity.

"There were other things to be done," said Williamson. He was conscious of the other man's attitude and knew Ramírez thought him to be an American.

"Are our instructions changed?"

Williamson shook his head. "Just modified. The exhibition still has to be protected. But now there's something else."

He gestured Ramírez to a chair. The Cuban sat, head to one side in the attitude of a man slightly deaf, as Williamson told him the result of monitoring Pendlebury's rooms.

"Ingenious proposal," said Ramírez. "They've taken a lot of trouble."

"Yes," said Williamson. "I suppose they have."

"Knowing what we do now, protecting the collection will be easy."

"I've given some thought to that," said Williamson. "I don't think we should oppose the robbery here. It's too public. There'd be little chance of our escaping undetected."

And therefore of me being able to remain in America, thought Williamson. He would have to be careful that his determination not to return to Russia did not become obvious to Moscow.

"Where, then?"

"There's a private road, leading to Terrilli's house," said Williamson. "There's sufficient cover for an ambush. When they get there, they will believe they've succeeded with the robbery. The timing will be right."

"The collection could get damaged."

"No more than it might if we confront them in the exhibition hall."

"Why is the man we have to protect so important?"

"Because Moscow says he is," said Williamson shortly. "I wasn't given a reason."

"Is he to know of the protection?"

"No."

"Do you want to brief the others?"

"No," said Williamson again, immediately regretting the urgency with which he spoke.

"No," accepted Ramírez, regarding Williamson thoughtfully. "I suppose there's no purpose. Are they to know of you at all?"

"There's no need that they should. And we'll finalize all the arrangements now."

"So we won't meet again?"

"Not unless I become aware of any changes you should know," said Williamson.

"What about afterward?"

"You were given your instructions in Moscow?"

"Yes," said Ramírez.

"Then follow them."

"This isn't going to be easy, is it?" said Ramírez. "Despite knowing so much in advance."

"No," agreed Williamson.

"We've been told we can stay. I'm very glad to be back."

"America is a good country," said Williamson.

"I've missed it," admitted the Cuban. "I've no complaints at the way we were treated, either in Cuba or in Moscow. But I've still missed it."

"I can understand," said Williamson.

"We all feel the same. That's why we want it to go well."

"We've got a lot of advantages," Williamson tried to reassure the man. "More than you could have hoped."

"The Americans told us that, before we set off for Cuba."

"This time it will be different," promised Williamson.

"I hope so."

Heppert had been the willing messenger from Senator Cosgrove, to inform Charlie that he was wanted in the committee room. Immediately, the man had stressed, in a carefully contrived afterthought.

"Their lawyers have given an opinion," said the Pinkerton's man, unable to get the satisfaction from his voice.

"Have they?" said Charlie.

"Yes. So the senator wants to see you..."

He paused, then repeated, "Immediately."

"Fifteen minutes," said Charlie. It was a small point, juvenile almost, but even if he were to be forced to capitulate he wasn't going to run cap-in-hand to the damned man.

"He said immediately."

Heppert talked like a programmed robot, thought Charlie.

"Tell him I said fifteen minutes," he said.

The politician had moved quicker than he had anticipated, conceded Charlie. There was a chance he could prevaricate until the following day, pleading the problem of the time difference between America and England, but they would have to restore cover within twenty-four hours. It was a bugger.

He was moving toward the door, to answer Cosgrove's summons, when the call came. He smiled, recognizing Clarissa's voice. He wondered why he was pleased to hear from her.

"How are you?"

"Fine," he said. "You?"

"Missing you."

"I thought all your friends were there."

"They are. I'm still bored. Hoped you might invite me up for the celebration."

"What celebration?" demanded Charlie.

"The one that Cosgrove is planning. Sally had a call this afternoon, telling her to come up. He said he wanted her with him; that it was important."

"When is it to be, exactly?" asked Charlie, feeling the beginning of the warmth spread through him.

"Tomorrow, I gather," said Clarissa. "Surely you knew about it?"

"No," said Charlie. "Apparently I'm not to be invited."

If the celebrations were planned for tomorrow, then he had a timing for the robbery. No wonder Cosgrove wanted him so urgently. Strange how the most difficult things were often resolved by the simplest of errors. He wondered if Cosgrove had overlooked his wife's friendship with Clarissa Willoughby or merely forgotten the tendency to gossip among the people with whom she mixed.

"Can I come up?" asked Clarissa.

"I'd rather you didn't."

"I see."

"No," said Charlie. "You don't see. I'd like you to be here, really I would. But the next couple of days aren't going to be safe."

There was an urgent knocking on the door of Charlie's suite.

"Wait a minute," he apologized to the woman.

Heppert stood in the corridor, trying to mirror the anger of the men waiting downstairs.

"It's been half an hour," said Heppert. "They're furious."

Charlie left the door open, returning to the telephone.

"Something has come up with the exhibition," he said. "I've got to go. I'll call you as soon as I can."

"Tomorrow?"

"I hope so."

Charlie didn't move away from the telephone.

"One more call," he said to the sighing man in the doorway. Because it was internal, within the hotel, it took less than a minute.

"There!" said Charlie. "Ready."

Still he did not immediately leave the room, lingering a

further few minutes ensuring he had everything in his pockets that he wanted and then, at last, moving out into the corridor.

Heppert was already hurrying off, leading the way and trying to speed Charlie toward the elevator.

"Christ," said Heppert. "They're mad. Damned mad."

"Yes," said Charlie. "I expect they are."

CHAPTER 22

THERE WERE eight men in the room, the first time Charlie had seen the organizing committee in a formally assembled group. The senator sat in the middle, as the chairman. Cosgrove was white-faced from what Charlie presumed was the anger of which Heppert had spoken, but appeared tightly controlled. Open annoyance from a politician would be unseemly, Charlie supposed.

He looked around, expecting Heppert to have followed him in, but the man had stayed in the foyer, near the closed entry into the exhibition. Pendlebury wasn't around, either.

"Sorry for the delay," said Charlie brightly. "Telephone call I wasn't expecting."

"It was discourteous," said Cosgrove.

"But unavoidable, I'm afraid," said Charlie. He saw the senator's body stiffen at his attitude. In the army Charlie had been able to make sergeants almost apoplectic by holding himself before officers just short of stiff-backed attention but insufficiently insubordinate to be put on a charge.

"We've called you here," began Cosgrove officiously, speaking with occasional glances at some papers before him upon which Charlie assumed he had written some notes, "to demand from you, as the representative of the British insurers, the reinstatement of full cover for this exhibition."

"I told you earlier today that I would have to get London's authority for any such action," said Charlie.

"And I told you I was having my lawyers examine the legality of what you have done. Their opinion is that the withdrawal of cover for the reasons you've stated are utterly specious and would not be supported in any court of law, either in this country or England. If you continue to refuse, then I shall tomorrow issue in London a writ against your company in particular and the syndicate as a whole, alleging breach of contract. I shall also officially complain to whatever professional governing body covers the activities of your company."

"The lawyers responded quickly," said Charlie, ignoring the threat.

"They were told to," said Cosgrove, his voice that of someone always used to having his orders obeyed unquestioningly.

"When?" demanded Charlie.

"When?" Cosgrove looked across the table at him, face creased at Charlie's question.

"When exactly did you receive this advice from your lawyers? The timing might be a legal issue."

Cosgrove smiled, glancing meaninglessly at his watch.

"Six-thirty this evening, precisely," he said.

"It's been recorded?" insisted Charlie.

"There seemed little point," said Cosgrove curiously. "But this committee will support that time, I'm sure."

From either side there were immediate nods and movement of assent.

"Good," said Charlie. "I'll accept that guarantee."

"And reintroduce cover?" said Cosgrove expectantly.

"No," said Charlie.

Cosgrove had been turning away, smiling his satisfaction at the imagined victory to the others at the table. He swung around to Charlie, his annoyance flooding back.

"Now, see here . . ." he started.

"This meeting was a little premature," interposed Charlie, so that Cosgrove remained with his mouth half open. "I am quite happy to continue it as an open discussion, but I would suggest to you, Senator, that it might be better if we had a private conversation."

The change in Cosgrove's demeanor, from anger to caution, was almost discernible.

". . . I see no point . . ." said Cosgrove, spreading his arms to include the men on either side of him.

"You will," predicted Charlie. "But I repeat, the choice is yours."

Cosgrove looked rapidly to the rest of the committee, their

backs to Charlie, who stood quite relaxed, wondering how the man would find a way out.

"Might it speed the settlement of this insurance?" Cosgrove demanded.

Charlie nodded at the man admiringly. "It might," he said.

Cosgrove went back to the other men, shrugging the shrug of a man prepared to carry burdens for the rest of them. There was a moment of uncertainty as first Cosgrove, then those around him, stood.

"Perhaps your rooms, Senator?" suggested Charlie.

Cosgrove hesitated, then nodded acceptance, striding from the room ahead of Charlie with no intention of being associated with the man, even walking across a hotel foyer. Charlie walked slowly behind, taking his time so that Cosgrove had to hold the elevator doors until he arrived.

"This had better be worthwhile," threatened Cosgrove, as the doors closed and the elevator snatched upward.

"Yes," agreed Charlie. "It had better be, hadn't it?"

"I intend making the strongest possible complaint to your company. Rupert Willoughby is known to us, you know."

"Yes," said Charlie. "I believe he might even regard you as a friend."

He had little justification for sarcasm like that, thought Charlie. When the elevator halted, Cosgrove strode ahead again, thrusting into the suite and then wheeling in the middle of the sitting room, legs astride and hands imperiously upon his hips.

"Well!" he demanded.

Charlie carefully closed the door and went unhurriedly into the room, so that the man had to remain in his exaggerated posture.

"Even at the risk of legal action, I do not intend restoring insurance protection to this exhibition," declared Charlie. "I have very good reason to believe that a robbery is to take place, with the knowledge of some people closely involved with it. In any court of law you choose to enter, I am prepared to put forward the grounds for that belief, and contrary to the views which your lawyers have expressed, I'm confident our withdrawal would not only be supported but vindicated."

Charlie was sure Cosgrove would never call the bluff. The American had no way of knowing that the possibility of identification made it impossible for Charlie ever to enter any court.

Cosgrove appeared to become aware that his stance made him look slightly ridiculous. He took his arms away from his sides and put his legs together.

"Those are strong allegations," he said inadequately. Much of the earlier bombast was leaking away, Charlie realized.

"They are," he agreed. "Reached after a great deal of inquiry during which I've discovered some very disturbing things."

Charlie thought at first that Cosgrove's concern was sufficient for the man to demand to know what they were. Instead, trying to recover his composure, the politician attempted to respond the way he imagined would be expected of him.

"...Well...we..." groped the man. "We'd better do something about it. The man Pendlebury..."

"...Wouldn't be a great help, would he?" cut off Charlie, wanting to keep the other man off balance.

"What do you mean?" challenged Cosgrove.

"I mean that I do not think Mr. Pendlebury is the proper person to whom this information should be passed on."

"Are you alleging something against the man?"

"Think carefully on what I've said," encouraged Charlie. "I've made no allegations against anyone that could be questioned in a court. What's the celebration you're planning tomorrow, Senator?"

Cosgrove took the question like a man emerging from an overhot sauna getting cold water thrown in his face. He actually gasped, then snapped his mouth shut.

"Celebration?" he echoed, trying to collect himself. "The restoration of cover..."

"Six-thirty tonight," reminded Charlie. "We established the time of the lawyers' call in the committee room. You were making arrangements with the banqueting manager this afternoon, long before that call. I checked, purporting to be your aide. I'd have hardly thought a restoration of insurance justified champagne and a gathering of at least a hundred...that seems to be the number for which the man is catering."

Cosgrove drew himself up, aware of his mistake and annoyed at its discovery.

"You've no right to put such questions to me," he said, striving again for his customary arrogance.

"You're quite correct, sir," said Charlie, the courtesy introduced purposely to stress what he was to say. "Perhaps we should leave that to whatever court will subsequently examine anything that might happen here."

Another expression began settling on Cosgrove's face and Charlie knew it from the previous occasions he had dealt with politicians who found themselves in difficulty. Cosgrove was responding as he had anticipated; it was invariably the way with ambitious men.

"What do you intend doing?" The man straightened and there was more control in his voice.

"Continue to suspend cover," said Charlie. "And then summon the police. Not that I expect they will respond as I hope, but for any further inquiry which might be held into what happens . . ."

"Sure that's altogether wise?" asked Cosgrove.

Unexpectedly he smiled and Charlie thought the expression was like that of a man practicing physiotherapy exercises after facial paralysis.

"I think so," he said.

"What do you think is the purpose for all this?" said Cosgrove.

There was always the pretense of being taken into confidence before the offer was made, remembered Charlie.

"The FBI entrapment of a known Mafia associate named Giuseppe Terrilli," said Charlie simply.

The face exercise smile came again. "You're very astute," congratulated Cosgrove.

"And therefore worried that something for which I'm responsible is going to be used as bait. Which is why I must protect it."

"*Nothing* can happen," said Cosgrove, utilizing the full depths of his politician's sincerity. "I give you my *word.*"

"It's an impossible guarantee," said Charlie. "And never one which any of the syndicate I represent would consider."

Cosgrove moved from his position in the middle of the room. His suite had a corner position, so there was a panoramic view from two sides of the room. He moved toward the ocean view, not looking at Charlie as he spoke.

"I am a man of considerable influence in Washington," he said.

"I know."

"And because of what is to happen, expect to increase that influence."

"Yes, I suppose you do," said Charlie.

"What if I call the British embassy and through them make an official request to the British government for cooperation?" suggested Cosgrove, suddenly turning back into the room.

It would bring to Florida in force at least ten people from the department who wanted him dead, Charlie realized immediately. He was sure he kept the anxiety from his face.

"You haven't time, have you?" he said.

"Reintroduce cover and I'll guarantee their agreement by this hour tomorrow."

Charlie disguised the sigh at the other man's desperation. Cosgrove had been a poor choice for a front man.

"That's not an undertaking you can give," he said. "And you certainly couldn't expect it to be made retroactive; by the time you were seeking agreement from London, the whole damned exhibition could have been destroyed."

There was the slightest indication of anger from Cosgrove at having his proposal exposed so immediately for its stupidity, but he curbed it.

"How much?" said Cosgrove.

Charlie smiled at the predictable demand. "For what?"

"Restoring insurance. And not involving the local police."

So the Palm Beach and neighboring forces *weren't* involved. Charlie wondered if Cosgrove would ever be aware of what he was disclosing.

"I don't think this conversation is going to achieve a great deal, Senator Cosgrove," said Charlie. After the other man's posturing over the past weeks, Charlie enjoyed the arrogance.

"A hundred thousand?" pressed Cosgrove.

"I'll not take a bribe," insisted Charlie.

"Two hundred?"

"Stop demeaning yourself," said Charlie irritably.

Cosgrove pulled up short again. "An honorable man!" he sneered.

"I suppose so," said Charlie. According to his own rules, that was.

"You'll do a deal," said Cosgrove, suddenly confident.

"I've told you . . ."

". . . shut up," said the white-haired man. "In return for your reestablishing cover and not involving the local police, I'm prepared to save your life."

"Save my life!"

"You might have worked out the robbery," said Cosgrove. "But sure as hell you haven't realized that there's to be a second indictment against Terrilli. And it's going to be your murder."

The politician smiled again. This time it was a satisfied expression.

"A deal?" he said.

Charlie hesitated. Stronger than any tenacity or vindictiveness had always been the need to survive. It was time to modify his rules.

"A deal," agreed Charlie. "What do they intend doing?"

Cosgrove shook his head, control resumed. "The undertaking in the committee room first. Then we'll talk about the killing..."

He smiled, enjoying the qualification. "...your killing."

He'd lost, conceded Charlie, trailing the other man from the room. He didn't like losing.

Saxby and Boella arrived first. They parked their car alongside the marked station wagon that Chambine had already placed in position, near the windows to the exhibition room. Leisurely they entered the hotel and strolled into the Alcazar.

Saxby ordered, while his companion looked around the bar.

"We've time to eat," said Boella.

"Why not?" said Saxby, unaware of the hand-over of surveillance from those who had followed them from Orlando to the men who had been moved ahead of their arrival, from Lantana.

Pendlebury had taken another set of rooms in the hotel, to act as his control center for the operation. He'd monitored the approach of the two men now ten floors below in the bar and on the map before him had marked the route of the four that were following, traveling through an avenue of observers.

In the corner but with an operator constantly before it, to check adjustments, was a closed-circuit television linked to two cameras that had been installed after the exhibition closed that night, of which Chambine's men would be unaware as they worked. Uncovered, they would provide an identifiable record later to link the thieves with Terrilli.

Pendlebury had had his back to it all for the past five minutes, frowning at Gilbert's report of the Englishman's meeting with Senator Cosgrove.

"I don't like it," he confessed to Gilbert. "I always felt that bloody politician was the weak link."

As he spoke there was a knock at the door and one of Gilbert's squad returned within minutes.

"It's Senator Cosgrove," he reported. "And the Englishman."

CHAPTER 23

CHARLIE MUFFIN sat unspeaking in the hotel control room, occasionally looking to the television screen and its pictures of the deserted exhibition hall but otherwise unmoving as the argument swung between the senator and the FBI man. Pendlebury was restricted, Charlie guessed, by his belief of the appointment the politician might receive if the robbery went as they intended. When they first entered the room, Charlie had thought Pendlebury was actually going to strike Cosgrove, so obvious was his fury.

"If I hadn't done what I did, the whole damned thing would have gone down," insisted Cosgrove. "He was going to bring in the local police. Terrilli's people wouldn't have come within a mile of the exhibition and you know it."

From the brief look that Pendlebury gave him, Charlie was sure he would never have got near any telephone; calls from his suite would be intercepted by now, he guessed.

"And we've got official insurance cover again," continued Cosgrove defensively. "If anything goes wrong, we're safe for the entire amount. Did your people get any government approval, to risk six million dollars of their own money!"

"It's weakened what we hoped to put against Terrilli," said Pendlebury, looking toward him again. Charlie wondered who had originated the murder idea.

"It's enough," said Cosgrove.

"It's going to have to be," said Pendlebury bitterly.

"They're at Lake Worth," said Gilbert quietly, and Pendlebury glanced away from the men before him. Pendlebury, who was not wearing a jacket, was sweating so heavily that dark crescents had formed beneath his arms and he occasionally wiped a handkerchief across his face. He looked back toward them, picking on Charlie.

"I never expected you to get as close as you did," said Pendlebury in begrudging admiration. "Funny. When we were setting it up, I said there was always the unexpected that fouled everything up."

"Flagler Bridge;" noted Gilbert at the radio.

"It's not fouled up," said Cosgrove as Pendlebury half turned at the position report.

"It hadn't better be," said Pendlebury. "Because now we've only got one chance."

"That's all you ever had," reminded Charlie.

Pendlebury smiled at him. "I was always sure of the robbery," he said.

Where, wondered Charlie, were the people whom he believed the Russians had moved in?

"They're here," said Gilbert.

Instinctively they all looked at the television screen, which remained eerily silent and empty.

"Saxby and Boella have gone into the dining room," said the radio operator, hunched over the receiver. "Chambine is still in his room. The other four are just moving about the hotel."

"I reached an agreement," reminded Charlie, addressing Cosgrove but turning to include Pendlebury. "I haven't heard you give any contrary instructions on that radio over there."

Pendlebury sighed, in apparent reluctance, then moved to where Gilbert had the communications equipment. Pendlebury glanced once toward Charlie and then curtly gave the all-units order, countermanding his earlier instructions about Charlie.

"Thank you," said Charlie.

"You're pretty cocky, for someone who's just learned how close he's come to death," said Pendlebury.

"It's a kind of nervousness, really," said Charlie. He wondered, with a detached objectivity, how he was going to settle with Pendlebury. The bastard had led him along, almost by the nose, set him up to be killed, and even now was treating him like a tolerant headmaster.

"No hard feelings?" said Pendlebury, just avoiding being patronizing.

"Of course not," said Charlie. It was like a bloody film script, he thought.

Cosgrove smiled, a politician who has succeeded in another compromise to suit everybody.

"I'll not forget your part in this," he said to Pendlebury.

"Thank you, sir," said the FBI man.

Cosgrove thrust out his hand and self-consciously Pendlebury took it.

There was movement on the television monitor and they all started toward it. Three uniformed guards had entered the room and were patrolling dutifully between the display cases.

"Eleven-thirty," time-checked Gilbert. There was a mumble from the radio. "Saxby and Boella have left the restaurant," the man added. "And the other four are moving into some sort of grouping, just outside the Alcazar. . . ."

There was a pause, then Gilbert resumed. "And Chambine has just left his room."

Pendlebury scooped a handful of ice into a glass and then poured from a full bottle of vodka that was on a small table. Appearing suddenly aware of the others, he said: "Help yourselves."

Neither Cosgrove nor Charlie took up the invitation.

". . . Saxby and Boella have gone out through the pool area," said Gilbert. "And Petrilli is making his way toward the anteroom. . . ."

That would be where he had stood, in apparent contrition, four hours earlier while Cosgrove had announced the resumption of insurance cover to the rest of the committee. The door leading from the foyer was in a small recess and there were parts of it where a man would be quite invisible to the general reception area.

". . . He's through. . . ." said Gilbert.

"His job is to bypass the electrical alarms into the anteroom and then the linking door into the exhibition hall proper . . ." said Pendlebury. He was looking at a clipboard. There were names written down a side panel and then tiny, identified figures inscribed on the paper.

"...Now the others are crossing," said Gilbert. "Bertrano first...now Bulz...Beldini's waiting...apparently there's been a sudden influx of people into the foyer...."

The Russians? wondered Charlie hopefully. They should have responded by now.

Cosgrove patted his pockets, located his cigarettes, and lighted one, staring throughout the entire operation at the radio set. Pendlebury stood with both hands held in front of his chest, with the glass against his lips but not drinking from it.

"...He's moving now...he's through...."

Pendlebury sighed, drinking at last, and Cosgrove exhaled a relief of cigarette smoke.

"...Eleven fifty-three..." recorded Gilbert.

"Two minutes ahead of schedule," said Pendlebury. "Now they wait until the midnight security round."

"You appear to know a lot about it," said Charlie.

Briefly Pendlebury smiled. "I know more about it than they do themselves," he said, moving toward the bottle.

It seemed he had been wrong about the people he imagined the Russians had installed, thought Charlie. He'd been wrong about almost everything else so far. He halted the self-pity. Not wrong. Just misunderstood. He'd still fucked it up, though, whatever qualification he tried to make in his own defense.

Williamson had lost his supremacy and because of it he was uneasy: insufficient to do anything not properly thought out, but still uneasy. From the moment Pendlebury had established his control room, it had been occupied by a minimum of three people, often more. They took no room service, because of the risk of disclosing the equipment inside, which had made it impossible for Williamson to establish surveillance similar to that of the earlier accommodation. Because of the conversation he had monitored from Pendlebury's original rooms, he knew the purpose of the move, which made Charlie's admission to it even more inexplicable. As confusing, almost, as the hour-long meeting the man had had in Senator Cosgrove's suite. Failing to install any listening devices there had been a bad mistake. His first; but still inexcusable. The only obvious conclusion was that Charlie Muffin had concurred with the robbery. It would be a remarkable about-face, having gone to the extreme of warning Moscow. But then his instructions had changed, just as remarkably. Williamson thought back to the conversation during which he had been appointed the man's protector. "Someone unusual for his deviousness" had been the warning. The man whom he now knew to be Charlie Muffin was certainly that.

Williamson, who was sitting in the foyer, glanced up at the wall clock and then expectantly along the corridor in the direction from which the security men would enter. Exactly on time, they approached the exhibition hall and three entered while a fourth remained on guard outside. How easy it would have been, reflected Williamson, to calmly walk up and alert the guard that four men who intended to steal the contents of the chamber behind him were at that moment crouched in the darkness of the anteroom, the alarms from which had already been nullified. The security people emerged within two minutes. Aware that Pendlebury wouldn't risk his people humping a dead body through the foyer, Williamson had decided that if an attempt were to be made on Charlie's life, it would be within ten feet of where he sat. And within the next twenty-eight minutes. He strained around, wondering if the Englishman had left Pendlebury's control center. On the far side of the reception area, Ramírez waited in the position Williamson had nominated. Aware of the man's attention, the Cuban looked up, anticipating some nodded instructions. Williamson stared at the man blank-faced, then looked away.

CHAPTER 24

THERE WAS something surrealistic at witnessing a robbery in which the participants were being operated, puppetlike. Visually, thought Charlie, it was a combination of an old silent movie and a moon walk. The cameras of which they were unaware were fixed and concealed, so there was not the complete view of the exhibition room and Chambine's men kept entering and leaving the picture, heightening the impression of a staged production.

Everyone in the control room was staring fixedly at the

television screen. Pendlebury and Cosgrove had arranged chairs, alongside Gilbert, from around whom came the only activity in the room. He was quietly commentating the identities into a tape recorder from which court depositions were later to be assembled, to accompany the film. Beside Gilbert hunched a second FBI man, counting aloud, allowing Pendlebury to time the robbery according to Chambine's own assessment and therefore gauge the risk to the 12:30 security patrol. To Pendlebury's left was the operator who had taken over from Gilbert the radio surveillance on Saxby, Boella, and Chambine. The man had already recorded the extinguishing of the pool lights by the time Bulz and Beldini entered the room. It was exactly two minutes past twelve.

"Sixty seconds early," Pendlebury had said. Until then Charlie had not realized that clipped to the front of the man's sweat-damp shirt was the pickup of a microphone connected to a second tape recorder.

The disguise of the first two men was excellent. It was impossible to discern where the black balaclava headpieces merged with their black track suits.

Their movements appeared almost choreographed. Going for the lights first, they scurried from fixture to fixture, one never impeding the other, each confident of the other's position and purpose. The light died on the picture, as if someone in the control room had turned down the brightness button.

"Twelve-six," intoned the timekeeper.

"Made up two minutes," calculated Pendlebury.

Cosgrove was hunched forward, hands against his knees.

The picture suddenly flared into light again as the coverings were taken from the illumination, and in the second it took for their eyes to adjust, Bertrano and Petrilli had entered the room. Bulz and Beldini snatched their hats off and there were isolated grunts of amusement at the silent picture of the two men puffing to indicate how hot the coverings had been.

"That'll convict you, bastards," said Pendlebury.

The four men began moving with the precision that Bulz and Beldini had earlier shown. Bertrano and Petrilli slid the rods beneath the display cases and then lifted, like operators of a miniature sedan chair, while the two who had entered first crouched with their bypass leads, clamped them into position, and then crab-walked side-ways to the adjoining cases, to make the connection to the linking alarm. It was almost an amusing sequence, thought Charlie, like a complicated morris dance. As the impression came to Charlie, Cosgrove sniggered.

"Twelve-nine," said the man alongside Gilbert.

"All display case alarms circumvented," Gilbert mouthed into his recorder.

"Two minutes, fifty seconds ahead," confirmed Pendlebury.

Maintaining the morris dance analogy, Bertrano and Beldini skipped back to the first case, repeating the sequence but this time lifting higher, so Bulz could cut through the immobilized connecting wires. As each display case became free, they ran to the window through which they intended to hand them to Saxby and Boella.

"Drive lights going," said the man in radio contact with the outside observers. ". . . first section . . . second . . . third . . . now Chambine is in the parking lot, moving toward the cars. . . ."

Nine of the twelve display cases were lined near the window. Bulz remained by it now, scraping the covering from the alarm wire beneath the sill and infusing the last bypass lead into the system.

"Twelve-sixteen," said the man with the watch.

"Saxby and Boella have entered the parking lot," reported the radio listener. There was a momentary pause. Then: "First lights gone . . . second . . ."

"Made up three minutes," recorded Pendlebury. The shoulders of his shirt were black with sweat.

"They're good," muttered Cosgrove, addressing no one. "They're very, very good."

"Parking lot completely out," said the radioman.

"Twelve-eighteen."

The four men were grouped around the window. There was a momentary pause, as if they were taking breath, then Bertrano unbolted the sash, paused again, and then jerked the window upward. Chambine and Saxby were just identifiable in the square of darkness.

"Marvelous," groaned Pendlebury, as if enjoying some physical pleasure. "Oh Christ, bloody marvelous."

"Boella's by the station wagon," said the radioman.

The cases were chain-handed through the window and into the car with the same efficiency there had been throughout the robbery.

"Twelve-nineteen..." counted the man. "Twelve-nineteen, fifty..."

"...Eight cases loaded..." said Pendlebury.

"...Twelve-twenty..."

"...Just one more to go..."

"...Twelve-twenty, fifty seconds..."

"...They've done it..." There was a note of personal triumph in Pendlebury's voice as they watched Bertrano vault easily through the window, turn professionally to close it so the brief sixty-second burst of light into the parking lot would not be investigated, and they were again looking at the unmoving but now empty picture of the exhibition hall.

"And we've done it," said Cosgrove, turning to the FBI man. His voice began softly, but rose as he got toward the end of the sentence. "We've done it!" he shouted, slapping out for Pendlebury's damp shoulder.

The FBI man grinned, almost shyly, as if he still found it difficult to believe it had gone as smoothly as he had planned.

"Yes," he said, controlling himself better than the senator. "It all worked."

"Moving off down the drive," said the man at the radio. "Quite undetected."

Appearing to remember Charlie Muffin, Pendlebury swiveled in his chair, the triumph that Cosgrove had earlier shown starting out upon his fat, reddened face. For a moment of incomprehension, the look stayed there, the smile flickering hopefully.

"Gone," he said, his voice broken in disbelief. "The son-of-a-bitch has gone."

Had Giuseppe Terrilli ever been asked, incautiously, what he considered the single most important reason for his success, he would have listed his control. It had been with him that childhood morning on the tenement roof, remained throughout his early career as a soldier determined to rise to the very top of the organization, and was with him now, subduing the excitement that was churning through him at the thought of feeling and touching and caressing the stamps that had once belonged to Tsar Nicholas II of All the Russias.

After his return from the beach and changed instructions to Santano had come news of two fresh interceptions, and because of the warning he had issued at their previous meeting and the displeasure which he had anticipated and received from the inner council of the organization, he had summoned both Santano and Patridge to a conference and reviewed the disaster with an ice-cold detachment which had worried both of them.

Able now because the robbery had been brought forward to release Santano immediately, he had ordered that a personal aircraft be made ready for the following morning to fly his lieutenant directly to Bogotá. So serious were the interceptions considered that he had ordered Santano accompanied by four others, physically to impress upon the Colombian organizers his annoyance at what had happened.

Santano and the accountant remained for dinner, not for any social reason, but because Terrilli was determined that neither would leave the house unaware that their own future employment and safety fully depended upon a higher rate of success. Throughout the meal, Terrilli never once consulted a watch or clock to establish how close the robbery was.

It was Santano who drew attention to the time, interrupting Terrilli at ten o'clock to ask if he could leave the room to check on the arrangements for relaxing the security precautions for the period that had been stipulated. Patridge was obviously curious, but refrained from any comment, instead continuing the conversation about the marijuana arrests and offering tentative suggestions at what could be done to prevent a reoccurrence. Terrilli sat nodding and occasionally intruding a question or observation, and all the time his mind was occupied with thoughts of the quality and texture of what was soon to be his and how he would rearrange his collection, to give the Romanov stamps the focal point of the display room.

Terrilli waited until Santano's return, and only then after they had had coffee, before pushing his chair away from the table to indicate the conference was over.

Patridge had released his driver, when he had been told to stay for dinner, and Terrilli nodded agreement to Santano's suggestion that he should drive the accountant home, seeing benefit in the frightened men carrying on the discussion further.

Santano rechecked the security instructions as he went down the driveway and then out into the private road leading to Ocean Boulevard. He turned northward and was almost to the point where the Flagler Bridge joins the mainland before the first of the Cubans moved quietly through the palms and shrubs bordering the approach to Terrilli's castle.

Before they had attempted the Bay of Pigs disaster they had been trained in the basic art of jungle warfare, because Langley had imagined Castro's overthrow would involve quite a lot of guerrilla fighting and considered it important. During their imprisonment in the Soviet Union, that basic instruction had been improved in the special KGB training forest bordering the Black Sea, even though its immediate advantage had not been guessed at the time. So they moved easily across the cropped lawns and through the clipped hedges, perfectly using every available cover and remaining quite unseen by Terrilli's patrolling guards nor detected by the Doberman dogs they restrained on tight leash.

The Cubans had been infiltrated back into America without any weapons, because such things were so easy to obtain within the country. They had been provided with .375 magnums, four carried Armelite rifles, and one had a Russian-made AK-47, which, if seized by the authorities, could be traced back to a three-term Vietnam veteran who had bartered it for his last three fixes of heroin and was now undergoing psychiatric rehabilitation in a New England sanatorium.

The Cubans' training had brought them up to British commando or American Marine standard. There were fourteen of them and they divided equally, dispersing themselves upon either side of the approach road and coming within twenty feet of the now secured, electrified gate. Their information was that when the cars they were to intercept came along the road, those gates would already be opened. If, for any reason, that failed to happen or the gates closed on them before they could get through, they carried sufficient grenades to blow it off its hinges.

It was always possible, of course, that the grenades would *not* burst the gates. So, confident there was still time before they had to spring the ambush, two crept undetected beneath the piercing searchlights and fixed plastic explosive charges to one of the concrete gate pillars, trailing the detonating wire back to where the main body were assembled.

They hoped the plastic wouldn't be necessary. The noise would obviously attract the authorities, perhaps before they had the opportunity of retrieving the collection.

CHAPTER 25

THE IDEA of quietly but simply leaving Pendlebury's control room had come quite spontaneously to Charlie. At the commencement of the robbery, he had been as intent as everyone else on what was silently unfolding before him and it was not until almost halfway through that his attention faltered and he realized the absolute concentration of those around him. And saw it as an advantage. The thieves in the exhibition room didn't know how they had been manipulated: Charlie did. And he wanted it to stop. It made him feel stupid.

He had risen slowly, remaining with his hands against the chair back for several seconds, then gradually made his way toward the door leading into the corridor, all the time tending toward the bathroom to provide an excuse if there were a sudden challenge. The monotone commentary had continued uninterrupted and their heads stayed fixedly toward the television monitor. At the doorway there had been the final hesitation, as Charlie had tensed against the sound of its opening and then, quickly, he had passed through and drawn it closed behind him.

Still without any clearly formulated idea of what he was going to do, the desire openly to run was overwhelming. But he had seen and learned enough about Pendlebury's operation to be impressed by its efficiency and so he had walked instead, aware that any observer whom he might not be able to see might become suspicious from any different behavior. It would only take seconds with the electronic equipment available to rescind that order against his assassination. And he needed all the time he could achieve against discovery.

Throughout an operational career as extensive as his, there had obviously been attempts against Charlie. Those that had arisen during assignments, people reacting against detection or arrest, he had regarded as nothing more than that to be expected, considering the profession he had chosen, and confronted them—and always succeeded in that confrontation—in a de-

tached, impersonal way. They weren't trying to destroy him,
Charlie Muffin: They were fighting his department and the
country he represented. Charlie thought that was fair.

But there had been other, isolated occasions when such
acceptance hadn't applied. Very early in his association with
the department, before Sir Archibald Willoughby had been
appointed its head, Charlie had been infiltrated into Poland and
halfway through the mission realized he was the front, the man
to be exposed for identification for the benefit of the real operatives in the hope of detecting an informant in the British
embassy. Two men he had drunk with in the Red Lion near
the old Scotland Yard building and with whom he had supported
Queens Park Rangers on a Saturday afternoon had suffered that
time, neither knowing even now how it was they came to be
recognized and snatched off a deserted Warsaw street, each to
face ten years' imprisonment. After the Burgess and Maclean
fiasco, when Charlie had been sent to Washington to close
stable doors after the horses had gone to the knackers' yard,
a first secretary at the embassy there had so resented the jus-
tifiable criticism of laxity that he invoked family relationship
to complain through the Foreign Secretary to Sir Archibald,
in the expectation of getting Charlie fired. And had never been
able to convince anyone that he had no knowledge of how
classified documents from the ambassador's personal safe came
to be in his briefcase during a cocktail party at his Georgetown
brownstone, which was why he had never risen further in the
diplomatic service and served his last eight terms in African
embassies. And then there was the episode during the east-west
border crossing, in Berlin, when he had been offered up for
sacrifice for those who had succeeded Sir Archibald. Resig-
nation had been the only recourse for both the English and
American Directors, after their humiliating capture and trade-
off in exchange for the Russian spy master. And not just the
Directors. A total of nearly a hundred operatives exposed and
identified and now only good for filing clerk duties at Langley
or Whitehall.

Charlie regarded each incident as personal. But there was
something more; worse, in some bizarre idiosyncrasy, than the
attempt at physical harm. Each time there had been people
treating him as a fool. Perhaps only Edith had come near to
guessing the cause of that; the resentment of someone whose

doubtfully widowed mother had charred and sometimes offered the men of the household additional services to earn the extra money to keep her son at the grammar school who had never been able to lose his conviction that the university graduates who were his constant companions were able to regard him as an equal.

Sir Archibald had come near, too. *"You're so good because each time you're proving yourself,"* the old man had said.

But he hadn't proved himself this time, reflected Charlie, entering the elevator and pressing the button for the first floor.

"Prick," Charlie accused himself as the elevator descended. "Made to look a thorough prick."

The first positive idea had come as Charlie emerged on the first floor, turned immediately left, and went down the last story by the fire stairs, which had an exit to the back as well as the front of the hotel. He had learned enough from the importance attached to timing in the control room to utilize it to his advantage. In one of the passages leading past the Alcazar lounge toward the beach, he'd checked his watch. Twelve-eighteen. Quite obviously, to avoid any confrontation with the security guards, it had to be completed within the next twelve minutes: probably within five, to enable them to clear the hotel before the theft was detected.

Five minutes, then, before his disappearance was discovered. What would be Pendlebury's reaction? Radio first. Seize and maybe even eliminate; there might still just be time to plant a body, to achieve the second, more serious indictment.

What next? Pendlebury was a professional and the professional response would be to attempt immediately to assess the damage Charlie could cause and then move to prevent it interfering with what still had to happen when the collection was delivered to Terrilli's house.

Charlie smiled, coming out near the oddly darkened pool area and turning back around the hotel. He was moving north, toward the private highway leading out onto the South County Road.

Had the situation been reversed, Charlie knew he would guess that Pendlebury had made for Terrilli's house. It was the only natural, logical conclusion to make: and Pendlebury was a natural, logical person.

Charlie took a shortcut across the lawn, gained the harder

surface of the private road, and sprinted down toward the better lighting of the public thoroughfare. He arrived at the junction panting, checking the time again. Twelve twenty-two. His chest hurt, but he forced himself to hurry, wanting the telephone booth near the junction with Cocoanut Walk. Breath was groaning from him when he reached it and he leaned out, grabbing at it and trying to recover. Twelve twenty-five.

He wedged himself into the booth, aware for the first time of the perspiration running across his back and chest and even down the inside of his legs.

He started up, at movement from the Breakers' drive. A Ford station wagon, with four men in it, came carefully out, checked for traffic in both directions, and then turned left. Immediately behind was a second vehicle, a Chrysler compact, with three occupants. Like that before it, the driver stopped for any cars on South County Road before turning left, spurting up to get into convoy.

His breath easier now, Charlie stood waiting, hand outstretched toward the telephone, his eyes unmoving from the driveway.

"Come on, you bastard," he said in quiet impatience. The sweat felt wet and uncomfortable. He shivered, despite the warmth of the Florida night.

The first car came out at twelve twenty-seven. It was a Dodge Colt. Behind it came a Plymouth, low against the ground because of the equipment Charlie guessed it carried. A thick-bodied radio antenna waved from the roof and there were two more aerials, mounted at the rear. A white Plymouth Fury was the third car. It was quite easy to see Pendlebury in the passenger seat.

Charlie had dialed police emergency before the lead car had come onto the highway. The police reception replied in a measured, unpanicked voice.

"There's a robbery at the house of Giuseppe Terrilli," said Charlie, speaking carefully but refusing any identification.

Charlie replaced the telephone before Pendlebury's car cleared the driveway. He remained in the booth, watching the man turn toward Terrilli's castle. He'd failed to get any response from an anonymous telephone call to the Russians. Charlie wondered if he would have any better luck with a warning involving one of Palm Beach's most respected residents.

As the taillights of the FBI squad turned toward Bethesda, Charlie saw the taxi flag and waved.

Four Cubans deputed as Charlie's protectors had been positioned in the foyer of the Breakers, in the belief that it would be around there that any violence would occur, but one had been positioned on the corridor of Pendlebury's second room and so Charlie had been identified as soon as he emerged. Charlie's disembarkation on the first floor, to walk down the last stairway, had caused a few seconds of confusion, but it had enabled the man to alert Ramírez and through him Williamson. They had located Charlie again by the time he got to the private road. Three stayed with him, while Ramírez returned to the Breakers for transport. Williamson took a second car and was actually driving slowly southward, along South County Road, when he recognized the surveillance team from Ramírez' parked vehicle and then saw Charlie get into the taxi and move off ahead of him. Williamson slowed further, letting Ramírez interpose himself between him and the taxi, checking the timing from the dashboard clock.

It was twelve-thirty.

At precisely that moment, Tony Santano turned his 350SL Mercedes off Ocean Boulevard into the private roadway leading to Terrilli's mansion. Ahead of him, unseen, waited fourteen Russian-trained Cuban guerrillas. One minute behind and only four hundred yards away came Robert Chambine, in the station wagon, with Saxby following in the Chrysler. Pendlebury, prevented from following too closely by the radio reports being constantly fed into his vehicle, estimated he was at least three minutes behind the Chrysler.

Pendlebury had evolved a code word which would activate the one hundred agents he had grouped within five miles of Terrilli's castle, pleased with the ambiguity of it. Everyone would move when he opened his radio channel and said, "Stamp."

At twelve thirty-one, Chambine went by the last of the FBI monitoring spots, placed one hundred yards away from the entrance to the private road to avoid detection. Pendlebury, who had been riding with his finger on the transmission button, depressed it and said, in a consciously controlled voice, "Stamp. I repeat, Stamp."

He turned the radio off, turned to Gilbert beside him, and added, "And I hope to Christ I find that Englishman, to stamp him, too."

A mile away, twenty-five Palm Beach policemen were activated in eight cars, with two backup vehicles, to investigate an anonymous allegation of robbery at the home of one of their leading citizens. For Palm Beach, where there is rarely violent crime, it constituted a major response, reflecting the importance of Giuseppe Terrilli.

It was twelve thirty-two and fifty seconds.

CHAPTER 26

TONY SANTANO had not intended to be so late returning. He had properly anticipated Terrilli's response to the marijuana seizures. And decided, too, that it gave him the excuse to come back, a loyal lieutenant apparently doing everything to ensure there were no further mistakes with the security and this private business, enabling him in fact to report the names of those involved for necessary action by those who were also going to censure Terrilli.

But he hadn't quite sufficiently gauged the true seriousness of the seizures themselves until that night's meeting. As he and Patridge and Terrilli talked, the full import had come to him and he had realized the concern initially would be more with the interceptions than with whatever Terrilli was doing on the side and that as the man who had established the Colombian operation in Bogotá, there was a danger of it personally reflecting upon him.

So he had sat longer than he expected in the car outside Patridge's home, trying to find the proper excuses to the inevitable inquiries and to evolve, too, the correct approach when he got to South America to guarantee it stopped happening.

He had been humming as he drove along Ocean Boulevard, happy with the solution. The affair with the stamps gave him the let-out here, just as it did with his return. If he were asked to explain, he would infer, because that would be the cleverest way to make the accusation, that Terrilli had been too occupied with this outside thing to devote his full attention to the shipments. Patridge, who was aware of his ambition and agreed that Terrilli's tenure of the top place was endangered, would support him, Santano knew. Because Patridge saw him the natural successor to Terrilli. Colombia would be easy. He'd create a few examples and tighten everything up through fear.

There was a bend in the private road, which meant that approaching vehicles had to slow, and until it was negotiated it was not possible to see the high main gates. Santano was halfway around and beginning to smile at the already open gates when the Cuban commando group mistook it for the first of the robbery cars and ambushed it.

They had concentrated at the bend, correctly recognizing it as the spot where vehicles had to reduce speed and were therefore easiest to stop.

Santano actually jumped, startled, at the sudden sight in his headlights of a man rising from the ditch at the side and about eight yards ahead. And then he realized the man was bringing his hand up and that the hand held a magnum, supported against recoil by the man's stance and left hand clamped to his right wrist. Santano had survived before upon reflex and his reaction now was almost automatic. He ceased turning the wheel, to complete the corner, instead straightening out and heading directly toward the gunman. The maneuver might have worked on someone less deeply trained, causing the man to falter or even leap aside. But the man didn't panic. He remained crouched, eyes screwed against the headlight glare for sight of the driver beyond, legs bent and pistol unwavering before him.

The Cuban managed one shot before the Mercedes struck him, carrying him spread across the hood until it hit a bordering palm tree, instantly crushing him to death. Santano did not have the satisfaction of seeing the man die. The .375 magnum has one of the highest muzzle velocities of any handgun. The bullet burst the windshield and completely decapitated Santano at the very moment when his car struck his killer.

After hitting the tree, the Mercedes toppled slowly to the left, nose-first into one of the bordering storm ditches with its rear wheels completely free of the ground. Santano's body was

not thrown out of the driving position by the impact, but rather
forward against the controls, so that his foot jammed down
against the accelerator and the engine howled at the continuing
thrust of power. Five of the Cubans surrounded the car, but
because of the way it was lying they were unable in the few
seconds available to realize they had the wrong vehicle. One
man was actually crawling in through the easiest opening, the
destroyed windshield, when Chambine's car came around the
corner.

Chambine's reflexes were every bit as good as Santano's
and he had the advantage of having almost half the interception
squad around the ambushed car and those that remained una-
wares and temporarily out of position. But initially he misunderstood it. He thought the Cubans part of Terrilli's personal
squad and assumed the upended Mercedes to be a car that had
been stopped penetrating that security. He did not imagine any
danger to himself or those with him. Nor did he decide it
concerned him; his function remained to get in and out in the
shortest time possible, particularly with the complication that
could arise from the crashed Mercedes.

He swept by, accelerating on the straight part of the roadway
leading to the open gates, and then the rear window exploded
in on first the stamps and then the occupants of the station
wagon as a bullet from one of the Armelite rifles ricocheted
off the edge of the bodywork and Chambine heard Bertrano,
in the rear, shout ". . . What the fuck . . . ?"

"They're firing," said Bulz incredulously. "They're firing
at us."

Chambine was only yards from the entrance now. There
were men grouped around it, gazing momentarily uncertain up
the roadway, but one had already activated the controls, so that
the heavy gates were swinging closed. Chambine pounded on
the horn and accelerated faster. The rear near-side fender
clipped the gate edge as he squeezed through, throwing the car
sideways into a skid, and as he fought to control it, Chambine
heard Bulz shout, "They've got Saxby."

The Chrysler had been less than three seconds behind the
larger vehicle, but the Cubans were ready now, concentration
fully back upon the road. Saxby had been driving, with Boella
in the seat beside him and Beldini at the back. Saxby had
slowed, because of the road, and then further at the sound of

the Armelite shot which shattered the station wagon window. Beldini had drawn his own gun, a Smith & Wesson, and when Saxby began coming out of the corner saw they were confronted by at least nine men, all armed. Beldini fired through the closed window, the sound so deafening within the enclosed car that Saxby screamed with the pain it caused in his ears. The shot did nothing except break the glass and then the Cuban with the AK-47 began firing, the weapon on automatic, so that the bullets sprayed the car, scything through the three occupants and killing them instantly. Out of control, the car plunged straight on, scattering the commandos and actually striking the rear of the Mercedes, knocking it further into the storm ditch. The automatic transmission raced on, adding to the howl from the Mercedes. One of its spinning rear wheels found occasional contact with the hood of the Chrysler, throwing up spurts of black smoke as the tires scorched the paintwork.

"The gates are closing."

The warning came, in Spanish, as the Cuban with the AK-47 opened the driver's door, hauled Saxby's body uncaringly into the road, and then thrust into the car. Before emerging, he switched off the ignition, at the same moment as someone else managed it in the Mercedes. They were momentarily disconcerted by the silence, shouting when there was no longer a reason.

"There's nothing here," said the man in the Chrysler, lowering his voice halfway through the sentence. "It must have been in the first car."

"We'll have to blow the gates."

The uncertainty of Terrilli's people went at the sight of more than a dozen men, all armed, approaching near enough to be seen in the searchlight's glare. Terrilli's guards only had handguns, which were ineffective for the range, but the firing split up the Cuban group, driving them into the bordering ditches. Two began answering with their Armelites, hitting two of Terrilli's guards with their first few shots and forcing the others through the small sidegate to the protection of the wall beyond. The return fire from the mansion was sporadic, because rifles hadn't yet been hurried to the gates and there was little hindrance to the men groping along the ditch toward the plastic explosives detonator.

Terrilli's mansion was about two hundred yards from the

gatehouse. The golf cart, which was the normal estate transport and which brought the rifles from the building where Terrilli's people lived, actually pulled in beside the gates when the plastic exploded.

A supporting pillar weighing ten tons was split completely at its base, lifted eight feet into the air, and then pulled sideways by its connection to the huge, splintering gates so that it fell completely on top of the golf cart and its driver, who had died seconds before anyway in the first shock of the detonation. The gatehouse, in which five men had been crouched, actually abutted the pillar. The shock killed three and crushing masonry a fourth. The fifth man was to be found three days later, deafened and blinded, his vertabrae, both legs, and an arm crushed. Incredibly, he was to live for a further five years, in a home for the incurably ill, with no memory of what had happened to him.

Terrilli had got the first warning from the gatehouse after the ambush of Santano's car, although the vehicle had not been identified as that of his lieutenant. He had ordered the gates closed and was still with the telephone in his hand when Chambine's station wagon was identified and reported to have scraped through.

The speed of Terrilli's reaction was that of an exceptional man. He depressed the receiver to clear the line and then dialed his lawyer in Fort Worth. The man knew better than to interrupt, accepted immediately there was a major problem, and promised to be at the house within an hour. Until which time, Terrilli was to refuse any interview with anyone in authority and certainly not consider making a statement on any subject whatsoever.

Terrilli had intended receiving Chambine alone in the study, where he had taken his calls, but decided that the changed circumstances now made that impossible.

Unaware of the surveillance, electronic monitoring, and photography to which he had been subjected in the previous days, Terrilli imagined his only provable connection with crime was what Chambine was bringing up the driveway toward his mansion. Which made it a pity that Chambine had succeeded in getting through the gates. A pity; but then again, not a disaster. Terrilli had little doubt that the interception had been carried out by the police, because of some mistake on Chambine's part of which he was yet unaware.

There might be doubts, he accepted, but none that could not be resolved, with sufficient persuasion. He'd invested a great deal of time and effort and money against just such an eventuality as this. Whatever the doubts, he was fairly confident there would be no serious questioning of his insistence that he knew nothing of Chambine and could only assume the presence of the man and his companions was nothing but a panicked attempt by criminals to find sanctuary down a darkened roadway when they realized they were being pursued.

Possible testimony from Chambine and whoever else was with him would upset that, of course. So Terrilli determined he would have to behave like the public-spirited citizen he had so often proved himself to be. What would be more understandable than responding forceably to the amazing and frightening situation of being confronted in your own home by a group of armed men? He would be able to show the proper reluctance and regret that they should all have perished in their attempts to seize his house or himself or whatever else their purpose might have been.

His real regret would be in having to return the Romanov Collection, but he knew there was no alternative. He might be able to hold it, for a few moments at least.

He missed Santano, Terrilli realized. He could have outlined the idea within a few moments and the man would have put it into effect, making sure there were no problems. Without him, Terrilli had to brief those at the gate. He stood at one of the interestate control panels, wall mounted beside the huge entranceway, jiggling the receiver to summon those who would have by now sealed the gate against any entry. He was looking through one of the side windows as he did so and saw perfectly in the estate floodlights Chambine's car coming too fast up the driveway; there was no way the man could negotiate the bend at the top of the drive without running over the neatly clipped lawn edge.

Because he was looking in the direction, he saw the explosion that tore away the gate. There was a sudden flare of white, then orange, and he heard the muffled crump and the windows and very fabric of the house seemed to shudder under the impact of the blast. A scratching, tearing sound came from the instrument in his hand and he knew it was useless. He replaced it neatly on the hook.

There were more of his people about the house and in the outbuildings. But there was no way he could assemble them in time to confront the occupants of the car which at that moment mounted the grass in front of the house, as Terrilli had feared, ripped a track through it as the brakes were applied, and slid into the steps before stopping.

Terrilli opened the door, trying to isolate a feeling he was yet to know as fear, more occupied with how he could create the opportunity to kill them all himself. He realized it would be almost impossible.

Chambine was out of the vehicle first, running around the hood in an awkward, crablike way as he tried to see what was following as well as what he was heading for. He hesitated, confused by the sight of Terrilli, glancing back curiously at the others who were thrusting out of the car.

"Get in," said Terrilli.

"The stamps..."

"Leave them."

Chambine entered first, then Bulz, followed by Bertrano and Petrilli, who came in side by side. Immediately beyond the door, they halted, looking uncertainly about them. Within seconds, there was a perceptible change in the attitude of Bulz, Bertrano, and Petrilli, as they recognized the man in whose house they were.

"What happened?" demanded Terrilli.

"Ambushed in the approach road," said Chambine.

"So the other three are dead or captured?"

Chambine seemed baffled by the question. Then he said: "They were *behind* us. They got hit, certainly. But there was another car, in front."

"Another car?"

"An ambush," Chambine repeated. "We went *into* an ambush."

"So someone knew... someone already knew...?"

Chambine shrugged. "How the hell do I know?"

Terrilli paused, then decided to ignore the sudden lapse of courtesy. With it came another decision. He couldn't kill them, not now when he didn't know what was happening. And then there was another thought. He'd disclosed himself, to others besides Chambine. The feeling came again, the unaccustomed fear.

"What about that explosion?" he said.

Again Chambine shrugged. "The gates, I suppose. Why don't you ask your own people?"

"None of them have come back yet."

"Men," reported Bertrano from one of the windows alongside the door. "There's men moving out across the driveway out there...."

As he spoke, there was a single shot, then another.

"... They're trying to take the lights out," completed Bertrano.

"The police wouldn't behave like this," said Terrilli, in sudden hope.

"Who, then?" said Chambine.

"I don't know," said Terrilli. If the interception in the private roadway *hadn't* been official, he was in better shape than he had thought. The explosion would obviously bring the police, but if he could contain whatever was going on before their arrival, there would be a way out; might even be able to get it officially regarded as a well-planned attempt at armed robbery of one of the community's better known residents.

"That room, to the right," he said, speaking generally. "The gun room. There are weapons. Stop whatever's happening out there and it's an extra fifty thousand apiece."

Bertrano and Bulz began running toward the room he had indicated.

"The collection," remembered Chambine. "We left it out there in the car."

"Get it," ordered Terrilli.

They had taken the legs off the display cases before loading them into the station wagon. There were twelve, each containing four albums and then some separate exhibits, and although not heavy they were difficult to handle. It was impossible for either Chambine or Petrilli to carry more than one at a time. Three were inside before the first shot sounded, caroming off the ancient brickwork around the door and spitting chips into Terrilli's face. He jerked back, hand to his cheek, momentarily dazed. Then he went to a control box near the communications panel, opened it, and threw one of the line of switches. The porchway area was put into sudden darkness.

Bulz and Bertrano arrived at the door at the same time as Terrilli. Bulz had a pump action Winchester. A figure rose, about a hundred yards away, and Bulz fired repeatedly, a man very practiced with a rifle, and in the middle of the burst the man crumpled, fell, and lay still.

Terrilli crouched low in the doorway, waving Petrilli and Chambine back and forth, uttering "careful" and "easy" every time either man handled a case badly.

Terrilli was waiting by the door, to close it, as Petrilli gasped forward with the last case. He was at the top step when he got hit, high in the back so that he pitched forward, his hands gesturing out as if he were offering the case to those crouched around the door. The case fell and smashed and Terrilli leaped out, snatching it up. Petrilli collided with him, knocking the older man sideways so that Terrilli ended hunched against the door edge with the broken case clutched to his chest. The shot had shattered Petrilli's lungs. He was already bleeding from the mouth and some had splashed onto Terrilli. He shuddered, disgusted, and then scrambled back through the door. Bertrano slammed it, as another Armelite bullet struck home, shattering a hole about six inches around.

"Heavy weapons," said Chambine.

"And they know how to use them," added Bertrano.

He wheeled at a sound from behind, but Terrilli held up his hand.

"My people," he said.

There were six, who had come from the outbuildings through the rear doors. Terrilli looked back to those at the doorway. Nine in all. That should be sufficient.

Another bullet smashed through a window, plucking the curtaining like a sudden wind.

"They're not police," Terrilli said positively. "Get out in the grounds. I want them taken away, every one...."

The men began turning, but Terrilli stopped them.

"Just a minute," said Terrilli.

They all stopped.

"These men will go with you," he said, indicating Chambine, Bulz, and Bertrano. "And I want just one of those people out there brought back, just for a moment. I want to know who the hell they are."

Terrilli was halfway back to the study when the idea came

to him. He stopped, openly laughing at it, then hurried on because the nearest telephone was in the room. He was connected immediately to the police emergency number.

"Giuseppe Terrilli," he said. "I'm being attacked. In my own home. For God's sake, hurry."

"We're already on our way," assured the policeman.

General Valery Kalenin had gone to particular trouble with the meal, wanting Berenkov later to realize that he had prepared the evening for the announcement. And not just the food; there had been two bottles of Aloxe-Corton and there was another in readiness on a sideboard. Kalenin knew it was his friend's favorite.

"You're an excellent host," thanked his guest, belching appreciatively.

"I've some news," said Kalenin.

Berenkov smiled at him over the table.

"Charlie Muffin is alive," said the KGB chief.

For a moment, Berenkov's expression faltered and then the smile widened.

"I never believed he'd died in that air crash," said Berenkov. "It was too neat and tidy."

He looked expectantly at Kalenin.

"In America," continued Kalenin. "Appears to be working for some insurance firm."

Berenkov nodded. "Sir Archibald Willoughby's son was an underwriter. Thought of attempting to compromise him, once. But his father had him too well protected."

"Yes," confirmed Kalenin. "It's his firm."

Berenkov sat back reflectively. "Charlie Muffin," he said distantly. "I *liked* that man. He caught me and I got a forty-year jail sentence. But I still liked him."

"It was because of him you got released," reminded Kalenin.

Berenkov shook his head. "He didn't do that for me. Charlie did that for himself. For revenge."

"He appears to be getting in the way of an FBI operation," said Kalenin. "They want to kill him."

"Does he know?"

"I'm trying to stop it happening."

Berenkov picked up his glass, gazing at the wine.

"It's a coincidence," he said.

"What?"

"This Aloxe-Corton. It's a wine I recommended to him, after he put me into prison. He used to drink rubbish before then...."

He sipped his drink.

"...It became his favorite, too," the former spy master added.

CHAPTER 27

WILLIAMSON HAD known it would happen, but because it was an unacceptable decision he had refused to consider it. Then he came to within fifty yards of the approach road to Terrilli's home, where he could ignore it no longer, and finally recognized he was going to disobey the completeness of his instructions because to do otherwise might mean capture and repatriation to Russia.

He had slowed and then halted completely, aware of the nearness of the turning he had already reconnoitered and correctly assuming that Charlie would go down on foot. The man must have paid while the taxi was still traveling, because the moment it stopped, Charlie left the car and went straight down the darkened private roadway.

Ramírez had also stopped his car, sufficiently far away for Charlie to be unaware of it. Williamson nodded with satisfaction as the five Cubans entrusted with the man's safety left their vehicles and went after Charlie. Williamson knew the completeness of their training and was confident that Charlie would not detect them. What about his own training? Far better and far more extensive than the five who had just dutifully and unquestioningly set off to do what they had been ordered. He should have been at the turning now, using the shadows as expertly as they because his was the ultimate responsibility for keeping the man alive and Moscow's instructions had been quite explicit.

Instead, he reached out and started the car, aware that to remain in the vicinity risked the very involvement he wanted to avoid. He continued south down Ocean Boulevard, around the curve and then along the section that runs parallel with the sea. After about twenty yards, the houses to the left stopped and he was looking beyond the palms to the open sea. It was a completely clear night, the moon silvering the gently lifting water. There were a few cars at the metered spaces, but Williamson easily found a place in which to put his vehicle. He stopped again, suddenly aware that he was perspiring and knowing, because psychology like everything else had formed part of his teaching, that it was because of the internal uncertainty rather than the heat of the night.

At the moment when he turned off the ignition, there was the thump of an explosion and he twisted around, in time to see the sudden glare from the direction of Terrilli's estate.

Pendlebury's tiny convoy had gone cautiously down the private road, stopping completely at the scene of the two crashed cars. Pendlebury's driver still hadn't turned off the engine when the explosion came. The Cuban commandos, who were expecting it, were flattened and quite hidden, sixty yards away, but the small FBI group were completely exposed. The Dodge Colt was still leading and caught the full impact of the blast. All the glass in the car shattered inward, blinding the driver and severing the carotid artery of the man sitting beside him, but no one realized it at the time and so he bled to death before help could be obtained. What was later to be judged the most serious effect was the damage to the radio car. The roof-mounted antenna was shifted from its mountings, giving from that moment only an intermittent signal, and the transistorized valves in the two backup sets were both broken. The windshield broke in Pendlebury's Plymouth Fury, but the only injury he suffered was a cut thumb, of which he was not even aware.

They were all stunned and sat unmoving for several moments. In Pendlebury's car, Gilbert was vaguely aware of what appeared to be some formalized movement some way off, where it was still dusty from the explosion, but his eyes would not focus for him to be sure in which direction the figures were going. He was too confused to associate it at that time with any danger.

"What in the name of Christ . . . ?" said Pendlebury. His voice croaked and he became aware from the cottonwool numbness in his ears that he could not hear his own voice.

"Did you authorize any explosives?" demanded Gilbert, re-covering first. When Pendlebury did not reply, Gilbert shouted the question again.

"Just grenades. And mace, of course," said Pendlebury. His ears were clearing.

"That wasn't a grenade," said Gilbert. "What the hell's happening . . . ?"

"I wish I knew."

Pendlebury got with difficulty from the car, his body aching as if he had undergone some strenuous exercise. The radio control man was sitting with the door open and his head in his hands, and when he looked up at Pendlebury's approach, Pen-dlebury saw that the man was bleeding from the nose and eyes.

He gestured the man from the vehicle, reaching inside to seize the microphone to warn the approaching agents. It wasn't until he had finished the message and demanded acknowl-edgement, getting instead a lot of static whine broken by the odd, unintelligible word, that he realized he had no radio con-tact with one hundred men converging upon the mansion.

"Fuck," he said bitterly, slamming the microphone against the seat. It bounced and fell onto the floor.

Pendlebury looked up as Gilbert ran from the crashed Chrys-ler. "Saxby, Boella, and someone I think is Beldini, but I can't be sure because the bullets caught him in the face," said the man.

"Terrilli's people had been told to let them in," remembered Pendlebury.

"Who, then?" said Gilbert.

Pendlebury shook his head, an almost weary gesture. "Who's in the Mercedes?"

"Impossible to say."

Pendlebury straightened, trying to clear the ache that had started around his neck and shoulders. He looked around. The man in the Dodge was moaning, hand to his sightless eyes, and the passenger unconscious. There were two in the radio car who appeared unhurt and another from the car he and Gilbert had occupied. He gestured one of the radiomen back into the Plymouth.

"Find a handset that works," he instructed. "Stay here and keep broadcasting. I don't know what's going on, so I don't want anyone taking chances. Understood?"

The man nodded, turning back into the vehicle.

"We've only got handguns," warned Gilbert.

"It'll have to do, until the backup arrives," said Pendlebury. The pain was going, so that he had almost completely recovered from the shock of the explosion. It had gone wrong, he decided. He didn't know how, but the whole thing had gone disastrously wrong. It didn't matter whether the Englishman had caused it or not. Pendlebury was more determined than ever to have him killed.

"Let's go," said Pendlebury. "Stay in a group. Anything else is hostile."

Hesitantly they moved off toward the entrance to Terrilli's house.

"Must have been a bomb," judged Gilbert as they climbed over the gate, which had been blown to form a ramp over the masonry and brickwork.

Which had been Charlie Muffin's assessment, when the blast reached him. The bend in the road had saved him almost completely from any effect, but there were still sufficient shock waves to knock him over. He landed awkwardly, thrown against the root of a palm, so that the wind was knocked from him. He rolled over, arms hugged around his body, and when he grimaced up thought he detected movement from the direction in which he had been walking. He pulled against the palm with which he had collided, sure of its cover. Twenty yards away the Cubans, three of whom had been knocked over, tried to reassemble, using less caution than before so that Charlie was able to confirm the first impression. Charlie stared around him. He was against the far edge of a ditch, dry and hard underfoot. He crouched, putting himself below the roadline, and scurried forward, one hand still against his bruised ribs, the other out to steady himself against the ditch wall.

Two crashed cars stopped him, a Mercedes blocking his path. He started to drag himself upward when he became aware, about five yards back along the road, of the vehicles that had formed Pendlebury's convoy. He halted, using the cars for concealment. Two men appeared injured in the Dodge and there was movement from the Plymouth, but he couldn't judge from it how many occupants there were.

As he watched, the Cubans came around the bend, jerking

to a halt at the roadblock. The man with the handset saw them and jumped from the Plymouth, waving.

"Careful, you guys," he warned.

Ramírez had been leading. He hesitated, recognized instantly the other man's mistake, and continued on, gesturing to the melee of cars and shouting as he approached. "What happened?"

Ramírez reached the operator when he was about to reply, but before the man could speak the Cuban shot him, once, in the head. The operator was hurled back into the Plymouth by the impact. Two of the group had gone to the Dodge. Both men in it were unconscious now, so they left them.

Charlie slid down, flattening himself and squeezing beneath the Mercedes. Once past the wheel, there was quite a lot of space at the bottom of the ditch. Something was dripping on him, he realized. He hoped it wasn't gasoline. After a few seconds, he had the limited vision of feet and legs as the Cubans stared inside.

"All dead," Charlie heard one of them call.

"We've lost him" said another. Charlie recognized the voice as that of the man who had shot the operator. Terrilli's men, he decided.

Distantly, but identifiably from the direction of Terrilli's house, came the sound of gunshots.

"We'd better get in there," said the voice of Ramírez again.

Charlie crouched where he was, listening to the sound of their footsteps and beyond that, more frequently now, the isolated cough of a shot; rifles, he thought.

He had become aware that there was more room between the wheel and the ditch bottom on the side other than that through which he'd crawled, but Charlie still left the same way, so that the Mercedes was between him and the direction in which the group of men would be. He peered cautiously between the ground and the upended wheels. A lot of the lighting was still in operation, despite the devastation around the gate area. The electrified fence had been broken, but there was a secondary source of power, so that occasional strands still sparked when the gentle breeze drove it against a contact. The explosion had settled now, so that Charlie could see just how much had been destroyed. Not only had the support pillar and the gate been flattened, but a gatehouse and about ten yards of wall.

"Christ," said Charlie softly. The Russians must have responded, after all.

Satisfied that for the moment he was quite alone, Charlie climbed from the ditch, feeling behind him and then bringing his hand out in front of one of the headlights. Oil, he saw. The suit was only three years old, too.

He looked up again, at the destruction of the wall and then toward the cars and their bloodied occupants. Very distinctly, he thought he heard the sound of police sirens, and the noise hardened his decision.

He paused, for the briefest moment, and then started to jog toward the exit onto Ocean Boulevard.

"Bugger a few poxy stamps," he said to himself. It was survival time again.

He was alert and the sweep of lights warned him, well in advance of the first of the FBI cars turning into the road. Charlie leaped to his right, confident of the ditch and its concealment. He waited until the first was past, then carried on, obviously more slowly but still with sufficient speed as the cavalcade went by in the opposite direction. The actual junction created a difficulty, because he could not just arise in front of the headlights, but the very congestion gave him the escape. As the cars jammed, blocked by the obstruction that Charlie had left minutes before, people began leaving their vehicles, to continue on foot, and in the confusion Charlie rose easily from the gully.

He was on Ocean Boulevard, going toward its turn into Flagler Drive, when the first of the police cars swept around the corner, siren wailing, roof cones lighthousing red and blue. Charlie walked unhurriedly, keeping close to the hedges and shrubbery, tensed against a challenge that never came.

Terrilli's telephone call for help had been radioed to all the converging units and the police chief alerted. The police operation was excellently coordinated, four cars sweeping through and then two others swinging across the highway either side of the slip road, creating a roadblock which effectively prevented more than half of Pendlebury's force ever reaching their objective.

The police were bewildered by the number of people involved in the attack upon Terrilli's house. The two officers in the first car snatched their riot pump guns from the rack between the two front seats, and the driver, a nervous man of twenty-two responding to his first major call, loosed off a burst scarcely over the heads of the scrambling FBI men. The following police cars did not recognize the shot as coming from one of their own men. Having been told by their dispatch officer to respond with force, they crouched mob-control fashion behind the protection of their vehicles and began shooting into the shapes they could see in their headlights milling in the roadway.

In that first flurry of shots, five FBI officers were killed and eight wounded, two with injuries from which they later died. When there was no answering fire, the two lead police cars flooded the entrance with their maneuverable spotlights, using their foghorns to tell everyone to place their hands against the roofs of the cars.

Thirty men did as they were told, which meant that less than forty managed to get by the blocked cars and follow Pendlebury and the other three agents into Terrilli's property.

Pendlebury was moving around the lawn that fronted Terrilli's mansion, knowing it was the long way but guessing they would need the cover of the border hedges. The floodlights brilliantly illuminated the area immediately in front of the castle, and the moon was so bright that it would have been like crossing the remainder in broad daylight had he tried to go straight over.

The years of indulgence slowed him, as well as his customary reluctance when faced with gunfire. The two operatives from the radio car were leading, Pendelbury next in line, and then Gilbert.

As highly trained as they were, the Cubans had left two men as rear guard, expecting the explosion to bring the authorities, who would have to be slowed while they made their escape along the beach, which was a decision they had reached in the ditch, seconds before blowing the gate. So close were Pendlebury's group and so powerful a bullet from an Armelite rifle that the first shot actually killed both the lead man and the one behind him and Pendlebury whimpered his fear as he plunged against the ground. He hoped Gilbert would think it was the sound of the breath being knocked from him.

"You all right?" whispered Gilbert.

Pendlebury grunted, to maintain the impression of being breathless.

"Can't see him," complained Gilbert, crawling up alongside.

Nearer the house there broke out a sudden snatch of firing, and from where they lay they heard the sound of breaking glass.

"Bloody war up there," said Pendlebury.

"But who?" repeated Gilbert. He could see figures ducking through the floodlighting, like some bizarre *son et lumière*, with gunfire instead of words and music.

There was the sound of movement behind, and both men twisted on their backs, trying to swing their guns around in time to fight off an attack, and then the shape said: "It's me," and they saw it to be Al Simpson.

"Where the hell have you been?" demanded Pendlebury.

"It's chaos back there," said the man who had headed the Boynton Beach group. "Police have fired into our guys. Some have been hit. It'll take some time to sort out."

"How many do we have here?"

"Maybe twenty. Perhaps a few more. I don't know."

From the darkness ahead, the Armelite fired again, stripping leaves off the nearby bush with a hissing sound, and then the second Cuban fired, driving their heads down against the grass.

"You got rifles?" asked Pendlebury. The grass got into his mouth as he talked.

"And a handset," said Simpson.

"Thank God for that. We're being held down by people in that clump over there, marked by the outline of that tall tree. I want fire poured in there. Tell everyone to keep down. There's fighting ahead but I don't know between whom."

Simpson twisted, repeating the instructions into his walkie-talkie. Other shapes began to materialize, grouping themselves around Pendlebury, and at his signal they started firing in the direction from which Pendlebury had identified the snipers. There was sporadic answering fire, and then, from Pendlebury's left, the group whom Ramírez had taken into the grounds started shooting at the perfectly identified target. Simpson and Gilbert were killed immediately and Pendlebury felt the thump in his left side and then numbness spreading from his shoulder to his thigh and knew he had been hit. He lay with his face against the grass, surprised that there would be a dampness to it, and wondered when the pain would come. He knew he wouldn't be able to stand it and hoped they got him back to an ambulance with morphine before it got too severe. He started trying to find the wound and then stopped; if he felt anything too bad he knew the hurt would start.

"Hit," he said to movement behind him. "I've been hit."

He was distantly aware of someone muttering into the handset that Simpson had carried and then another crash of shots as Ramírez' group was flushed out. Ramírez tried to run toward the one Cuban who remained as a rear-guard, but was mistaken and caught full in the chest with a burst from the Armelite. Marked by the flash of the explosion, the last sniper was killed in the crossfire of two groups that had managed to get on either side of the tall tree coppice.

Terrilli's house was actually built upon a slight, man-made elevation, and with the floodlights he was able to see perfectly what was happening outside, like a Caesar watching an ancient Roman spectacle. Bulz had gone down within seconds of coming around from the side of the house, and as he watched he saw Bertrano suddenly jerk upward, crying out, hand cupped to his head. Terrilli strained to see the figures darting from cover to cover, trying to isolate Chambine. He thought he had him once and smiled as the figure toppled sideways, but then he realized it was someone attached to his own staff. He was aware of more people entering the grounds, far away beyond the reach of the floodlights, and tried to detect above the firing the sounds of the police cars. They couldn't be much longer.

He saw Chambine at last. He was with three others, crouched behind some ornamental masonry that marked the very front of the house. Initially it formed good cover, but then two groups managed to work their way around either side, so that it became a trap. Chambine appeared the first to realize it. He looked hurriedly around, saw that the front door of the house was the only escape, and darted toward it. The station wagon in which he had arrived, so very few minutes before, was pockmarked with bullet holes and only one side window remained unbroken. He crouched against it, using the cover. One man still by the stonework went down and the other two at last came to the same conclusion as Chambine. One was hit as he tried to dash to the car, but the one made it.

Terrilli saw Chambine turn, toward the house.

"Is the door open?" Chambine yelled.

"Yes," Terrilli shouted back, sliding the huge securing bolts into position and then twisting the key in both the locks. He fled back to the gun room at the very moment that Chambine and the other man made their run for the house. They were perfectly silhouetted as they reached the door. Chambine thrust against it so hard that the breath went from him as he shouldered the woodwork. He stood back, frowning, jerking at the door handle and shoving again, and then the Cubans opened fire, cutting into Chambine and Terrilli's man like amusement park targets.

Terrilli had not waited to see what would happen. He was on the telephone to the private house of the mayor of Palm Beach, shouting for protection and repeating what he had said earlier to the police control room about being under attack.

As he replaced the receiver, he heard the sound of the first siren and went back to the hallway. The gunfire that had shattered the windows and splintered the door had caused a great deal of damage, pocking the marble balustrades and puncturing several of the oil paintings with which the entrance was hung. Falling debris had smashed some more of the display cases, but Terrilli was still able to locate the case he had handled. He took a handkerchief from his pocket and carefully wiped away any trace of fingerprints. Satisfied, he crouched, just five feet from the treasure he had coveted so much but now couldn't even touch. He became aware of the handkerchief, still in his hand, and took it gratefully to his face, blowing hard. He wasn't surprised at the emotion.

The sirens were louder now and there were more of them. There was still sporadic shooting, but it no longer appeared directed toward the house. Terrilli allowed a lot of hammering against the door before he moved to open it, assembling an air of bewilderment about him. He opened the door at last, just slightly, then peering through the opening as would a properly frightened man. There were five police officers grouped on the step, around the police chief. Beside them stood Terrilli's lawyer.

"Thank God you're here," said Terrilli, managing just the right catch in his voice and opening the door wider. "I've been terrified."

Police had summoned to the scene ambulances from every one of the seven hospitals serving Palm Beach. Pendlebury was carried to that from the Good Samaritan Hospital in West Palm Beach, but by the time he got to it the emergency morphine supplies had been exhausted. The pain came, even through his unconsciousness, as the vehicle slowly maneuvered its way through the car-littered private road. Pendlebury began to scream, because the bullet had practically severed his left arm and then gone on to penetrate his lung, and the medic had to hold the writhing man down in his stretcher. Williamson, driving a circuitous route back toward the Breakers, heard the ambulance siren and slowed allowing the vehicle right of way across Cocoanut Walk. By that time the attendant wasn't having to remain beside Pendlebury's cot anymore, because the man was dead.

The police cars in the driveway of the Breakers initially alarmed Williamson, but then he remembered the robbery and what would have had to be the official reaction to it and continued cautiously toward the entrance.

As he got from the car, he identified the figure of Charlie Muffin, walking with his jacket folded and carried across his arm, and felt a lessening of the tension bunched inside him. How soon would it be, he wondered, before he discovered what had happened to the Cubans?

The foyer was thronged with people. Near the exhibition, Charlie saw Cosgrove in the middle of a group of men. Some were uniformed and others were not; police, guessed Charlie.

He hesitated and in the pause Cosgrove saw him. He thrust through the men around him, hurrying across to Charlie. He appeared to have forgotten Charlie's exit from the control room.

"What happened?" he demanded urgently, his voice soft and head forward, so that there were only inches between them. "Did it all go okay . . . as we planned . . . ?"

Charlie remembered how he'd lost his last encounter with the man and then had a recollection of the unsuspecting FBI agent getting from the radio car in the private roadway and the fleeting second of shocked surprise as the Cuban had shot him and then of the destroyed gatehouse and wondered for the first time just how many men had died.

"Terrific," he assured the senator. "Couldn't have been better."

Cosgrove smiled, looking past the waiting policemen. Charlie became aware for the first time of technicians assembling television lights and then of cameramen.

Cosgrove hurried back toward the exhibition entrance, but before he got there called out, so that the journalists as well as the police would hear. "Excuse me . . . I've an announcement. . . ."

The noise in the foyer subsided.

Cosgrove spoke directly to the reporters now.

"There'll be a statement almost immediately," he promised. "First I must discuss some developments with the detectives in charge of this case and then I'll address you. Just a few minutes, please."

Charlie politely pushed his way through toward the elevator, suddenly feeling very tired. He was too old to spend nights running up and down ditches, he thought.

The idea came to him upon impulse when he got to his suite. For a moment he considered it, then picked up the telephone, dialed Clarissa's number, and asked for her extension.

It rang several times, and Charlie realized it was past one o'clock and began regretting the call. Then the receiver was lifted at the other end.

"Who is it?" demanded a man's voice.

There was the briefest of pauses from Charlie. "Wrong extension," he said, putting down the telephone. Which it was, but he was never to know it.

CHAPTER 28

BOWLER HAD stationed his secretary in the corridor to learn when Warburger returned from his conference with the Attorney General and had wondered at the hour it had taken for the summons to the Director's office. As soon as he entered, he guessed the reason. Warburger sat hunched behind his desk, as if he were in physical pain, and when he looked up at his deputy, the man's face was colorless and ill-looking.

"Nothing," he said flatly.

"There must be *something!*" insisted Bowler.

Warburger shook his head. "Terrilli's lawyers are claiming entrapment and the ruling is that they're right. We've got nothing we could bring before a grand jury."

"Son-of-a-bitch," said Bowler bitterly.

"Everything is in Terrilli's favor," said the Director. "Cosgrove really ruined it, with that goddamned press conference at the Breakers. If he'd kept his mouth shut until he'd known what was happening, we might have stood a chance. But that gave Terrilli the complete let-out. Then there was the man's own call, to the police. And the mayor . . ."

"What about Cosgrove?"

"Terrilli is threatening to sue, in a civil court."

"Could he win?"

"Easily, if he wants to press the case. Cosgrove's only hope is that Terrilli will hold back because of awkward questioning."

"Think we've frightened the bastard?"

Warburger spread his hands in an unknowing gesture. "May have fouled him with the organization for a while, but it won't be permanent. He's too good. He'll be careful, obviously, but within a year everything will be back like it was before."

"Son-of-a-bitch," said Bowler again. He hesitated at the question, then asked: "What about the CIA?"

"They won't admit a damned thing," said Warburger. "But they screwed it: sure as hell they screwed it. At least they got the shit in their own laps."

"What were they doing, moving in on a thing like this? It was *our* operation . . . an internal thing, for God's sake."

Warburger laughed, a sneering sound. "Know what they say! They say it wasn't them . . . that they know nothing about it and that they thought the Cubans had been killed, in the Bay of Pigs invasion."

"Do they think we're stupid?"

"I don't know what they're trying to prove," said Warburger. "But if it's a war they want, it's all right with me. A lot has been leaked already, but I want every file detail that's known about those Cubans released to the media. I want it to stink worse than a skunk in heat."

Bowler nodded, accepting the instruction. "Saw Mrs. Pendlebury," he said.

"How was she?"

"Broken up," said Bowler. "Apparently they didn't have any savings. She'll have to let the house go...asked if we could help?"

"What did you say?"

"That there'd be a pension, of course. But that we couldn't make any *ex gratia* payments."

"Right!" agreed Warburger immediately. "Do it once and there'd be a queue a mile long."

"There's the expenses," reminded Bowler. "I suppose she's entitled. You held them all back."

The Director nodded in recollection. "They were very high," he said defensively. "I was going to have him cut them by at least twenty-five percent. On the first week, the cocky bastard charged eight lunches, for Christ's sake!"

"He's dead," pointed out the deputy.

Warburger hesitated. "We'll compromise," he said. "Reduce them by ten percent."

"Pity about Jack," said Bowler reflectively.

"Yes," agreed Warburger. "Good man...."

He looked up. "They were *all* good men," he said, suddenly angry. "I'm damned if I'll let the CIA get away with it. I want them fixed. Do you hear me? Fixed!"

"I hear you," said Bowler.

The two men were silent for a long while. Then Warburger said: "We've come out of this badly, even though all the blame is on the CIA."

"I know," said Bowler.

"It'll take a long time to recover."

"Yes," said the other man.

There was another silence, but this time Warburger remained staring at his deputy. "He showed me," said Warburger at last.

"Showed you?"

"The Attorney General. He showed me your report, saying that you opposed the operation from the start."

"He *demanded* it," blurted Bowler anxiously. "He said he wanted personal reactions, throughout the executive."

"I know," said Warburger. "It still wasn't loyal, was it?"

"I said I came around to supporting the operation," attempted Bowler.

"Under pressure," qualified Warburger. "And because you hadn't much of an alternative."

"I didn't intend any disloyalty," insisted Bowler.

"I know you didn't. You intended to guard your own back. I understand that, Peter. It's a natural enough reaction. I'm still disappointed."

Bowler accepted if the Attorney General had shown Warburger the file, the man had talked his way out of any personal blame. He wondered upon whom the Director had managed to shift the responsibility.

"I'm sorry," he said.

"So am I, Peter. Very sorry. I'll expect a change, in future."

"Yes," said Bowler. Desperate to move Warburger on, he said: "Do you want men assigned to this Cuban thing?"

"Yes," said the Director. "And I don't give a damn if the Agency discovers it, either."

"What about Terrilli?"

Warburger leaned back in his chair, head tilted upward, considering an answer. It was several minutes before he came forward, reluctantly shaking his head.

"No," he said. "We daren't try anything more."

"So we failed?"

"Yes," agreed Warburger. "We failed."

There was another pause and Bowler realized the Director had spoken looking directly at him. At that moment Bowler answered his own question. He knew exactly who had been blamed for the disaster.

Williamson had know that if Ramírez had been captured then he risked identification and so he had lingered in the foyer, anonymous among the other residents, trying to discover what had happened. He had listened to Cosgrove's impromptu press conference, devoted almost entirely to the man's boasts of involvement and commitment against organized crime, then actually risked asking one of the reporters, who hadn't known any more than he did.

Sleep had been impossible, of course. Williamson had sat in his room, fully clothed, alert for any sound in the corridor outside, suppressing the desire to run because of the possible attention it would draw from any investigation. It wasn't until the early radio bulletin the following morning that he heard all the Cubans had been killed and finally learned he was safe. Relief had trembled through him and with it came the awareness that Moscow would regard it as a completely successful mission.

He had slept at last and by the time he had awakened, at midday, the radio, television, and newspapers had the CIA connection and Williamson smiled, admiring the speed at which Kalenin had moved.

There was still a great deal of police activity. By midafternoon they had reached him, working on a floor-by-floor check of the rooms. A fresh-faced uniformed policeman politely asked him if he had been aware of anything unusual around the exhibition the previous night, and equally politely Williamson assured him he had not. The policeman thanked him, drew a line through his name, and moved on to the adjoining room, and Williamson realized the wisdom of not panicking.

It was five o'clock when Williamson went curiously down to the foyer, to make his booking for San Diego, wondering about Pendlebury. He found the man's name in the official list of FBI dead in a late edition of the Miami *Herald*. There was an officially released picture, which must have been taken soon after Pendlebury joined the Bureau. He hadn't been as fat then and his clothes seemed neater. The newspaper said he was forty-two. Williamson would have guessed at another five years, at least.

When he was making his reservations he became aware of Cosgrove's flustered departure. There seemed to be a dispute about the responsibility for a canceled party, ending with the senator's shouted insistence that the account be sent to his Washington office. The man's wife seemed tight-lipped and angry, too, Williamson thought. Their attitude toward the surrounding reporters had changed overnight.

Williamson caught the early plane to San Diego on Thursday, reported his return to his employers, still sympathetic over the death of his father, and with three days before he had to return to work decided to make a weekend of it. He drove up to Los Angeles. The Aztecs beat the Rowdies three goals to nil in one of the best games he had seen that season.

CHAPTER 29

RUPERT WILLOUGHBY had sat unspeaking and without movement as Charlie recounted the story, and even when Charlie stopped talking there was no immediate response. Then he breathed out, noisily, an almost disbelieving sound.

"Good God!" he said.

"It almost worked," said Charlie.

"So Terrilli escaped?"

"It might appear so, from the outside. I suspect he'll be handled by his own people."

"But that won't stop the drug-running?"

"No," agreed Charlie. "It won't stop that. It might hinder it for a while, that's all."

"Thank you for keeping Clarissa out of it," said the underwriter unexpectedly.

"She seemed annoyed."

"Did she?" said Willoughby. "She's got over it, if she was."

"Good."

"She wants you to come for dinner. Asked me to make arrangements with you today."

Charlie stretched elaborately. "I'm still jet-lagged," he avoided.

"Wednesday?"

"I'll call you," promised Charlie doubtfully.

"Make sure you do," urged Willoughby. "I'd love her to hear what really went on...as much as she could be told, anyway. And she seems to have helped, even though she didn't realize fully what she was being asked to do."

"You tell her," said Charlie.

"Something wrong?" frowned Willoughby.

"Of course not," said Charlie. He had not expected to feel the degree of guilt, confronting Willoughby for the first time.

"Telephone tomorrow?"

"All right," agreed Charlie.

Since his return from America, Charlie had been more alert

than normal for any surveillance, fully aware in retrospect of the risk he had taken involving the Russians. He changed underground trains three times after leaving Willoughby's City office before he was finally satisfied, at last getting out at Oxford Circus for the Victoria Line connection to take him to Vauxhall. The evening rush hour was over and the crowd was thinning, making his checks easy. He approached the anonymous apartment complex confidently, convinced his anxiety was unfounded and thinking back to Willoughby. He wondered how Clarissa would behave when they were both in her husband's presence. Quite relaxed, he guessed. She'd be more used to it than he was. He realized with surprise that he wanted to see her again.

A graffiti artist had been busy in the elevator, warning of God's impending arrival to purge the earth of sinners, Jews, blacks, and homosexuals. Charlie was glad he wouldn't be around; whoever was left would bore the ass off him.

He stopped short, immediately outside the elevator. The package was tight against the door of his apartment. The corridor was deserted. The only noise was the distant sound of music, from one of the apartments. Debussy, he thought.

He moved carefully forward, holding himself to the wall opposite to that against which the parcel had been positioned. The shape was oddly familiar and Charlie frowned at it. He remained about two yards away for a long time, crouching twice in an effort to see any wire leads. Then he went nearer, taking a pen from his pocket and gently tilting it, trying to discover any connections at the bottom. At last he reached out, recognizing the outline and smiling tentatively.

Unmarked brown paper was taped tightly around it. Still gently, he peeled away the sealing, then cautiously unwrapped the paper. As the bottle became obvious, a small square of card slipped out and fluttered to the ground. He bent, picking it up.

"Glad to learn you survived" was printed in block capitals.

Charlie took the last of the paper away, cupped the bottle in his hand, and saw it was vintage Aloxe-Corton.

"Shit," he said.

ABOUT THE AUTHOR

Brian Freemantle was a foreign correspondent in London for the *Daily Express*, the *Daily Sketch*, and the *Daily Mail* before taking the career of a novelist. He has worked and traveled in thirty countries, including the Soviet Union, the United States, and Czechoslovakia. His books in the Charlie Muffin series include *Charlie M, HERE COMES CHARLIE M, and THE Inscrutable CHARLIE MUFFIN*. Mr. Freemantle lives in Winchester, Hampshire, England.

MURDER...
MAYHEM...
MYSTERY...

From Ballantine